DESTINY
AND
DECEPTION

ALSO BY SHANNON DELANY

13 to Life
Secrets and Shadows
Bargains and Betrayals

DESTINY AND DECEPTION

Shannon Delany

St. Martin's Griffin

New York

DESTINY AND DECEPTION. Copyright © 2012 by Shannon Delany. All rights reserved. Printed in the United States of America. For information, address St. Martin's Press, 175 Fifth Avenue, New York, N.Y. 10010.

www.stmartins.com

Library of Congress Cataloging-in-Publication Data

Delany, Shannon.
    Destiny and deception : a 13 to life novel / Shannon Delany. — 1st ed.
        p. cm.
    ISBN 978-0-312-62446-0 (trade pbk.)
    ISBN 978-1-4299-2556-3 (e-book)
    [1. Werewolves—Fiction.   2. Supernatural—Fiction.
3. Mafia—Fiction.]   I. Title.
    PZ7.D3733De 2012
    [Fic]—dc23

                                                    2011032803

10 9 8 7 6 5 4 3 2

Dedicated to all my friends and readers
who have stuck with me unflinchingly. I love you all!

DESTINY AND DECEPTION

PROLOGUE

Long after the fight with the company imprisoning the Rusakovas' mother is over, the smell of gunpowder and smoke still lingers, hugging the figures gathered in the dining room of the old Queen Anne house in the town of Junction. Like the stain of blood, the sharply sweet scent is hard to be rid of even after thorough scrubbings in showers, and it clings like a ghost to a life recently lost.

"A toast," the rescued woman, Tatiana, suggests.

Around the dining room table the Rusakovas and a few others they've brought into their family willingly—some with far better results than others—raise their glasses in response.

"To brave young men and women who give a bit of themselves so others may profit." Copper and silver twining in brown curls that tumble around her shoulders, Tatiana looks at the girl her youngest son calls Jess, the girl whose arm still stings from the cut allowing Tatiana the blood needed for her cure.

They all reach forward in unison, glasses touching together, the clink of crystal a merry sound announcing their
success. To have taken down their enemies—so many at
once—and freed Mother . . . to now be able to provide her
with the cure to her genetically engineered and fiercely abbreviated life . . .

The group watches, transfixed, as Tatiana drinks, pulling
the thick, dark red liquid past her teeth and into her throat.
She blinks, wobbling a moment, the remaining cure slosh-
ing in the glass, which her youngest, Pietr, catches and sets
carefully down before taking her hand in one of his and cupping her elbow with his other.

The elder of her biological sons, Max, leans toward the
redhead seated beside him.

Amy's become quieter since Marvin, a trait Max is determined to reverse. His willingness to show her his alternate
form—that of the wolf—has certainly given her plenty to
contemplate, and to potentially talk about. But for now,
Amy is lost deep in thought. Having dinner with a family of
Russian-American werewolves when one's Halloween cos-
tume was that of Red Riding Hood tends to give anyone
momentary pause.

"This may get messy," Max warns, redirecting Amy's attention with a point of his chin as he remembers when his
sister, Cat, took the cure.

The same sister who suddenly dares not meet his gaze
but exchanges a brief and pained look with Jessie before
settling her eyes on Mother once more. Only a handful of
people know what Jessie and Cat do, and only two of that
handful are seated at this particular table on this particular
evening. They know that the cure can be broken—pushed
past—in moments of extreme stress.

It seems the only thing that never changes is the very existence of change in Jessie Gillmansen's life.

Tatiana sways in Pietr's grasp, her eyes losing focus with memory and something more.

"Mother?" Pietr's voice rises as he steadies her.

"*Da*," she says, eyes glinting. "Have I told you the tale of how I first met your father?"

The entire group stiffens at once, knowing the story well. Tatiana has only recently told it, lingering on its details while barely holding back the wolf within during the course of the telling. For her to have forgotten something so freshly related . . .

"I had only just left Eastern Europe—running through the wild remnants of state forests and national parks, driven west for no better reason than my desire to watch the sun set off the ragged western coastline," she begins with a tremble.

"Pietr," Cat murmurs, her voice high in warning.

There is not one among their number who doesn't realize something is wrong. Somewhere—some*how*—something has failed them.

"Mother," Pietr whispers, pressing his strong and slender body to her side to better wrap her in his powerful arms.

The tremble becomes a shiver that shakes her narrow frame. "Where, precisely, I was, and when," she continues, her voice going soft, her glossy eyes witnessing a scene none of the others can see as it unfurls before her like the petals of a rose opening for the first time, "I do not know—what did I care for political limitations?" She smiles, the flower of memory blooming before her, inviting her to indulge in a time years past. "He was such an amazing man . . . Just"—she focuses a moment, spears her sons with a suddenly sharp look, fiercely proud—"just like my boys. . . ."

And with a shudder, she collapses, falling limp into Pietr's arms. Her chest heaves once before it stops rising and falling, the bright glow of life falling out of her still-open eyes.

Clutching her to him, strangely clumsy beneath the weight of death, Pietr stares at Jess, horror carved into his features beside complete disbelief. "Mother . . . ?" His knees give way beneath him and he tumbles to the floor, dragging her body onto his lap.

From the opposite end of the table, the one grudgingly called "Uncle" Dmitri because of the assistance he and his mafiosos offered rises, solemn and cool. His posture speaks of a dignity of sorts, but one that somehow lacks an under-standing of grace. "Her time is over. Now yours begins," he says to Pietr.

Quivering as rage and terror war within him, Pietr lifts his mother's body, crying out, "Do you not see *this?*"

Her head lolls to the side, hair falling across her face.

"She was as much our future as our past!"

Jess's feet become unstuck and she runs to Pietr, her chair tipping over and clattering in her wake, forgotten as the stunned people at the table spring to action. Cat, Max, and Alexi press in, crouching or kneeling, hands reaching for the woman who loved them, raised them, protected them as long as she could. But the only action that seems logical to Jess is to wrap her arms around her boyfriend—her love—and hold on.

It is Alexi who gently touches Mother's eyelids to finally close her eyes.

"Oh, God," Pietr whispers, cradling her in the crook of his arm. He tenderly sweeps the hair back from her face. "You tell them, Dmitri—tell your masters—tell your *dogs*—" He breaks free of Jess's grip and sets his mother reverently down to take her abandoned wineglass from the table. "Tell them there are no more werewolves in Junction—" He downs a dose of the cure in one large swallow, grinning at Dmitri with bloodstained teeth. "That time"—he reaches around and, grabbing Max's stubbly jaw, forces his mouth open, spilling the cure inside and along his face—"is over!"

Pietr springs to his feet and, pushing past his siblings, grabs the stunned mafioso. Dragging him to the front door, he shoves him into the cold outside. "Our deal has ended. I have nothing left to give you. We are all just men here, Dmitri, damaged, damned, and dangerous men. Leave. Do not come back—there is nothing to come back *for*. There are no werewolves in Junction," he repeats before slamming the door.

He leans against the door a moment, chest heaving as he catches his breath and realization spreads across his features. He has broken ties with the Mafia man who trained him, marked him as his second and threatened to ruin his relationship with Jess. He has finally and ironically cut himself free of his mother's rescuer and the man who would be his master. The leash has come off, but beneath its control there is no longer a wolf—just a young man feeling the cure race through his system eradicating the wildest parts of him.

Sinking to his knees, a smile twists across his lips despite everything and he embraces it: the pain, the strange "noise" Cat spoke of, the panicky death of the wild beast, and the freeing of the mild-mannered man who has struggled to correctly define himself as either man or monster since the noticeable parts of his change began at age thirteen.

Suddenly Jessie is beside him, one arm slipping between his back and the door, the other stretched across his chest to hold him tightly to her as he prepares to make his final change.

From the dining room come the sounds of Catherine, sobbing before she races through the house and out the back door, and Max as he gags and coughs, spitting before he launches away from them all and races up the stairs to lock himself in the bathroom and away from all curious eyes.

CHAPTER ONE

Jessie

I wrapped myself around Pietr, holding him while the cure tore through his body. Together we tumbled the rest of the distance to the floor; my arms never once relinquished their hold on him. Within the human halo of my grasp, his clothing ripped and fell away in shreds and tangles of cloth. Fur sprouted in thick tufts, filling in awkwardly and obscuring the way his muscles slid beneath his sleek human skin as he became the wild-eyed wolf.

One last time.

His fingers curled tight into the meat of his palms, bones slipping free to re-form and reshape into broad paws that thrust out claws and scrabbled weakly against the hardwood floor of the foyer, catching in the rug's long fringe. Frantic at knowing its time was over, the wolf struggled, whining in my grasp, and I adjusted my grip—glad the cure already weakened the beast. I would have never been able to hold back Pietr in his wolf form if he'd been himself.

The thought spun loose in my head, seeking traction like wheels slipping in mud. *If he'd been himself* . . . I laced my fingers together and buried my face in his thickly furred side, breathing in deep the scent of pine forests and winter's vast chill—the scents I'd come to recognize as *his*.

If he'd been himself . . . Closing my eyes tight, I dragged in another breath, my arms burning at the stress of holding on. Wasn't this Pietr, human and free of the beast always clawing at his heart and shortening his life span—wasn't *this* Pietr as himself?

He'd been at my side when things were undeniably dangerous—the least I could do was embrace the danger that plagued him since he became a teen. I loved him. And I had promised him I always would.

This was only one small test.

The wolf snapped its wicked teeth threateningly, closing inches from the top of my head—toasting my scalp with its fiery breath. I felt it twist, struggling to escape by dragging us some other direction. The bones in its spine and ribs wiggled against my rib cage, wobbling between wolf and man. I pulled my nose out of his soft fur to glimpse his eyes. They glowed the red of some dangerous sun setting the laws of gravity in a distant galaxy, and I knew we were close . . . close to a freedom he'd wanted but had never been free to choose.

There was a sound like a clap of thunder as his wolfskin ripped brutally in half. Pietr, completely and undeniably human, slipped free of the animal to rest nude and slick with sweat on the foyer's Oriental rug. His body heaved with the effort of being nothing but human after four fast and hard years of being so much more.

I released the damp pelt, empty and strangely like the husk of some alien lifeform as it cooled, and I scooted forward on the floor to embrace him—*my Pietr*—once again.

After everything—all the fighting, the danger, and the drama—finally, we were going to have our chance at being a normal couple. Everything was going to be okay. I was going to get my happily-ever-after after all.

"Jess," he whispered, his voice ragged. Worn.

I squeezed him gently, tucking my head into the curve of his neck. "I'm here, Pietr."

He sighed and pulled back from me, slowly opening his eyes.

They seemed different somehow, a softer blue, like the sky after a summer storm washes the darkness away, leaving nothing but a gentle, flat shade perfect for institutional clothing. I looked away a moment, shoving the thought back. When I refocused on him I noticed his forehead had wrinkled, a crease settling at the end of one dark eyebrow. He blinked and looked at me, cocking his head; puzzled. Pulling completely out of my arms, he sat straight up and rubbed his ears.

"What?" I leaned forward and stroked his hair. Odd. The red highlights—such small and seemingly obscure bits of color that sparked within his nearly ebony shock of hair—seemed dull now. I glanced up at the light hanging above our heads. Of course. The trouble had to be with the lighting. Or the fact I was still shaken. I was imagining things. I was seeing differences everywhere because I wanted him to be as different, *or as much the same*—I wondered now which it truly was—as he wanted to be. "Is something wrong?"

My heart sped as soon as the idea formed words.

Was it possible the cure killed his mother—that my blood

or some other ingredient in the gruesome mix had somehow poisoned her and now was taking hold of Pietr?

"What's wrong?" My eyes scoured his lean form.

"What time is it?"

"What?" Pietr always knew the time—it was as close to him as breathing, as regular as his rapid heartbeat.

He grabbed some anonymous shred of clothing and threw it across his lap.

My eyes narrowed at his suddenly discovered modesty, but I pulled out my cell phone and told him the time.

He blinked.

"Talk to me, Pietr—tell me what's going on."

He shook his head, and his eyebrows tugged together as he fought for words. "I don't . . . I can't . . . I can't hear the birds."

"What?"

He straightened and leaned his head back against the door, eyes wide and darting.

I shifted, twisting one arm around his while I stroked his bare shoulder with trembling fingertips.

"There were birds," he insisted. "Before . . ."

I brushed the hair out of his face. "There were birds singing outside?"

"*Da*. But now . . . there's nothing. God," he whispered. "Mother is dead. . . ." His voice cracked.

The only thing I could think to do was redirect him. "I didn't hear them," I admitted. "The birds."

A vein near his hairline twitched, and I knew my words did nothing to reassure him. But if they distracted him from the greater loss . . .

From upstairs the sound of Max's change taking hold of him threatened to tear the bathroom door off its hinges.

"Maybe the birds left?" I tried.

Pietr twisted in my grip and stood, hauling me up with him to peer past the lace curtain and out the small window of the porch door. He pointed.

I saw them then, a few stubborn sparrows animated as if song was bursting from their fluffy breasts. Still, I heard nothing.

"Is this it then?" he breathed. "Is this how quiet it is when you're only human?"

What sparked in his eyes was part wonder and—my heart stuttered in my chest recognizing the emotion—part fear.

"Yes, I—" I stroked his cheek and he shivered. "I think it must be."

"I had forgotten. I feel so . . ." His Adam's apple bobbed in his throat as he swallowed hard. ". . . so alone?"

I held him tighter, my joints aching with the effort. "You aren't alone."

He nodded, sticking his chin out like an obstinate child being brave just for me. "Hmm. Okay then." But he clutched me to him, winding my arms tightly around him. "Jess?"

"Yes?"

Closing his eyes, he leaned down, resting his head on my shoulder, and whispered, "Just—don't let me go."

"Never," I promised as my eyes lifted to catch Amy watching us, propped against the dining room's doorjamb, arms crossed, tears edging out of her eyes.

I realized we'd all lost something precious. And not just with the loss of Mother's life. Because in the end, it's not love—or werewolves—that breaks us. It's the choices we make—the cures we scramble to find, to take, both good and bad—and the lack of time we get to study and make better choices. Because it's always our choices that either save us or screw us.

So I chose to make sure Pietr knew he wasn't alone and would never be alone again. Maybe there were other werewolves—*oboroten*—from the experiments that made the Rusakovas, and maybe not. But there would never be another Pietr, never another *us*. So as long as we stayed together, neither of us would truly be alone again.

Marlaena

We were *so* screwed.

The winter wind pulled me along, claws dug deep in my nostrils, dragging me toward destiny. With hunters barely two states behind and snow hemming us in on all sides, our choices had been limited since we lost Harmony by the Ferris wheel on Navy Pier. The gunshots still rang in my ears like they'd been fired yesterday, although Chicago was far from the mountains we now raced across.

I wanted to shake free of my humanity—the stain seeping through the wolf in me and reminding me I'd failed, that I'd made the choice to leave the Windy City too late. That my failure had cost my pack.

In lives. Every human cell in my wolf body whined, weak and slow, sluggishly processing our loss.

Lingering over worthless emotion.

Muscles burning with effort, I pushed on, clawing into thickly frosted ground, my eyes slitted against the sting of the snowflakes threatening to blind me. Warmer weather wouldn't have narrowed our options. My snout wrinkled. We should have gone south with the migrating birds.

I should have known better. As alpha, *I* should have been smarter—more prepared. I glanced around the fur rippling across my shoulders and counted the wolves fighting to keep pace.

Eleven stumbling, bleary-eyed wolves with bellies rattling like beggars' bowls followed me. And one ran ahead, laying down our path with nothing but scent, a thinning reminder of his red hair and fox-like features. All together twelve wolves looked to me to keep them all safe.

All we had was one another.

And that amounted to next to nothing with hunters on our tails.

Jessie

Closing the door to Pietr's room, I leaned against it and caught my breath. Only a few hours had passed since Tatiana's death. Inside, Pietr dozed on his bed, exhausted from the impact of the cure and the emotional strain of losing someone he'd only just won back. Disbelief and anger at our failure warred within him.

The same way they'd battled inside me when I lost my mother.

Over the past months I'd dealt with my grief (certainly not gracefully), but it didn't make me any better at helping Pietr through his pain.

I was failing. I should've known the right thing to say or do to make things better. But every time his eyes met mine, my throat clogged and all the words stopped.

There had to be something I could do.

The temptation to have Dad come get me was strong. I could head home and saddle up Rio. A ride in the crisp wind might help clear my head.

I closed my eyes. What would a ride do for the Rusakovas? *Nothing.*

Now was not the time to be selfish. Now was the time to buckle down and do whatever I could for the people who needed it most.

Even if most of those people were werewolves.

. . . *were* werewolves. Past tense.

With a groan I pulled away from the door and stumbled down the hall. I paused by the bathroom to assess the damage Max had done: towel racks torn from the walls; tile broken; chunks of plaster and a coating of white dust covered a floor that wallpaper brushed, trailing raggedly from the walls in long shreds. The mirror over the sink was shattered—by fist or paw, I couldn't tell.

What had he seen to make him lash out, intent on destroying his own reflection?

The sink, tub, and shower were still intact. That was good, at least. I'd talk to Max about cleaning up a little later—but before Cat decided to talk to him and the tension between them grew even more difficult to control.

Or . . . I stepped into the bathroom, glass grinding between my sneakers and the tile. Maybe I'd just clean it up myself.

"Jessie."

I jumped, but breathed a sigh of relief seeing Amy in the doorway.

She held a bucket and mop in her gloved hands. "I can't do nothing," she said. "I'll do the physical cleanup, and you handle the emotional. You understand this better." Her eyebrows pulled together, and she looked at the bits of glass sparkling on the floor. "I just don't know what to say," she admitted, squeezing past me.

I nodded, although words seemed just as elusive to me.

Out of the bathroom and down the stairs I went. I paused on the last step. I could straighten up the sitting room. Remembering that was where Alexi had Max move Mother's body, my stomach twisted, deciding there'd be no straightening up there after all.

Not yet, at least.

Thinking I could clear the last things off the dining room table, I turned toward it but stopped short when I caught Cat reflected in the china cabinet. Her back to me, she focused on the wineglass that had held the cure—a wineglass that seemed even emptier than before.

What could I say to her? *I'm sorry it didn't work—but we knew there was a risk when you broke past the cure? Maybe we should've said something right after that . . . ?*

I backed away as quietly as I could and made my way to the kitchen.

Maybe I could cook something so Cat wouldn't have to, and Max wouldn't make some comment that'd hurt her already battered feelings. It was a small gesture, but better than doing nothing. Tugging open the refrigerator, I saw the casserole Wanda had brought over only a little while ago. And the pie. Even though almost no one knew about Tatiana's death, it seemed the few who did felt a need to feed the mourners.

And in record time.

My cell phone buzzed, vibrating against my hip. I yanked it free. *Sophie.* I let it go straight to voice mail. If I didn't know what to say to Cat, I sure didn't have a clue about what to say to Sophia. She'd been instrumental to our temporary success but she'd also made it clear she wanted a normal life.

Just like I did.

The phone buzzed again and I shut it off, reaching over to turn on the radio instead.

Maybe if Soph and I never talked about any of this, it'd just go away.

A girl could dream.

"The first large snowfall of the season is expected to make its way into our region late tomorrow night," the DJ announced. "We're expecting between three and six inches in the course of twelve hours."

Opening the fridge again, I discovered my mission, lame as it was. Snow was coming, and the Rusakovas were nearly out of milk. And bread. I dug into my jeans and counted my assortment of bills and coins. Yes. I could get supplies at the Grabbit Mart two blocks away and not bother anyone to drive. That'd clear my head almost as much as a horse ride and it'd get something they needed.

I shrugged into my coat, pulled on a knit hat, and wrapped the scarf that made Hogwarts standard-issue scarves seem bizarrely short around my neck.

Five times.

With a final glance toward the stairs, I shoved out the front door, plunged down the porch steps and into the wind.

CHAPTER TWO

Jessie

The snow glistened, peppering down in slow-spinning eddies, just starting to stick to the grass and moisten the sidewalk. At the first intersection I paused as a car went by. Ignoring the light, I crossed the street and suddenly found myself on the other corner clinging to the light post, my vision blurred and my breathing ragged.

Something twitched in the thin space between my brain and my skull and I let go of the light post and grabbed my head. A centipede ran prickling feet through me, setting my brain on fire. . . . My knees quivered and I stooped over, determined to keep my balance.

My vision wobbled and my stomach matched it. In an image bubble-thin and nearly as transparent I saw a hand before me—not my gloved one, but a small, bare hand with chubby fingers. It reached out to a dainty and cooling teacup, something that wriggled and squirmed pinched between its fleshy fingers. A face reflected back at me as I edged closer to the cup: soft child's features contorted in glee, blue eyes grinning as much as his mouth.

He seemed familiar. I squinted, tried to get closer to him. . . .

"Derek!" a woman's voice cried out, and I reeled back as the centipede he'd held dropped, writhing, into the cup and the image burst into a thousand glittering drops that evaporated and left me panting at the street corner.

I shuddered as the tickling sensation scuttled from my head and slithered in slow circles before settling into the base of my skull. Finally regaining control, I sucked down a sharp breath and stood straight again.

Derek. Dead, but not so gone.

Breathing deeply, I freed my cell phone. Alexi knew Derek had shot something into our heads during his death throes and he'd said we should tell him immediately if anything strange happened.

That little episode totally qualified as strange.

I pulled up his cell's number. And drew down another breath. Steady, my finger hovered over the call button. But I didn't press it.

Instead, I searched my brain for lingering weirdness—any other strange sensation. And I reminded myself that Alexi's mother—well, his *adoptive* mother—had just died even though he'd done his damnedest to concoct a cure and save her.

How would he feel knowing I needed his help now? Besides, it was the first time it'd happened. It could be a fluke—maybe the only time. With that hope in mind, I hurried the rest of the way to the Grabbit Mart.

The Grabbit Mart on the corner—a little place that existed because of convenience, not competitive prices—was nearly empty. A man worked behind the counter handling the occasional gas customer and glancing at the domed security mirrors out of habit probably more than interest. He nodded at me as I pulled the door closed and adjusted my hat and scarf. Then he returned to swapping glances between the mirrors and the pumps.

I'd only been in once before, so it took me a minute to find their sparse stock of bread. Studying my choices, I was startled by the sudden appearance of someone else in the aisle. Slender, with close-cropped red hair, the guy approaching me had pinched features and a nose that pointed in a way that made me think he was as much fox as anything. I froze, and he looked in my direction as if he'd overheard my thoughts. He cocked his head. "Hey."

I nodded and snagged an anonymous loaf, my eyes stuck on him.

He locked gazes with me and reached over to the opposite shelf. He grabbed three candy bars.

And shoved them into his coat pocket with a sly smile and a look that clearly dared me.

My eyes must've widened because as soon as my mouth opened, his smile slid to one side of his face and he whispered, "You wouldn't rat me out, would you?" He tilted his head in the opposite direction and studied me, eyes bright. Taunting. "We all have our little secrets." With a wink he spun on his heel and walked back down the aisle and out the door.

"Dammit." Why'd I hesitate? I took three candy bars my-self and headed to the refrigerator section.

Milk, bread, and candy bars in hand, I set everything on the counter in front of the cashier and paid.

"Want a bag?"

"Yeah," I said, my eyes lingering on the door. I wondered where he'd disappeared to. "Oh, wait." I pulled the candy bars out. "Put those back on the shelf for me?"

"Uh—okay. . . . You wanna return them?"

"Yeah."

"Hold on, lemme do a return." He groaned at the effort even the thought of doing a return evidently took.

"No. You don't have to do that. Just put them back—and leave the money in the till."

He squinted at me, confused.

"Please?"

"Yeah, whatever." He placed the candy bars behind the counter, and I headed for the door. "You meet all sorts of weirdos in this place," he muttered even before the door began to shut behind me. "Shoulda stayed in Farthington. Nice and normal there."

Alexi

Dealing with death, every family faces unique problems. Some war over possessions the dead left behind. Some squabble about unanswered questions and fight out their inner turmoil, won-dering if there was something they still should have done, if there were words left unsaid.

There always are.

My family was no different in those things. We all had

doubts and questions. Worldly possessions came into none of it—they never had mattered when we thought Mother was dead before, so why should they now?

But the unique problem we—*nyet, I*—was faced with was how to dispose of the body of a woman who never seemed to truly exist. Even in life, Mother had been more ghost than alive—at least when it came to open and public government documentation.

Pietr did not want to think about it—not any of it. Having seen his haggard expression after the cure took hold, I could only imagine what it was like to lose two such amazingly important things so close together. I dared not ask him to help. The mere idea of suggesting we get rid of Mother's body, not give her the burial, the respect, she deserved, would be too much for my youngest brother.

I raked my hand through my hair, tugging at its roots; For nearly a month I had not wanted a cigarette like I did now. But Cat found every last one of them and emptied the last of the vodka, saying so many things had changed so fast, perhaps a few more dramatic changes were in order.

It seemed wrong for my little sister to be smarter about life than I was.

Standing before Mother's carefully wrapped corpse, I decided there was nothing left to do but make a call.

"Allo?" a voice rich as the finest cognac said, and I was too easily drunk on the mere sound of Nadezhda again. *"Allo?"* she repeated, this time the cognac slipping away and the word sharpening like the sting of a wasp. "Alexi, I know it is you. Talk to me or hang up. I am a busy woman."

"Nadezhda," I whispered. "I need you—" I coughed and stuttered out a more acceptable truth. "I need . . . *your help.*"

"Of course you do," she snapped. "Everyone needs my help. 'Day in and day out,' as they say. I am a popular girl."

I envisioned her in some fancy hotel, checking her meticulously managed blond hair in a gilt-framed mirror far away from me. Far away from the trouble her associations with me brought.

The distance did not matter so long as she was safe. I had to remember that and believe that.

"Alexi," she said again. "I have no time to chat. If you have merely called to hear the sound of my voice . . ."

"*Nyet.*" It was true, but it felt like lying, listening as intently as I did.

"*Horashow.* Then what is it, boy?"

I blinked. She did that sometimes, called me *boy* though we were nearly the same age. *Sometimes*, she had joked to me at a party in Moscow, *you surprise me by being the more mature one.* I sighed so deeply she had to hear. "She is dead, Nadezhda."

"What?" Although she felt a million miles away, I heard the shock as plainly as if I had seen it on her face as her breath brushed out in surprise. "Who?"

"Mother."

"Oh, Sasha—dear, sweet, Sasha . . ."

The back of my throat burned at the shift in her tone and attention. I coughed to keep from strangling the words fighting to get out. "It will be all right," I assured her, though I knew I was bluffing.

"Shhh," she soothed. She knew I was bluffing, too.

Damn it.

"Breathe, baby."

But how could I when she was being so gentle with me? Damn the woman. I needed guidance, not tenderness. I needed logic and calm, the cool of rational thinking and emotional distance.

How would she respect me if I let grief overwhelm me and I buckled now?

"I simply need to know how to . . ." My breath caught, wedged around a lump swelling in my throat. ". . . how to dispose of her body."

Nadezhda sighed.

I pushed ahead, using the awkward momentum the words helped build.

"She cannot be found . . . by anyone. . . . Is there a place? A method?"

"*Da,*" she whispered. "There is always a method."

Carefully and quietly she explained the most efficient way to destroy all physical traces of the only woman who'd truly known me and still loved me—knowing all.

Jessie

I shoved the milk into the fridge and tossed the bread on the counter. Knowing all that I did still didn't help me know how to help Pietr. I wanted to go home—back to the farm and the horses and the regular rhythm of what some people in Junction still called "city folk" presumed was a simpler life.

Normalcy. The sweet lure of an average life.

I wanted that. And *now.*

But I couldn't leave because the thought of going home so soon after Tatiana's death made my stomach twist. I'd be abandoning Pietr.

And I couldn't do that.

But I was no good to him as some shadow occasionally

wrapping its arms around him and muttering soft and soothing noises. My contribution to his happiness was utterly
lame. I'd lost my own mother and I still didn't know what he
needed now that he'd lost his.

Propping my elbows on the counter, I rested my head in
my hands. It felt heavy—oddly foreign. Maybe something
more was going on inside some deep recess of my brain. . . .
The hairs on my arms rose in warning. Fumbling for my phone,
I considered calling Sophie. Maybe she'd had some weird vision
thing, too. . . .

The phone rattled in my hand.

New Message.

Dad.

I returned the call. "Hey."

His tone made it clear that my greeting didn't mask my
worry. "How's everyone holding up?"

"As well as can be expected?"

"Come home, Jessie," he suggested. "You can't do more
than you've already done."

"I know . . . but . . ."

"Would a curfew help? I can make one right now."

I'd never really had a curfew—I'd never been enough
trouble or been *in* enough trouble to need one. But that'd
changed. Like everything else. "No, I don't know what'd help.
But I need to stick around a little longer. I'll have Max or
Alexi drive me home tonight, okay?"

Dad got quiet, considering my suggestion. "Give me a call
when you're on your way."

"I will. I love you."

I slid the phone back into my jeans and looked up the
staircase and toward Pietr's bedroom.

Resting my hand on the banister, I wondered what I still

needed to do before going home. And I weighed that against what I *wanted* to do with my boyfriend in order to forget everything else.

To just forget for a little while . . .

I felt so stupid. I should have been exactly what he needed. And putting together the need and the want, I wondered if I could successfully combine the two and provide Alexi with the time he'd quietly requested for the removal of Mother's body.

The Queen Anne–style house echoed with emptiness even as full as it was with inhabitants. Amy was tucked away in the basement; Cat had disappeared upstairs to her room; Alexi stood in the parlor as silent as the unmarked grave he prepared to fill; Max sat at the dining room table staring at the same glass that had briefly held the cure—the glass no one wanted to touch again.

And me?

I was as hesitant and heartbroken as the rest.

Pitiful.

We had been so close to success. . . .

A shiver shook through me, and I forced my feet into action. As quiet as things had become, I had the nagging sense trouble wasn't far away. And that at least part of that trouble was the filthy film lingering over my brain with Derek's fingerprints all over it.

Marlaena

I vaulted over a broad rock dusted with winter's white and gasped at the way my shoulder clenched on landing. Locking my jaws, I fought past the pain and whipped down a deer trail, my pack close behind.

Dodging between the bare bushes, my sluggish humanity stuttered over the first lines of books I loved. J. K. Rowling's Dursleys would've gotten along great with my parents—though Phil and Margie were as much my *parents* as the Dursleys were Harry Potter's.

Yeah, so, not at all.

That book kicked off a great series, but a totally unrealistic one, if you asked this particular werewolf. Far too optimistic. No one ever came to *my* rescue. Living under a staircase? I'd be left there until I clawed my way out. Suffering with whiny, neglectful relatives on a windswept island? I'd be abandoned to my fate until I built my own damned boat and sailed away.

But I was no *chosen one,* so who'd blame a hero who never arrived?

I was nothing special. Phil and Margie made sure I knew that.

Springing across a busted tree trunk, the breeze ruffled my fur, leaves crunching crisply under my paws as I landed on the log's other side and I spun in a tight half-circle, determined no one would spot my weakness or my pain. I paused for a breath and a few heartbeats on the pretense of watching them catch up. Absorbed by the sight of them—beautiful beasts, glorious monsters—*my pack*, the throbbing in my shoulder dulled to a slow pulse of pain.

They were my family—spelled with a capital F. And they were *so* much better than blood.

The adults—Justin, Terra, Tembe—came first, trailed by the pups, all younger than I was: Kyanne, a tawny thing who in her human skin was blond and dreamed of being an author—the stories she'd write after time with us; Noah, one of the few boys; Darby, a polite redhead sparking with attitude;

Londyn and Jordyn, the blond twins; Beth, the youngest, a clever brunette; and Debra, whose fur was as springy as her coffee-colored hair.

Bringing up the rear was Gareth. Almost always last, he made sure everyone was taken care of. He'd quoted some Scripture to me—something about the *last being first and the first being last*. . . . It hadn't been a first line of anything and certainly not from any of *my* favorite books. I'd barked out a laugh saying I was looking out for *number one* right now and I'd worry about how things'd reorder themselves later.

He hadn't been impressed.

Gareth muscled up beside me, carefully keeping a few inches between our heaving sides. He stretched his legs, each ending with a broad paw that swallowed the ground when we ran. His dark coat was full and thick—a chocolate color as rich as his human voice and as smoky as his howl. That coat of his was so luxurious you'd never guess the structure of the wolf beneath—how much lean muscle and broad bone built him up.

He was all powerful shoulders and sleek hips, with a thick neck, heavy snout, and ebony nose, his nostrils flared to drink in the night. And his eyes—lavender snarled with red—glowed with the promise of something like the sanctuary I sought.

He was by far the prettiest of all of us. And the most noble. Amazing what a little prison time had done for him.

Gareth paused beside me, knowing the others panted nearby, for a moment watching anything but us and our classically awkward interactions. Boldly he stepped forward and nuzzled my shoulder. I blinked and snapped my teeth at him—the only warning, and *answer*—he needed. I was still wounded. He whined so softly only my ears caught the sound, translating it to *sorry*, and I hardened my heart against him, reminding myself he'd show the same affection to any pack member.

I couldn't afford to mistake his tenderness as anything else but Gareth being Gareth. And giving to the extreme like some saint.

Sainthood was only good for two things: pissing me off, and making the saint a target for sacrifice.

I stared him down and counted the milling wolves. Twelve of us jumped that rotting log—only one was still absent.

Gabriel. No angel.

I tasted the air, skimming their scents and appraising their vitality. Everyone was in good health. In good spirits? What could be expected when you were running for your life?

We were tired. Frustrated. Above all: hungry.

Raising my head, I howled, my heart thumping faster when they joined in without question, making a wild and richly raucous chorus.

The rumble of a car pulled me back from our music-making, and with a snarl I pressed my nose to the ground and snapped up Gabe's trail. Together we plunged into the sparkling and spinning flurries.

Alexi

I had done well, considering. I glared at my hand as it shivered like a panicking animal caught in a trap. *Stop shaking.* It shook harder. Shoving it into my coat pocket, I looked toward the house, the porch and turret shrouded in a swirl of growing snow and gathering gloom.

A shadow moved, darkness smeared over darkness, and

Max appeared, cradling Mother as carefully as if she slept in his arms. The car's trunk glowed in the dark, and I watched him lay her in the back, careful to not knock her head against the trunk's edge. He hesitated, staring, as I slowly closed the trunk, shutting Mother away in darkness.

"I should come," he said, his voice as rough as the stubble that marked his jawline.

"*Nyet.*" Max and I might war over little things, but regardless of the fact he tried to kill me once—and nearly succeeded—I did not hate him. So I would spare him this if I could. "*Nyet.*"

"You cannot do it. Not by yourself."

I glared at him, wondering if the cure had dulled his superior night vision. Could he read my eyes even now? I considered the task and my abilities.

"Alexi. I am right. You hate it, but you need me to come along."

He was correct. On all counts. Mother was a . . . How could I say it without lessening the fact it was *Mother* in the trunk of the car? A burden? *Nyet.* A difficulty? Never. A . . . I struggled to put a name to it until it occurred to me that Mother wasn't involved in this at all. Not anymore. Mother was gone. This was her body—something her soul (presuming such things existed)—had shrugged off.

"Sasha." He invoked my nickname as only Max could: like a boy who still looked up to his big brother. The same way he used to say it when we were all just little scraps of flesh with no idea of what we were or what we were destined to become.

"*Da*, Maximilian," I conceded. "Will Pietr . . . ?"

"*Nyet*," Max assured. "Jessie has him—*occupied*—in his room."

"Lucky Pietr," I muttered, sliding into the car and trying to not think about what we were going to do. And where.

"*Da,*" Max said with a sly grin that somehow still came easily to him. "Lucky Pietr."

CHAPTER THREE

Jessie

Lucky me, I was alone with Pietr. In his room—one of the locations my father still held as taboo when it came to where Pietr and I spent our time. And yet, lucky Dad, nothing was happening regardless of location or proximity.

I wanted to scream.

Although I'd been sent to distract Pietr, just being close to him was distracting *me*.

He'd crawled out of his bed (and a bit of his depression) and made himself busy. *Already.* Maybe this was denial: Counselors say grief comes in stages, and denial is one of the earliest. I didn't care, because Pietr—climbing out of sorrow so fast—was amazingly encouraging.

But even as encouraging as it was, there was still something odd about Pietr after the cure—something softer, something quieter, something . . .

Less.

What if the alpha wolf had been such a big part of Pietr's makeup that removing the wolf reduced him to something much farther down the food chain?

Something simply human.

"I do not know if I can respect a school that believes we have such a great need for upper-level math," Pietr muttered, bent over the papers on his desk. "What time is it?"

That question—asked with increasing frequency—shook me. Pietr had been born with an internal clock that began ticking obnoxiously in his ears with his first full change. To know that his last change deafened him to it—or wiped it out entirely—was frightening. But on the edge of his bed, my fingers twisting in the bedspread, homework and the time was far from my mind. Pietr—*alone*—was the only thing on it. "Seven . . . ish?" I guessed.

"Seven-ish?" he snorted, and pulled a watch out of his desk drawer. A watch I'd never seen before.

"Is that new?"

He nodded, examining the small clockface. "Seven-ten," he said with a tone just short of authority.

"You're not sure?"

He rubbed a thumb across the glass. "*Nyet,*" he admitted. "It says seven-ten . . . seven-eleven now. But I don't feel it. I see it, but it doesn't seem real. Like time no longer connects to me. It sounds crazy, *da?*"

"Not when you consider recent events." Like the fact werewolves existed. And I'm dating one. Well, I *had* dated a werewolf. Now I was dating just some normal guy.

Nice and normal. No prickle of heat between us when he pressed his body to mine, no roasting breath heating my lips when he paused just before a kiss . . . *Snap out of it, Jess.* "How much math do you have?"

"Enough that an apt description of the quantity should include the phrase *bordering on the ridiculous.*" He shook his head. "There is no need to drown us in numbers."

I nodded, watching him. "I guess it depends on what you plan on getting *into* . . . ," I whispered, watching the back of his strong neck where his hair ended in slight curls.

"What?" he asked. He pinned me with blue eyes that pierced straight to my heart even as they sent it racing. *Think, Jess.* But the hair that usually tumbled into his right eye was swept back, giving him a very studious look. A look that made me want to do things that'd mess it all up . . .

His fingers drifted along the chain at his neck and he suddenly sat up straighter. "I don't need this anymore, I guess," he mumbled, slowly unfastening the necklace that had been specially designed to keep his animal magnetism in check. He set it on the desk beside his textbook. "Any different?" he asked, his eyes soft, his voice sweet.

He knew I hadn't been affected before, but now my reaction seemed even more important. I cleared my throat. "No. You're still Pietr to me. My beautiful Pietr." I leaned forward, but he'd already turned back to his jumble of books and papers.

Dear. God. How had he turned me into *this?* Unable to focus on anything but *him* . . .

His mother had just died, and I was imagining touching him. What sort of monster had *I* become?

I straightened on the bed and folded my hands in my lap. *Focus.* He'd been slow to touch me ever since he'd made his final transformation. Modest—*shy.* Something between us had changed, something I wanted to fix. "What are you go-ing to do—after high school? Maybe math will count."

His mouth quirked in a smile. "Math always *counts.*"

"So what do *you* want to do?" I asked, feeling the heat rise in my face as my eyes raced along his body, observing his long, lean lines.

"After high school?"

"Yes. *That's* what I was thinking. Precisely. What do you want to do after high school?" *Not right now. With me. In the quiet privacy of your room.*

"I hadn't really thought about it. Until recently"—by which I knew he meant after the cure—"the idea of a career, complete with eventual retirement, never crossed my mind. Things are different. *Da,*" he added, a note of sadness creeping into his voice. "Very different. I have a future to plan for."

I used that as my cue. Pushing to my feet, I crossed the floor and stood before him in two quick steps, my hands on his muscular shoulders. "I hope you mean a future with me . . ." I breathed deep, qualifying my request. ". . . at least for a while." I didn't want to sound desperate.

He wrapped his arms around me and pulled me onto his lap. "Of course I want my future to include you. You're the reason I *have* a future."

Winding one arm around his neck, I played with his hair, letting the contact calm me and hoping it soothed him, too. But he took my hand in his own and drew it back around to his front, kissing it gently.

Just once.

"Don't *you* have homework?" he asked.

With a groan, I stalked back to the bed and my book bag.

"I'm sure there's something I could be doing," I muttered, rummaging through its contents.

I pulled out my history text and flopped onto the bed with a sigh. Alexi said to keep him occupied—he didn't specify how. And although I knew how I *wanted* to occupy Pietr, doing my homework and watching Pietr do homework at least still accomplished somebody's goal.

Marlaena

My goals changed with the region's weather. Wincing, I shoved Tembe into the bushes and dove after him as the car rolled by, its headlights dividing the night sky from the inky road with burning white light. Laughter and curses poured from the car's open windows along with a heavy bass line of some metal tune. The sharp scent of alcohol—and vomit—scalded my nose.

Grain alcohol. Nasty shit. It'd blind them faster than anything else they could do in a dark room alone. . . . The last thing we needed was some group of dumb-ass country teens reporting seeing a pack of large wolves roaming the mountains.

That'd be enough to get every guy with a gun on our tails. We should have never come this way. What the hell was Gabriel thinking?

I nipped Tembe, making him whine and focus. The noise of the car faded into the distance, and in the dark I saw the hot red glow of wolf eyes as the pack ringed us. Only my saliva softened the sound of my snapping teeth, and I sucked down the acrid scent of Tembe's growing fear.

Fear made me hungrier. Reminded me we were all either predator or prey. The difference was marked by a narrow margin based on choices: smart or dumb.

Whimpering, Tembe flopped to the ground, sending snow up in a puff of white. Belly up and throat exposed, he submitted.

Totally.

His will? *Mine.* His life? Mine to take or leave. Life or death. *My* choice.

Mind-blowing. Knowing where I'd been—how helpless I was . . .

The sharp sound of a train in the distance flattened my ears and pulled my lips away from my teeth, wrinkling my snout in a growl as my tongue curled.

A breeze tickled my fur, and I spared a glance for the valley below, filled with a bustling town that crawled awkwardly away from its heart, stretching toward the crest of the mountains. The difference between where I'd been two years ago and where I'd led my baker's dozen werewolves was startling.

From deserts and plateaus in the southwest where grit ground our fur short and left us chasing lizards and holding up liquor stores to some white-bread town where the junction of railroads lay and where ice crusted sharp and fierce between canine toes like glass from a busted windshield prickling in a driver's hair. Every place brought its own special pain, its own subtle needle prick to tender flesh.

The heat pumping through our veins and singing through our blood combined with our thick coats and temperature-moderating paws shielded us from the worst of the northern wind and weather.

It only stung at unexpected moments . . .

. . . and reminded us we were still alive.

I'd take this particular prick of pain over the pricks we'd encountered two states back: men calling themselves *hunters*. Outwitting them was much more a need than a want.

Sure, we were trouble—but *a plague upon humanity?* Words like that easily offended an entire pack.

Sticks and stones may break my bones, but names will never hurt me. . . . Bullets, though—bullets that sizzled in the skin and sat too long in a busted and burning shoulder—they could kill. My shoulder ached with more than memory. Chicago had sucked for me.

My teeth snapped shut like a steel trap on the ruff of fur at Tembe's neck. He yelped and whined and wiggled in my grasp. I shook him so hard *I* hurt, reminding him *this* pain, instead of death, was the extent of my mercy.

Life was a bitch. And for them, I *was* that bitch. For us, the wolf: the pleasure, the pain, the fear, and the exhilaration of the change—*that* was the Way.

Alexi

My hands trembled holding the phone, but my breathing steadied and my pulse slowed, the sound of Nadezhda's voice filling my ear. "Did you find a way?" she asked, her voice yielding and worried.

"*Da*. She is gone."

"She was gone long before you made her body disappear, Sasha," Nadezhda assured.

My voice caught, dragging roughly across my question.

"Where are you?" I could hear her, true, but I wanted to see her, hold her. Although remembering how she'd held a gun to my head during our most recent carriage ride together cooled my baser impulses.

"Does it matter?" she wondered aloud. "I am too far for you to see me easily and too busy to make more time than what we have now—on this phone call."

"So you will not give me your location?"

"You know I cannot." But something in her demeanor changed, becoming nearly wistful. "Have you ever heard the nightingale sing outside your bedroom window?"

The nightingale . . . She was giving me a hint to her location.

"*Nyet.* Tell me what it is like."

"They can be very loud if they are lonely," she said, her words as soft as the snow falling outside my window. I imagined following the trail of that voice all the winding way to wherever she rested without me. "They have a journey they make every year. I do not know why this one still sings, and stays—he should be gone—he should have given up finding love this year."

"He is a stubborn bird?"

"*Da.* Stubborn, or persistent. I like to think of him as the latter."

"Do you think he will find his love?"

"Persistence should pay off, *da?*"

"*Da.* In a perfect world."

But our world was far from perfect.

She wished me good night, knowing I did not know what to wish her—was it morning, afternoon, evening, or something stretching in between where she was? Was her day coming to an end or a new beginning?

I set down the phone and laid my head on my pillow. Leaving Mother's body as we did—losing her so completely—seemed the fiercest of endings, but doing precisely *that* I prayed would somehow give us all a new beginning.

CHAPTER FOUR

Marlaena

In the beginning God created the heaven and the earth. And the earth was without form, and void; and darkness was upon the face of the deep. Straining even with my superior night vision to avoid running into bushes and brambles, darkness surrounded us. Perhaps *this* was the void.

And maybe, beyond it, there'd be a new beginning.

I wanted that. A fresh start where no one knew our names, our faces, or our pasts. Where we could be what we wanted to be. But those were things all the members of my pack wanted. I might be alone in many ways, but I wasn't alone in wanting a redo.

The B-I-B-L-E, yes, that's the book for me . . . A snatch of the Sunday school song invaded my brain. *The Bible* was the book I should have been most familiar with because of Phil and Margie, but, thanks to them it was also the one I avoided the most.

A year after I'd run away a man in a bookstore pressed a copy into my hands after catching me trying to steal *The Catcher in the Rye.*

"Do you know what book is most frequently stolen?" he asked, his eyes solemn as only the faithfuls' could be.

"*The Joy of Sex?*" I'd quipped.

But instead of shouting at me, he simply took *The Catcher in the Rye* from me, stepped across the aisle, and gently nudged the Bible—King James Version—at me. "The Good Book," he whispered as if imparting some big secret. He corralled me toward the cash register and set both books on the counter. "Please ring these up," he instructed the girl watching us with great curiosity. "At some point everyone wants answers. At some point everyone wants a bit of grace, a bit of peace. And forgiveness. That's why people steal the Bible. They'll commit one more sin to gain the knowledge to be rid of a lifetime of sinning."

He paid for the books and set the bag in my crossed arms. "Go," he instructed, "and don't come back until you've read and understood both."

I flipped him the bird and left the store. But the bag was heavy. And for some reason I thought back to all of the books I'd stolen. All the knowledge I'd sucked down in rebellion seeking something I doubted even existed—but something he seemed to know the location of with certainty. He understood the need for sanctuary: something it seemed no one and no place could provide for me yet.

But maybe that could change.

Gareth loped up beside me, his look assuring me that everyone was fine—and that he was checking up on *me.*

I clenched my jaw against the lingering pain in my shoulder and lengthened my stride, giving him a challenge as we dodged and wove our way through the trees lining the mountain's top.

As much as I wanted sanctuary, safety—*security*—I knew enough about life at twenty to know *I* was the only one I could truly depend on.

And sometimes even *I* let myself down.

If there was a rescue to be had—figuratively or literally—it would be made by me. I had no one else to depend on. The pack understood that. They recognized my independence—my dominance—and knew that if I could somehow save myself, I would do my damnedest to save them all, too.

That was why we all worked so well together. They understood me.

They wanted and needed me.

And because of that, I needed *them*.

Sometimes my depth astounded me. Mostly there was so little depth to me I was the wading pool of personality: shallow and easy to get to the bottom of. I had to give credit where credit was due, I thought, glancing at Gareth. Any depth there was to me was in part—*in large part*—due to Gareth's late-night talks. Or Gareth's stories told around the campfire at any odd place we stopped along our way to wherever.

All *his* tales had some deep meaning or moral.

All *mine* came with a punch line or a lesson from the school of hard knocks. Gareth had only been enrolled in *it* a few years—*I* was born into it.

A sudden dip in the ground and I stumbled before catching my stride. But it was enough Gareth noticed. He looked at me, eyes narrowing. I ignored him and kept my focus ahead. He swung his heavy head toward me, hinting I should slow down, maybe stop.

I pushed on. Sped up.

He turned his face back to the path ahead, settling into the rhythm of our run.

Then he lunged in front of me, cutting me off, and I plowed into his ribs with a *whuff* as the breath tore out of me.

We tangled on the pathway, our packmates swarming around, nudging us with soft noses before stepping back and whining softly. They shifted their weight from side to side, flared their nostrils to try and smell some clue they couldn't see or hear, and watched us with great curiosity.

I came up fighting, my teeth filled with Gareth, my growl the rumble of a Harley. I bit, I tore. His fur littered the snowy ground, and I spattered the white by our paws with bursts of bright red, my snarl bubbling through the coppery taste of his blood.

The pups plowed backward into each other in surprise.

But Gareth just stood.

Still.

Stoic.

Shit.

I froze, the growl still rattling along the length of my spine.

Nose-to-nose, puffs of cocoa-colored hair floated on the breeze around us like fuzzy clouds.

So surreal.

Gareth tossed his head, looking over his shoulder and down the waiting trail.

He wanted to *lead?*

His eyes drifted to my sore shoulder and I realized the pain I saw in his eyes wasn't him hurting from my attack—it was him hurting *for me.*

Damn him.

Me? Follow Gareth? The wolf I'd just attacked? We had no alpha male in our pack—though Gabriel was hungry for it—Gareth had never wanted a leadership position of any sort. He'd been fast to turn down any hint I made—and quick to question my every move and plan.

He was my conscience, he once joked.

As if I didn't have one.

Phil and Margie would have agreed with him wholeheartedly.

And why not? That Bible I'd been given? I read it cover to cover. Nothing but smut, violence, and vengeance. The afternoon soaps Margie lied to Phil about watching had nothing on the content of The Good Book.

It was as dirty as Shakespeare.

When Gareth saw me reading it, he asked: "Just what did you think of it?" I slapped it into his chest. "I think it oughtta be yours."

I went back to reading *The Catcher in the Rye, The Bell Jar,* and *The Merchant of Venice.*

And anything by Poe.

There was a balance we somehow maintained—me being embittered and cynical, and him being . . . Jesus with dreadlocks? All at once peace, love, and forgiveness—like some savior with fish and loaves, and yet there were moments he was still all claws and teeth: Jesus in the Temple.

I licked my lips, tasting him on my tongue.

Following him was laughable, but feeling the muscles spasm from my shoulder to my back, following seemed somehow smart. Besides. Who would question if *I* decided following him was best?

Ironically, the only one who'd outwardly question me changing my mind was Gareth.

The only one who'd *outwardly* question. Gabriel was a different matter. But that quiet dissenter was nowhere in sight.

But. I couldn't just *give* him power.

So I lunged, snapping and pushing, shoving him down the trail, pushing him into a punishing run, nipping at his heels, dogging his every turn. Only he and I knew what was really happening as the pack fell in behind us.

I itched, handing over so much control, but Gareth was right: I needed to take it easy. Heel and heal up.

My stride slowed, wolves slowly overtaking me. A bumbling and confused mess, they passed me by, each dipping their head briefly to note my frustration with Gareth. Or perhaps checking to see if they could find the weakness—the fault or flaw to exploit later. . . .

No. I reminded myself that wasn't the way of my pups.

Even if I suspected it might be Gabriel's way.

But, as Gareth so frequently pointed out, I was the one in control. The decisions I made could come back to bite us, too. But they were always decisions that allowed our survival. I'd been a teenage miscreant. A vandal, a thief, and a liar. But I did it all to survive and keep the rest of us alive, too.

I hung back, watching for stragglers.

And trouble.

The hunters were bright, deadly, and impossible to understand. Catch us, try us, imprison us, but . . . there was no reason to come after us so hard and so fast. . . .

. . . and with such a willingness to kill.

Someday I'd turn the tables on them. Payback was a bitch, and I was willing to *be* that bitch for them.

But right now the smartest thing was running. Nose to the ground, Gareth trailed Gabriel—his scent softening as he ran far ahead of us, the falling snow dampening and cooling his trail.

What might lie ahead of us was as much a lure as what lay behind us was a prod.

What if the hunters were closer than we thought?

Jessie

I scouted the kitchen and the little breakfast nook and sneaked into the hallway to get my coat. The fact it was Monday didn't matter. Outside the door's small window and just beyond our small porch, snow fluttered down in large, soft chunks of feathery white.

"You're not going over there when you've got a snow day." Dad's voice made me jump, and coat in hand, I shook it out instead of immediately putting it on.

He stood on the steps, watching me with curiosity. One eyebrow rose in challenge.

"Three and a half inches of precipitation already for our region, with more expected between now and noon," Annabelle Lee's voice added from behind him.

She was always so helpful.

"That just means plowing is already a priority," I retorted.

Dad and Annabelle Lee finished their descent and split paths, Anna heading to the breakfast nook to pour some cereal, Dad making a beeline for the coffeemaker.

He and I shared that particular early morning priority.

He poured a cup of steaming black goodness and looked at me as I stood there in full-idiot mode, coat hanging from my hand like an admittal of my guilt. "Mmm-hmm. Plows may be out, yet," Dad said, casting me a glance over his coffee mug, *"our* driveway—our *long* driveway—hasn't been plowed."

I stared out the door and down the long, pristine swath of white. Damn. He was right. Why hadn't I thought of that?

"Let me guess," he said slowly. "Right now the question on your mind is: 'When must Dad be at work—afternoon or night shift? When does that mean he'll have plowed the driveway?' Are you racking your brain remembering?" he teased.

I turned and spoke through a clenched jaw. "Yes, Dad."

"Night shift."

Something buzzed inside me like electricity at the idea of spending an entire day away from Pietr *because of* snow. It wasn't fair. I wanted to spend time with Pietr—*needed* to spend time with Pietr—especially on the day of the first real snow of winter. . . . I'd promised we'd do so much during winter the night he'd lain dying after the gun fight when they'd tried unsuccessfully to free Mother.

And now winter was here, proven by snowfall, and I was stuck. And frustrated. In every sense of the word.

I never used to need anyone like I needed Pietr. I hadn't dated many guys, and the ones I had never affected me the way Pietr did. I wanted to be with him. Already. Darn the fact I'd never paid attention to Dad's occasional attempts at giving me a snowplow tutorial. The easiest way to avoid a chore on the farm (and I did plenty of chores already) was to be ignorant or incompetent. Who would've guessed it'd finally prove to be a real disadvantage?

Dad set down his mug. "I'll call Wanda."

For once I didn't inwardly cringe at the mention of her name. She'd been a dangerous and daunting figure—a member of a group parading as the CIA but with a much darker agenda. But she'd become more deeply involved with my father than any of us could have ever expected. They loved each other.

And love—even a love I still found creepy because it involved my father and a gun-toting research librarian— seemed to have helped her see the light and make the break away from the company that had employed her and tried to imprison the Rusakovas so they could be used as lab rats.

"I'll have her see if the roads look clear out her way. And I'll plow as soon as I'm off the phone with her. If it's safe, you can go," he assured me.

I ran to him, wrapping him in a grateful hug.

Annabelle Lee rolled her eyes.

Sticking my tongue out in return, I busied myself with the dishes while Dad took the phone, put on his coat, and stepped onto the porch for a little privacy. I tried not to stand close to the little space where our coats and boots rested— the spot between the kitchen and the front door that was much more mudroom than foyer. I wanted to know what Dad said to Wanda nearly as much as I *didn't* want to know.

Nearly.

He was done in nine minutes. Odd how now that Pietr had seemed to lose his sense of timing, mine sharpened—at least when it came to the amount of time Dad and Wanda spent chatting.

He glanced from me to the empty dish rack and nodded approval. "Says the roads look pretty good. So I'll plow. I'll even drop you off if Max or Alexi can bring you home. Sound like a plan?"

"It sounds like an excellent plan!"

As soon as he was bundled up and out the door to plow, I got on the phone to Max, making plans for a ride home.

Marlaena

My stretch ended in a yowl and a yawn, and still fully furred, I peered over Gareth's healed-up shoulder and toward the mouth of the cave. Gabe's head on my hip, he twitched in his sleep, one paw flicking as he dreamed of . . . rabbits? Red-headed women? I slid free of them both and padded to the small opening, ducking my head to look outside.

Snowflakes skittered across the lip of the cave, and outside the world was white and thick with a fresh winter coat. Pure and beautiful.

As unstained as a virgin bride.

If I didn't ruin it, someone else would. And I liked to leave my mark.

I trotted out and took a piss, only returning to flop down on the furry pile of my packmates after I'd fouled up perfection.

CHAPTER FIVE

Jessie

Snow fell in wet clumps, covering the roads nearly as fast as the plows kicked it out to the blacktop's edges and spread their salt and grit behind them. Dad dropped me off in front of the Rusakovas' large Queen Anne and watched me climb the steps to the wraparound porch and wave before entering the house.

The door—which seemed locked and unlocked randomly now—slammed shut behind me, blocking out the crisp and surprisingly cruel brush of winter's fingers. I found myself in the foyer, surrounded by the warm scents of old woodwork and furnishings and the distinct pine forest smell that seemed to be part of the Rusakovas' natural makeup. The pine warred with the other scents now, not as sharp and powerful but sadly muted since they'd taken the cure.

Lower lip pinched between my teeth, I knew much more than just scent had been muted by the cure's power. It seemed all of Pietr's personality—if it could be viewed in decibels— had its volume turned down. The intensity in his eyes, the grace in his movements, the power in his kiss . . .

I tried not to think of it.

Alexi greeted me and pointed up the stairs with a thrust of his chin. "He's up there. Studying," he added in explanation.

"Good god. What do we have to study on a snow day?"

He shrugged. "I have no idea. It seems now that he studies everything."

Everything but me. I brushed my hands over my arms and fought back a belated chill. Before, Pietr would have heard me—or smelled me—coming and been waiting at the bottom of the steps to greet me, whether with good news or bad.

But I'd become the least of Pietr's priorities. And I was determined to change that. I knew I loved Pietr and I knew that Pietr loved me, so it only made sense—in a most logical way—that if I was smart I could somehow regain his attention. I swallowed, fighting down the idea that love and logic seldom worked together.

I am in love with a werewolf after all, a small voice in the back of my head pointed out. *That defies all sorts of logic.* My life, it seemed, defied logic as well.

I started toward the stairs, but Alexi's voice stopped me. "Boots."

"Right," I said, seeing the slush that coated their sides and knowing their treads would be full of the stuff. Hopping, I tugged them off and dragged my socks back up so their toes no longer flopped loose thanks to the suction from my boots. Setting my boots in the nearby tray, I shrugged off my coat and left it there in the foyer, folded and resting across my boots' tops.

Alexi merely leaned against the wall and smiled. "Hardwood floors are miserable to maintain," he said apologetically.

"No problem," I assured him, though I suddenly noticed the worn condition of my mismatched socks. I tugged at my jeans, getting the cuffs to settle lower. As much as I wanted to regain Pietr's attention, I didn't want it to be because he feared I'd gone color-blind.

Cat paused in the foyer to greet me, and Alexi's smile became a smirk, spotting my sorry socks.

Cat caught the look.

"Do you not have something better to do than be a load-bearing structure for that wall?" Cat asked, raising an eyebrow at him.

He chuckled, but the sound didn't reflect fully in his eyes. "And what would that be, Ekaterina?" he asked. "Worry about the dangerous antics of my werewolf siblings? *Nyet*. There are no werewolves in Junction, as Pietr so gladly informed Dmitri. Should I struggle with translations and formulas trying to find a cure for my siblings' abbreviated lifestyles? *Nyet*. Thanks to Jessie, we have our cure."

My stomach tossed, knowing what Alexi still did not: the truth.

Cat looked away.

"What if you paid your mother a visit?" I suggested.

"My mother is dead," he replied, all the joy drained from his voice and expression.

"Your *biological* mother," I clarified cautiously. I had the sudden feeling I was walking on eggshells. "Hazel Feldman."

He blinked at me as if the name didn't even register.

Something hit the door behind me, and both Cat and I jumped.

"Excellent," he muttered, brushing past me. "The newspaper's here. *Now* I have something worthwhile to do."

My eyes squeezed shut a moment as I regained my composure. Alexi still had a mother—unlike Pietr, Max, Cat, Annabelle Lee, and I—and he didn't bother with her. Regardless of the mistake she'd made in giving him up, it seemed somehow wrong to me that he'd just ignore her now that he knew. Couldn't he forgive her? To me, it seemed that, after everything, there was little that was unforgiveable.

Feet dragging, my hand trailed along the top of the smooth wooden banister as I headed upstairs. My feet in slow motion, I reached the top of the staircase.

Pietr's bedroom door wasn't even open.

It was as if he had forgotten I was coming. As if I wasn't as welcome as I had hoped.

I wandered to his bedroom door, giving more attention than ever before to the knickknacks and pictures that helped fill the space between the Rusakovas' rooms that lined the top of the stairs.

My socks crackled, crawling with sparks, static popping between my feet and the slender rug. *Electricity.* That's what I wanted to feel between Pietr and me again—that's what we seemed to be missing.

But how did I get it back?

I reached out to touch his doorknob and saw the electricity arch and leap free a moment before it shocked me.

"Yow," I whispered, looking at my fingertip.

But more importantly than how I got electricity back in our relationship was how I could do it and not get zapped.

Slowly I turned the knob and pushed the door open, again finding Pietr stooped over his studies, every bit the perfect student.

On a snow day.

My mind rebelled at the idea. A snow day. There was something verging on the sacred about such days and the way one spent them. Snow days were meant to be enjoyed—they were gifts Mother Nature gave students to bolster us against the oppressive crush of too many worksheets and projects and days without sunlight. A snow day should never melt away in a fit of studying.

I cleared my throat.

He turned to look at me, his expression of intense concentration sliding into a gentle smile. "You're here already?"

Even at such simple words, my heart faltered.

He glanced at a clock, and a frown line folded the distance between his eyebrows. "Of course," he said with a sigh. "You're right on time."

I decided I was also right on time to change the subject. "So. What are you doing?" I asked, trying to keep the note of reprimand from my voice.

I failed.

He arched an eyebrow, and his smile broadened. "Studying."

"It's a snow day."

"Precisely. It's like a bonus day to get organized and get extra studying in," he explained proudly. "I may even Skype with Smith later and review some notes from a few classes. . . ."

Words bubbled out of my mouth awkwardly. "I'm sorry, Pietr. I won't tolerate this. I've dealt with you dating my sometimes best friend, learning you're a werewolf, your nearly selling your soul to the Mafia, but this . . . Oddly, wasting a snow day with studying is where I choose to draw the line."

"What?" He tilted his head, quirking an eyebrow at me. "*This* is where you draw your line?"

I grabbed him by the wrist and tugged. "Ugh," I protested

when he didn't budge. "What did you have for breakfast—lead?"

"So many things are made in China today . . . it's possible. . . ."

"Shut up, Pietr. And stand up."

He obeyed hesitantly, standing and towering over me, a distinctly amused look lighting his eyes. "And now what?"

"Now get your boots and your coat and we'll take real advantage of this amazing day." I cleared my throat and specified. "This amazing *snow* day."

"Fine," he conceded.

"Where's Max?"

"In his room, I guess."

"Dear god—not studying?" But the thought of Max studying on a snow day was absurd. The thought of Max studying at all . . . "Sleeping in?"

"Of course."

I snorted. We walked up to his room and I banged on the door, announcing: "Up and at 'em—we're going to have a snowball fight to beat all snowball fights."

Max's door opened a crack and he peered out, disheveled and bleary-eyed, his hair a mess of soft rioting curls. "Jessie." He opened the door wider to stand boldly in only—

"Heyyy," I said, ignoring how Max looked in just boxers as he scrubbed a hand across his broad bare chest, ruffling a bit of dark hair. The only other thing he had on was the shorter-length chain he'd worn as a choker—a chain made out of the same material Pietr's had been. And with only one purpose to its construction.

"Still wearing the necklace?"

He blinked and rolled the links under his index finger, his lips sliding in thought. "*Da.* I've gotten used to it," he added a little quickly, watching me. He yawned and leaned forward in the doorway, his hands on the top of the doorjamb, his powerful arms above his head. "You mentioned a snowball fight?" His lips slipped into a grin.

"Absolutely."

"I'll be there," he grumbled, smacking a hand solidly against the door's frame. "Kicking ass is a great way to start the day."

"Kicking ass?" I asked.

He nodded. "I'm coming for *you*," he said to Pietr with a nod and a dangerous glint in his eyes.

Cat climbed the stairs out of curiosity. "Jessie—*pravda*—really? A snowball fight?"

"Yeah—come on, Cat. . . . It'll be fun," I guaranteed. "Max intends to kick everyone's ass," I added as incentive.

"He does, does he?" Her demeanor changed a few degrees, a touch of the sibling rivalry I often saw sparking in Annabelle Lee's eyes lighting in Cat's. "Perhaps I should help teach him a lesson in humility?"

"Max and humility . . ." I rolled the offer around in my head. "Huh. Do those two words even work together grammatically in a sentence?"

But she slipped past us and into her room to change into warmer clothes and join in the upcoming fray.

Pietr's hand rested on my shoulder, a temperate reminder of the heat his body used to harbor. "Are you certain this is the most productive use of our time?"

"There is nothing more productive on a snow day than making time to have fun." I turned to him, pressing my body against the length of his and waiting for a reaction.

None came.

Sighing, I said, "Look at it this way. We take the day off,

relax and have some fun, and tomorrow we go back to school refreshed and more able to pay attention and focus on our schoolwork."

He weighed me with his eyes, considering my words. He could surely see through me—in that moment I didn't give a rat's ass about being more focused on schoolwork, I just wanted Pietr more focused on *me*. But he chose not to second-guess my intentions and simply nodded, following me down the stairs to pull on his boots and coat as he waited for me to make one last stop.

I pounded on the basement door. It didn't open. Instead a loud growl rose from far below—the only invitation I'd get into the space serving as Amy's bedroom now that her father was in rehab and she had no desire to return to the trailer she'd grown up in.

The same trailer where her boyfriend attacked her.

It was a thin invitation, but I did what I always tried to do now and made the most of whatever I was given.

"Morning, Sunshine," I greeted, pounding down the long line of wooden steps.

Her long red hair a mess of tangles, she looked as if she would have been just as well rested if she hadn't bothered sleeping at all. Dark spots like thumbprints rested right below her bloodshot green eyes and shadowed her even more than normally pale complexion.

Unable to help myself, I sprang forward and hugged her. "Hey," I said. "We're going to have a snowball battle. An epic snowball battle. Max has this idea that he's going to kick some major ass."

"So, Sarah's here?"

"What?" I pulled back and looked at her. Maybe she wasn't fully awake.

"You said Max was going to kick some major ass, so I presumed that the major ass had to be Sarah." She stuck out her tongue, and I knew she was more than conscious. She was even briefly verging on dangerous. And seeing that attitude of hers thrilled me—even if the joke came at Sarah's expense.

I laughed. "No, Sarah's not here."

"Maybe it'll be a good morning after all."

"Of course it's going to be a good morning. *I'm* here." I did a little spin, as if my presence were all that was needed to rally a celebration. "Now get dressed. You can't go out for a snowball battle wearing those pajamas."

"*These* pajamas?" She pressed down their front with her hands. "I have *other* pajamas."

"Ugh." I rephrased: "You can't go out for a snowball battle wearing pajamas."

"I can't, can I?" she asked, a note of challenge rising in her voice.

"Okay, okay—you *can*, but you really shouldn't. How's that?"

"Better," she said, a touch of the old fire burning in the depths of her eyes. "I like to think I can do whatever I want," she reminded me.

But as quickly as it had sparked, the fire in her eyes smothered out and I wondered if she'd realized that although she liked to think she could do what she wanted, some things were still too difficult.

"If anyone can, Amy, *you* can. You're a tiger."

"Glad *you* still think so," she muttered, turning her back to me and straightening out her bed. She fluffed the pillow by whacking it hard against the bedpost and admitted, "Most days I just feel like a pussy."

"It'll get better," I assured her, although I wasn't certain it would.

"How do you know? You haven't been through what I'm going through." Crossing to her dresser, she tugged open a drawer so it squeaked in protest. Clothing was shoved aside and shaken out as she rifled through the drawers.

"You're right," I conceded. "I have no idea what you're dealing with. Or how. But by the same token, you understood what I went through losing my mom the way I did and yet your mom is still alive."

"Might as well be dead to me," Amy said firmly.

My fists clenched at my sides. "But she's *not*. She's not dead. But you understood; you felt my loss and my pain even though it was totally different from your own." I glared down at the floor, toes in my mismatched socks twitching in frustration. "Give me a chance," I requested. "I'm *trying* to understand what you're going through. And to support you. The way a good friend should."

She nodded, a stiff yank of her head, keeping her back to me as she meekly pulled off her pajama top and replaced it with a loose-fitting sweatshirt that would have never before found a place in her wardrobe. Amy never claimed she had a perfect body, but once she'd been proud even of her small imperfections.

And certainly proud of her generous curves.

Lots of girls who ran cross-country and track, like Amy did, complained the first thing to shrink was their boobs and the last was "asses and ankles." Amy maintained her shape and flaunted it.

At least she *had*.

But since Marvin's attack, things had changed. Before, she'd worn tight tees, halter tops, and belly shirts, making her a frequent violator of Junction High's dress code; now her wardrobe was mostly turtlenecks and baggy sweats. Before, she'd walked with her shoulders back and her boobs out, enjoying the attention. Now it seemed the less attention she drew to her body—to her *existence*—the more comfortable she felt.

She dug around for socks and sat on the edge of the bed to tug one on. She didn't look at me. "How bad do I look?" she finally whispered. "I didn't sleep. . . ."

"You're fine."

Finishing with her second sock, she stomped her foot. "I thought you were done lying to me."

"I . . ." I shook my head. "You look rough."

Her head lolled forward on her neck. "I know." She heaved a sigh. "He'll notice."

There was only one "he" she could mean. Only one guy she still cared about looking good for. *Max.*

"Look. We'll brush out your hair, put it up in a ponytail. . . ." I grabbed her brush off the card table that acted as her night-stand now, but she raised a hand between us.

"It's more than my hair. A lot more than my hair. It's everything about me."

"He won't say a thing," I promised. Max wouldn't. As much as he blustered and bulled his way through life, he was care-ful around Amy.

Now.

"That's almost worse," she confessed. "Him noticing and not commenting. . . ." She thrust a hand out. "Gimme that."

I handed over the brush and watched her fight and curse her way through the tangles and snarls. She caught my eyes at one point as she panted between tugging the brush through her red mane and paused in a particularly long string of curses. "I could make a sailor blush," she proclaimed. *Proudly.*

I snorted and refused to ask what Cat would think of such a thing.

When Amy was done she seemed oddly satisfied. Like she'd just won a battle with herself. I hoped this one would be the first of many.

"How dark are the circles under my eyes?"

My mouth opened, and she just shook her head. "That bad?" She flopped forward, reaching under her bed, and dragged out her purse to fumble for concealer.

"Don't," I said as she untwisted its cap. "It's okay for him to see. It's better if he knows."

She blinked and swallowed once, then twice, and shakily put the cap back on, tucking it all away again. "I guess all that's over anyhow."

"What? What's over?" I joined her on the bed, wrapping one arm around her shoulders and gently giving her a squeeze, doing my best to ignore the way her body still stiffened at anyone's—even *my*—touch.

"Him seeing me . . . *that* way." She shook her head, red hair cascading around to cover her face.

"What way?"

"As pretty—as *sexy*." She croaked out the last word, her spine going loose as she leaned against me.

I propped her up.

"No," I returned. "Max is a dork sometimes, but he's not an idiot. He's not done seeing the sexy side of you. . . . I think you're the one who's struggling with it, and that's okay."

She sniffled and rubbed at her suddenly running nose. "Oh, god," she said, sucking in a breath, "I'm getting even more disgusting. . . ."

"Stop it," I demanded, giving her a little shake. "You're having more of a problem with this than Max is."

She pulled back and I struggled to unwedge my foot from my mouth. "As you should. I mean, it only makes sense. . . ." I groaned. "Don't give up. Not yet. Max cares enough about you to show you who he really is—was . . . Hell. You know what I mean. That level of honesty: the hey-by-the-way-I'm-a-werewolf level of honesty? The when-they-say-he's-a-sexy-beast-they-mean-it-in-more-than-one-way level of honesty? That's huge." I stroked her hair with a trembling hand. "Don't give up on Max. And don't you dare give up on *you*." I let go of her and stood. "Now get up."

"What?" She looked up at me, her hair falling across her face and obscuring all but a few bits of her damp eyes.

"Get up," I commanded. "We have a snowball battle to fight. To *win*. And I say we take no frikkin' prisoners."

She pulled the hair out of her eyes and back from her face, tying it up in a crisp ponytail with practiced hands. "Fine. I'll pull my ass out of the dumps for a while. Just. For. You," she emphasized.

"Geez. That's *all* I was asking," I teased, rolling my eyes. "Let's go. Cat wants to teach Max humility."

"Is that even possible?" Amy mused. "Have you explained to Cat the concept of setting *achievable* goals?"

I laughed and together we climbed the stairs, shrugged into our coats, pulled on our boots and gloves, and prepared for a battle.

Of epic proportions.

CHAPTER SIX

Marlaena

I shifted forms to start the campfire. Though I reveled in the wolf, the human bits of me didn't always stomach what the wolf greedily gulped down. *Not that there was much food to have,* I thought, looking at the squirrel we'd dug out of a rotting tree and the assortment of nuts that had been stashed by it.

Beth changed, too, seeing the way I retained parts of my wolfskin to appear human except for an amazingly well-fitted fur suit. She mimicked me, adjusting the sleeve length, neckline, and midriff for a more modest look. She might have been the youngest of our crew, having only turned seventeen a month before we found her outside Chicago, but she was a fast learner. As long as she remembered her place in the pack, she'd stay.

But if anyone ever forgot their place . . .

My gaze settled on Gabe. "We can't stay here. We need a

better den." I focused on my index finger and watched my fingernail pinch together and sharpen into a claw. Knowing we were all desperate to eat every bit of it, I gutted the squirrel and skewered it on a pointed stick.

Debra nosed a flat rock to the fire's edge, and I dumped the guts onto it to sizzle as it warmed by the fire.

Gabriel rose and sniffed the air.

"Have a bite, then go," I ordered. "We want better than this. We *need* better than this."

He nodded, and we all scooted closer to the fire and the scent of roasting meat.

Jessie

Pietr had begun constructing a snow fort by the time Amy and I stepped off the back porch. He hadn't gotten far— probably his overthinking of the structural integrity of its architecture (instead of just slamming snow together) took its toll.

Snow still fluttered down around the house, big soft flakes like fat feathers falling from the sky.

Amy and I were barely off the lowest step when Max charged us, hurling snowballs as Cat screamed from her position near the tree and frantically returned fire to cover our stunned advance.

Pietr watched, dumbstruck, and I scooped and balled snow, throwing as fast as I could.

And loving it.

"Pietr!" I screamed.

"Man-up, Jessie!" Max shouted.

Pietr lobbed a snowball at him, and Max staggered back

at the impact. Cat pelted him with a few, shrieking each time she tossed one and Max yelped and dodged away, keeping the tree between his sister and himself as he returned fire.

Amy screamed, balling snow as fast as she could and tossing snowballs indiscriminately at everyone.

Except Max.

"Hey!" I protested. And got a loosely packed snowball to the thigh in response. "Whose side are you on?"

"There are sides?" she asked, hitting me again.

"Yeah—aren't there?"

"I thought we had a whole grand mêlée deal going on!" she called back, taking cover behind Pietr's fort.

"*Grand mêlée?* Are you goin' medieval on our asses?" I laughed.

Amy roared, bending over to hold her sides at the absolute indignation in my tone.

I barreled over the wall of snow and took her to the ground with a *whuff!*

Giggling, we tried to untangle ourselves from each other and each other's scarves. We got to our knees and peered over the wall, watching Max and Cat still heaving snowballs at each other around the tree.

Every time Cat got hit, she screamed. And every time she hit Max, he mimicked her scream so well she shouted at him. In Russian.

Pietr started stockpiling snowballs and I thought back to social studies class and the arms race. My face ached from grinning in the cold.

His back to me, Max made a lovely target. I tore into the top of the densely packed snow wall and freed a nice chunk of snow.

Max stumbled when my snowball thumped right between his shoulder blades.

He turned and snarled out my name. "Jessssie . . ."

"Wuh-oh," Amy squeaked.

Ignoring Cat, he raced straight for us, and I pitched snowballs so fast and hard my shoulder tightened.

Some went wide, but a few nailed Max.

Right in the chest and gut.

One accidentally went a bit lower.

He growled—but didn't slow down.

One of his snowballs hit me in the shoulder so hard I spun partway round.

Stooped and repeating, "Ow, ow, ow . . . ," I felt him rush past and heard the *ooof* as someone lost their breath. I whipped back just in time to see Max barrel over Amy, wrapping an arm around her as he took her to the ground and stopped her fall as fast as he'd started it, dropping into something like a push-up position, boots and one gloved hand holding them both up, one arm keeping her just suspended above the blanket of snow.

"Give her back, you beast!" Cat shrieked, raining snowballs on Max's broad back.

He seemed not to notice; his nose a hairsbreadth from Amy's, he said, "Good morning."

She just stared up into his face, her heart surely pounding after it'd dropped so quickly into her stomach. "Good morning yourself."

He turned his head and looked at all of us. He grinned, a stretch of his lips making him boyish and brazen at the same time. "Battle's over," he announced. "I win."

"What?!" Cat demanded, furiously pressing snow between her gloved hands.

"*Da*, I won." He looked back at Amy and kissed the tip of her nose as he smoothly brought them both back up to a standing position, his arm staying tight around her. "I rescued the princess."

"What?!" Cat socked him with a snowball and he pushed Amy behind him, shielding her with his broad body, and nearly doubling over laughing at his sister.

"Rescued the princess from *trolls!*" he roared, scooping up a discarded snowball. He hurled it at Cat and roared even louder when it pulled her hat right off her head.

"You brute!" she shouted. Her face was frozen and pink in a strange balance of outrage and laughter.

Max looked over his shoulder at his willing captive. "Come with me?" he asked, his voice dropping. Going suddenly serious.

She nodded and he scooped her up easily, sprinting around the far side of the house, away from our curious eyes and ears.

Alexi

I heard them on the porch before I saw them. Setting down my coffee mug and the newspaper that announced "Stray Dogs Become Problem for Junction," I moved my chair closer to the window.

His voice was low—dark.

Hers was soft. And more vulnerable than ever.

"If you aren't sleeping well, maybe you need to do something differently," he suggested. "Change a habit. Get some help."

"What habit? Or help?"

"How you sleep. When. Maybe where?" He paused. I imagined Max was as deep in thought as he could get. Probably rubbing his forehead because that most important part of him—well, not the part he did most of his thinking with, but the part he should engage more regularly—was pounding against his skull at such sudden and intense usage.

"I don't sleep. Not much," she retorted. "That's a habit I'd definitely like to change. I fall asleep as soon as I can. As soon as I . . ."

There was a stretch of silence.

"As soon as you . . . ?"

"As soon as I can stop thinking about him. And *you*."

I shifted to peer between the curtains, catching a sliver of their two forms, huddled together, him in a denim jacket—stubborn against the cold—her bundled in a thick coat, scarf around her neck and covering her chin, knit hat pulled down to cover all the way to her eyebrows. Their breath pooled out in soft clouds of steam, mingling and fading into nothing as winter tore all warmth apart.

He reached an arm out to rest around her shoulders. She leaned back. Away. Far enough that he hesitated and dropped his arm down, sitting back to watch her, to wait for some clue to what he should do next.

Max being awkward yet attempting to be something—*someone*—better was fascinating.

"What do you dream about?" he asked, his voice hoarse.

She straightened, going stiff at the question, and shook her head. "No," she said. "You can ask me almost anything else—but not that."

He narrowed his eyes. "Okay," he said. The next words blurted out. "Do you trust me?"

Amy watched him a moment, knowing the question was

loaded and that no matter how she answered it'd potentially change everything between them.

"Yes," she finally said. "Yes. I trust you. Completely. I want no walls between us. Ever. That's how much I trust you."

"*Da*. No walls. So sleep with me."

She shot back from him, her body language all angles that read like a line of exclamation points. "*Sleep* with you?"

He raised his hands. "I don't want sex—"

"You don't *want*—"

"Just sleep beside me. Maybe knowing someone you trust is right next to you . . ."

"Ha."

"What?"

"You must think I'm stupid. Or easy." She stood, straight and sharp and, placing her hands on her hips, glared down at him.

"*Nyet*," he protested. "Why would you think that?"

"Because guys—especially guys with the sort of reputation you've *earned*, Maximilian Rusakova—don't just sleep next to a girl and expect nothing else will happen. And nothing else *is* going to happen, do you understand? *Comprende?*"

He stared at her, stricken. "Nothing else . . ."

But she turned on her heel and strode away, into the foyer, the door slamming behind her.

". . . *was* going to happen," he concluded. "Damn it."

I sat still as a rabbit waiting for the hunter's hound and wishing I could tell him to go to her, to tell her exactly what he'd meant to before she'd cut him off.

Jessie

I brushed the snow off my coat and followed Pietr inside. "So." I looked him over and did my best to smile. *Suggestively.* "Wanna try and warm me up?"

He nodded. "I'll heat some water for tea."

"That's not what I was thinking about," I countered, putting a hand on his arm. "I was thinking about something we could do *together* that would get my blood pumping." I glanced toward the upstairs as plainly as I could.

"Oh," he said.

"So . . . shall we?"

He nodded slowly and, taking my hand, we climbed the stairs together and headed to his room. The knot I felt in my stomach eased as the door to his room clicked shut behind us. We had our privacy.

The knot doubled when I sat on the bed and he sat a healthy distance away. "Kiss me, Pietr," I said, leaning toward him.

His response was a firm closed-mouth kiss that was cool in every way except the good one. Carefully, he put an arm around my waist and I scooted closer so our hips and legs touched.

Oblivious, he just looked at me. Blankly. I pressed myself to him and pushed my lips against his until he responded.

Awkwardly.

Romance is supposed to be awkward, my mind whispered. *He was just a late bloomer when it came to the awkward, stuttering, and clumsy part of it.*

We flopped onto his bed together, kissing, my heart pounding against the cage my ribs formed.

His lips were too soft or too wet or . . . They never managed to find my own frantic ones as my hands raced across his back.

Or maybe he's just been an idiot savant and now we are more firmly in the realm of idiot than savant. . . .

"Pietr," I whispered, surprised by the need I heard in my voice and hoping it was enough to silence the sniping voice in my head . . .

. . . or to help him home in on my lips. . . .

Damn it.

Then he said, "Jess," and snuggled me into his arms, holding me so politely and carefully, his chin resting on top of my head, that I wanted to die.

And as long as we lay there together—twenty-seven minutes precisely—that was as far as Pietr was inspired to go.

It felt perfectly like rejection—although I knew it wasn't; it was the result of the cure, an effect of the very thing my own blood caused.

Like so much else, this was my fault, too.

So I rolled over and placed my head on his chest and tried to enjoy the slower rhythm of his heart at rest.

When I finally gave up on our time turning romantic and tugged free of his gentlemanly embrace, I kissed his forehead and left the room.

Amy sat on the bottom of the steps, staring at the door to the front porch.

I plopped down beside her. "Hey."

"Hey." She continued to stare straight ahead.

"What's got so much of your attention?"

A shadow moved on the door's other side, and I instantly recognized the silhouette.

"Oh. Not what. Who. What's Max done now?"

"He asked me to sleep with him."

A year ago I would have needed to pick my jaw up off of the ground after hearing a statement like that. Now? I barely stopped myself from nodding. "The . . . *bastard?*"

She glared at me. "He thinks I'm easy."

"How do you know?"

"Why else would he suggest that I sleep with him if he didn't think I was easy?"

"Because maybe he actually meant *sleep* with him? Not *sleep* with him. Like, the passive form of the verb, if there is such a thing, compared to the"—I cleared my throat—"more *active* form?"

She snorted. "So you actually think Maximilian Rusakova, stud of Junction High, just wants to have me in his bed to hold me like some lame body pillow—or teddy bear?"

"It happens," I said with a sigh.

"Really? Max actually means sleep as in *sleep?*"

"Why not?"

"I never thought . . ." She stared even harder at the door and the small window set into it covered by thin and lacy curtains.

As if by her wish, the door opened and Max appeared, pausing on the Oriental rug, his boots shining with snow and slush. He saw her instantly and hung his head, his tousled curls falling into his eyes.

"Hey," she said.

"Hey."

How was it that between the two of them that single word had so much more intimacy and immediacy than I'd ever heard it have used in any other way? The weight of those three letters felt totally different stretching across the air between them.

Amy shifted beside me and tugged at her ponytail. "I may

owe you an apology," she said to Max. "It might just be possible I misinterpreted your words."

Without raising his head, Max lifted a single eyebrow, his eyes darting from one of us to the other and back again as he tried to figure out what she actually meant. "Want to talk about it?"

Amy pulled me close and said in a whisper loud enough for Max to hear, "It freaks me out when he suggests we talk and it doesn't mean he's breaking up with me." Then she turned and looked at him again. "You're not like most guys, are you?"

He raised his head, straightened his shoulders and back, and gave her a cocky grin. "The werewolf thing didn't give you a hint?"

She blinked at him, nonplussed.

The grin faded back to a simple smile, and he cleared his throat and tried his answer again. "Undoubtedly not."

"Good," Amy said firmly. "Because most guys suck. Let's talk."

She rose, pausing to rest her hand on my shoulder. Then she left, taking Max's hand in her own and leading him down the basement steps so they could be alone and discuss what *sleep* actually meant.

CHAPTER SEVEN

Alexi

I sat in the car, my eyes drifting over the large brick building at the opposite end of the parking lot. The sign reading GOLDEN OAKS ADULT DAYCARE AND RETIREMENT HOME was in need of a fresh coat of paint, and what used to be sharp lines of architectural detailing had blurred slightly with time or acid rain. Its window ledges were softened by smudges of snow, but the facility looked respectable.

And I had been here before.

Once to bring home a wayward retiree and once when Pietr called after falling from the second story chasing a kitten and mystifying the onlookers because he walked away with barely any bumps or bruises.

Then I'd returned another dozen times or so since learning my biological mother was a resident. Just to circle the parking lot, look up at the windows, and wonder which one was hers. And if she had ever peered out and noticed a red convertible.

Leaving.

As the sky began to darken at dusk I started the car again, remembering Max had promised to take Jessie home. Pulling out of my parking space, I counted the rows in the lot between the building's entrance and me.

Twenty-two. The same as my age. A dabbler in the paranormal, as I knew Feldman to be, thanks to Jessie's descriptions, would have thought there was some significance to such a coincidence.

I knew better. So I left without meeting her or even seeing her.

Again.

Marlaena

The truck rattled, bits of green flaking off its wheel wells. "Jesus, Gabe. Next time you grab a vehicle make sure it's not gonna shake itself to bits."

"Want something flashier?" he asked. "I've been eyeing other options, but the locals aren't big on sexy cars."

I jabbed a thumb in the direction of a gleaming red convertible leaving the school parking lot.

"There are exceptions to every rule," he noted.

I looked in the rearview mirror. "Got what you need?" The truck heaved and bucked its way to the edge of Junction High's property.

Fictional supernatural creatures abhorred holy ground. Me? I wouldn't step foot on school property. Traditional education wasn't my thing.

Gareth had already signed the appropriate enrollment papers as their guardian. The alpha that always ghosted around his edges made it easy to bluff his way into and out of situations like that.

In the rearview mirror Jordyn and Londyn rested their heads together and peered at me, a smile starting on Londyn's lips and spreading to Jordyn's. The twins were amazing. And a touch creepy.

"Bagged lunches—" Jordyn began.

"Full of preservative-rich foods—" Londyn continued.

"That Gabe acquired for us."

"Acquired?"

Gabe mimicked their lazy smile and shrugged, a movement more innocent than he had any right to portray.

"Got pencils and paper?"

They nodded.

"We need more than supplies," Gabe pointed out. "Instructions."

"Stay quiet and out of trouble. Below the radar. Sniff around a bit. There's more going on in this little town. I don't want us falling into something we can't fight our way out of."

The twins nodded again, but Gabe's eyes narrowed. "When will the rest be enrolled?"

"We'll go in stages. Play things carefully here. More carefully than in Chicago. The last thing I want is to attract more attention or—"

"More trouble," Jordyn concluded for me.

"Exactly," Londyn agreed.

Gabe watched and said nothing.

Jessie

Junction High was swathed in black to acknowledge the latest of what had been dubbed by local newspapers the "Teen Train Track Suicides." The suicide of Marvin Broderick was one of many. If any of the others *had* been suicides. Wrestling with the last textbook wedged in the bottom of my locker, I struggled with the fact there probably hadn't been a single suicide among the list except for Marvin's.

Even that one left doubts in my mind.

Had there been murders? Yes. Probably every death on the train tracks between Farthington and Junction had been the result of one twisted teen.

My head ached just thinking about him and I wondered how long someone that screwed up could maintain a hold on someone's mind. Even after death.

"I can't believe Derek's still missing," someone said to their friend as they walked down the hall. I shoved the last of my supplies into my book bag.

"It's so awful," the other agreed.

I sighed. Presumed missing was the team captain of the Junction Jackrabbits football team: hotshot jock, social manipulator, remote viewer, and energy transferer, Derek Jamieson. A psychic puppet master of sorts. And the guy I had moronically crushed on for years.

But "presumed missing" equated in this case to "dead and *not entirely* gone" since part of him still ghosted through me, skirting my brain and sharing memories. And although my mother had raised me to forgive people, I was finding some of her expectations for me were set a bit too high, considering current circumstances. Derek topped my list of the probably unforgivable.

He had been psychically feeding on both friends and competitors, a vampire of sorts without the need for blood—and most recently feeding on me—his hunger growing along with his other powers. He had also been one of the Rusakovas' greatest obstacles in freeing their mother from a group believed to be CIA. And he had nearly . . . I stood, glancing at Amy, who waited patiently by my locker. He had nearly done to me what Amy's ex had so willingly done to her.

The one thing that made the difference in my case?

The guy who was sure to have wanted to have made the same difference for Amy: Maximilian Rusakova—Pietr's biological brother, Russian-American werewolf, and the guy with the reputation of previously being Junction's stud and number-one player.

Max sidled over, careful to stay in Amy's view and not spook her. Max did that now, taking extra precautions, being calmer and cooler, on her behalf. "Hey," he whispered. Leaning over, he kissed her forehead.

She smiled at him, a hint of what used to be her old self showing in the tilt of her lips before it faded away.

"Yeah, it *is* awful," the other anonymous friend agreed. I turned to take a look. They had stopped in the middle of the hall, the crowd of students passing on their way to homeroom thin at best because of the odd illnesses striking down student after student. "I mean, what are we going to do for a football team next year?"

I snorted and rolled my eyes at Max and Amy. Small-town priorities still overrode reason. It was oddly reassuring. We may have werewolves, Mafia, and all sorts of weird phenomena showing up in Junction, but we still obsessed over the success of our football team.

I shouldered my backpack and looked up and down the hallway. "Pietr?" I asked.

"He'll be here," Max responded mysteriously. "He's just . . ."

Amy glanced at the clock in the hall. "Running late?"

What could I say? Not long since his final change and Pietr had *definitely* changed. Pietr had lost the ability to hear the invisible internal clock he had become so attuned to because it was so rapidly ticking down the time until his inevitably early death.

That countdown had ceased with the taking of the cure. Pietr's life span had increased once more to normal parameters—whatever normal parameters really were. I wasn't the best to ask about normal life spans since my mother's life had been cut short, because of the actions of one of Derek's more amazing puppets.

"Oh, great," Amy hissed, pressing into Max's side. "Here she comes."

Flouncing her way down the hall in a short skirt and heels came my ex–best friend and recent nemesis, Junction's self-appointed Queen Bee and head of the mean girls: Sarah Luxom.

Other than the tiny scar marring her forehead as proof of her involvement in the car crash that stole my mother's life and had threatened to wreck my own along with it, Sarah looked perfect. As always.

She walked straight up to me. "Hello, Jessie."

My lips puckered at the usage of my name. She had called me Jessica for so long now it seemed odd we could get to the point of Jessie. Amy called me Jessie; Max and Cat and their adopted oldest brother, Alexi, called me Jessie; as did my father; his girlfriend, Wanda; and my pesky little sister, Annabelle Lee. To Pietr, I was (and always had been) Jess.

The same name my mother used for me.

But to the troublemakers in my life, I was Jessica. As Shakespeare wrote: *what's in a name?* So accepting Jessie from Sarah's carefully colored lips would take some getting used to. But somehow . . . I looked at her and thought about the night we destroyed the company and watched Derek die. Somehow I thought I could adjust to it, knowing what I did now about who had been pulling Sarah's strings all along.

Like a shadow cast across my brain, he was there, ghosting through me like he still watched my every move. Derek. Even dead, he was still around, stuck in the heads of those of us who had been close enough to catch the psychic backlash of his death throe. That bound us together more tightly than anything now, Sarah, myself, and Sophie: the fact that something of him lingered within us even though his hands could no longer touch us and initiate his powerful manipulations.

"Hey, Sarah," I replied.

"So where's Pietr?" she asked a heartbeat before covering her mouth with her hands. "Not that I'm looking for him—I mean, I *am* looking for him—but just because he should be here, shouldn't he. . . ." Her voice trailed off to a whisper as she looked away, chewing her lower lip. "I'm not looking for him for any *wrong* reason . . . ," she tried, blowing out a puff of breath in frustration.

Amy clicked her tongue, grabbed Max by the hand, and began towing him down the hallway. She looked over her shoulder at me, giving a distinct signal to follow.

"I know," I assured Sarah, seeing how she brightened again. It was just a little white lie—what could it possibly hurt? I had lied much worse recently. Besides, just because I was having trouble believing the big bad bitch of Junction High had finally been cowed enough to follow instead of lead . . . It wasn't a lack of faith in people's ability to turn their lives around and become better—just prudent behavior, right?

Max and Pietr had definitely agreed to the idea of keeping your friends close and your enemies closer. What did you do with someone you could no longer accurately judge? Keeping Sarah under my watchful eye seemed far smarter than letting her be too long out of my sight. Though keeping her around pissed Amy off.

Massively.

Sophia joined us, muttering about some issue with the school newspaper that had somehow escaped my attention as a fellow editor. Again. I nodded, made the appropriate guilty noises, and tried to act like I cared. But after everything I'd survived since meeting Pietr and his family, my opinion about what was truly important in life had changed. Whose photo wound up above which caption about proper study habits on page three really wasn't anywhere on my personal radar anymore. Although caring about the school paper was a wonderfully normal pursuit, I had to wonder if normal was somehow beyond my grasp.

I was briefly jealous of Soph's ability to regain a normal existence.

Maybe it wasn't my destiny to have normal—no matter how much I craved it.

A shout of "Holy crap!" from down the hallway made us all jump.

"Ohhh, god—not again . . ."

We turned in unison toward the noise. By the math wing someone wobbled and—

"I got her!"

—was barely caught by a friend.

"*What* is going on?" I hissed at Sophie. Didn't reporters always have the story?

Sophie twitched, one eye wider than the other. "Just more weirdness," she assured. "We seriously need to rethink the school motto."

The lockers lining both sides of the hall trembled, rattling on their hinges.

"Daaamn—" Amy whispered, transfixed, her hand seeking Max's.

Metal creaked. Every locker door quivered.

Teachers flocked around the student who now convulsed in her friend's arms.

The quivering became shaking.

A radio crackled and the nurse was called.

The lockers flew open all at once with a *clang* so loud we grabbed our heads to cover our ears and watched, stunned, as a barrage of books, papers, magazines, and shrapnel of the school supply variety was vomited free.

Vice Principal Perlson was on the scene, following a crew with a stretcher. Teachers stepped back and began ordering students to "help clean up this stuff" or "get to your classes."

We stood dumbly in the midst of the mess.

Some heroes.

I cleared my throat. "Is this more about the school food?"

A blond head bobbed through the crowd, and I recognized Counselor Harnek snapping orders at Counselor Maloy. If anyone could handle a problem this big, it was Harnek. She'd handled the mess I'd made of two cheerleaders easily enough. She looked in our direction, and Sophie straightened.

The janitor appeared, dragging a huge trash can on wheels and delegating volunteer responsibilities. Yes. Our janitor liked to think the people she chose had volunteered. Only the cheerleaders ever cared to argue.

Sophie, kicking a textbook that had stopped a few inches from her feet, smiled at me. She glanced toward the gradually clearing chaos. "I need to be going," she said softly in apology. "I'm working on this *thing* . . ."

"What thing—?" But I was nearly knocked off my feet by Pietr racing around the corner.

"Jess," he exclaimed, grabbing hold of my arms so I didn't fall backward and take Sarah with me.

Sophie drifted away without answering.

"Hey!" I blinked up at Pietr, smiling as I noticed both of his eyes at the same time: his normally rebellious hair had again been tamed and instead of his right eye being shadowed by a few riotous strands, his hair now framed his face.

My eyebrows rose.

It wasn't necessarily a *bad* look for him—I doubted Pietr had a bad look. . . .

"Uh—what did I miss?"

I shrugged. "An important new equation: convulsing student equals exploding lockers. There was already a test of sorts."

"We failed," Amy muttered, shaking off her backpack so someone's stray paper fluttered free.

Max cleared his throat. "Later," he said with a nod. He led Amy to her classroom's door before pressing one chaste kiss quickly to her lips. She frowned and left me in the hall with the boys.

And Sarah.

"Sorry. I'm running late. Again," Pietr apologized, the words blurring together in his haste. His normally faint Russian accent was more pronounced with stress and he glanced from Max to Sarah to me and back to Max.

Not like the Rusakova alpha at all. I shifted from one foot to the other. "You look different," I commented, heading to the door of my class.

His eyes were wild, but not in the way that spoke to me of his wolfish background. More like . . . He dodged in front of me, almost nailing my shoulder in his haste to open the door for me.

"Uhhh . . . thanks." I studied his face. I cast a questioning glance toward Max and only got a shrug in answer before he turned away.

Sarah grinned vapidly at Pietr and also thanked him for opening the door.

He nodded and followed us into the classroom. Sitting at the desk next to mine, he pulled up one sleeve to check a watch against the clock on the wall.

I reached across the aisle to touch his arm. "Seriously?" I whispered, looking at his wrist. "Another watch?"

"We are not supposed to have our cell phones on in class, so, *da*. A watch."

"*Another* watch," I prompted.

"*Da.*"

I widened my eyes at him.

"The other one did not keep good time."

I stayed perfectly still, waiting.

"I think." He sighed. "I need to know the time," he said sadly. "I no longer sense it, so I need to see it. And it must be accurate."

My lips pressed together, I nodded and turned back to the front of the room just in time for class to start. Class passed me by as I stole glances at Pietr. Pietr sitting still as stone in rapt attention, only occasionally looking away from the teacher or up from his notes to glance at his wrist and check the accuracy of his watch. Pietr, studious and involved in the same classes that months earlier had paled when compared to his adventures in Europe or his powerfully animal-like abilities and aptitudes and his desire to live life fully—to live life fiercely and love courageously—and to do so every exciting and dangerous minute.

Pietr twitched and glared at his newest watch when the bell rang, releasing us from class.

I gathered my things, dumping them into my book bag, and asked, "Is it a little off?"

He frowned, and I knew the answer was yes—well, *da*— before he even opened his mouth to say it.

In silence we left the classroom and were bombarded by the anxious chattering of Hascal, Jaikin, and Smith just outside the door.

Pietr was immediately involved in their conversation.

And I was quite simply stunned.

Words that would've made Sarah's head spin—even when she *was* Little Miss Vocabulary—were being tossed around by the group of them like they were nothing.

Finally the talk of time-space continuums, parsecs, and the anomaly of a sudden surge of graffiti in Junction died down and Smith glanced in my direction. In a very pointed way.

"We're all bright people. We should get together on a weekly basis to play some variety of game. Something that strengthens our strategy and mental acuity. What do you think, Pietr?"

"I think that sounds like a reasonable idea."

Smith rubbed his hands together, a smile on his face.

I wondered if Pietr realized he was being put to a challenge. That a game night to Smith might very well equate to a potential opportunity to show he was mentally superior to Pietr. I stepped closer into the group of them, my curiosity piqued.

"Chess?" Smith suggested.

Pietr shrugged, seemingly unimpressed by the prospect of squaring off against Smith using a chessboard.

"Dude," Hascal warned, "he's *Russian*. . . ."

I turned away for a moment to keep from choking on a laugh. Even I had heard of the legendary chess rivalry between the USSR and the United States. But if your heritage determined your capabilities or your destiny . . .

I paused, considering. My family was a mix of many backgrounds. German? Check. Italian? Check. French? Check. A little Native American mixed in for good measure? Supposedly it got a check, too, along with some mysterious Asian influence from the 1800s. Whenever someone asked about our ethnicity, we jokingly claimed "mutt." If my heritage determined my destiny—if I had no free choice—I would still do okay because my very mixed heritage allowed for all sorts of opportunities. I was as American as Americans got.

And that was definitely okay with me.

Smith's eyes narrowed, and he studied me until I took Pietr's arm and looked away, made self-conscious by his staring.

"A game that encourages intellect and creativity as well as a bit of freedom of expression is D&D."

Pietr tipped his head. "Dungeons & Dragons?"

Smith's smile widened. "Indeed. Have you played?"

"*Nyet*, but I have heard of it."

"Then we must teach you. And the rest of your family. And of course Jessie would be invited as well. . . ."

"*Da*, of course," Pietr agreed.

"Then we shall have a grand and glorious game of Dungeons & Dragons," Smith proclaimed, his small eyes, greatly enlarged by his thick glasses, wide with anticipation. "Friday at seven?"

Pietr nodded. "At our house. I'll e-mail you details."

"Excellent. If we don't see you before then, Jessie, I hope to see you then."

I just snuggled more tightly against Pietr's side and nodded politely as they turned and walked away.

It was then I realized what was bothering me.

Pietr had surpassed settling in as a student and had tumbled right into being content as a . . . My mind balked at the term that kept presenting itself. I swallowed and thought of my frequent flirters club—the smartest and most well-intentioned guys at school. Hascal, Jaikin, and Smith held doors open for me all the time. Not a bad thing. And they took excellent notes (this I knew from having borrowed from the best). And just because they all had their little—quirks . . .

That was it.

My Pietr, the ex-werewolf with special tattoos marking him as a captain in the Russian Mafia, was now studious, polite, and concerned—to the extreme? My hot, dangerous Russian-American boyfriend who'd finally taken the cure I provided had flown right by *normal* on his way to embracing *nerd*.

CHAPTER EIGHT

Marlaena

I'd picked my way down the slopes surrounding the small town to better investigate what Gabe had led us into. And create a little havoc.

Everyone needed a hobby.

Running through town was more invigorating to me than loping through the wooded parks. Racing across streets and dodging down alleys in daylight meant I might be seen—I might get caught.

It kept my feet swift and my senses sharp.

I zipped down side streets and jumped over fences. I prowled yards and dodged down alleys. If the area around Junction seemed relatively quiet at night, it was nearly as dull in the daylight. The most exciting moment came when I was greeted by the shout of a child proclaiming, "Doggie!"

At least, I thought that was all the excitement the town had to offer.

Until I smelled *him*.

Along the edge of town, where one railroad ran, I stopped short. There was a scent I recognized. Not intimately, so this wasn't my family, but the scent of pine was clearly out of place in the nearly naked deciduous forest. *One of these things is not like the other,* my mind sang as I pressed my nose to the snowy ground and I began tracking.

Yes. It was a wolf. Big. Male.

And not running with a pack.

We didn't always run as a pack—I sometimes preferred being alone.

Maybe he was wired the same way.

So . . . I snuffled around, following the trail until it muddied outside of a pool hall on the outskirts of town.

Interesting.

I eyed the place, reading a bit difficult in my wolfskin. JOHNNY BEY'S.

A wolf who knew his way around a pool cue.

I stared at the business hours scrawled hastily on a sign hanging on the door.

We might meet if I started showing up. And if he was *truly* alone . . . A new recruit who understood the lay of the land—such as it was—could be beneficial.

Could at least give me a view of the area beyond Gabe's.

But a wolf who couldn't be recruited . . . ? *That* would be trouble.

Either way, I needed to meet him.

And deal with him.

Alexi

"A family meeting?" Max grumbled. "How very civilized." The last to join us, he scraped his chair out, sat heavily, and glared in my direction.

I ignored his attitude and set the stack of bills and their corresponding envelopes on the dining room table before them all. "We have an issue, you see? All of these bills *must* be paid—in order for us to continue living here."

Pietr and Cat nodded in agreement—but not yet in understanding the crux of the problem or, as my people would sometimes say, *the place where the dog is buried.*

Max just watched me, daring me to teach him something.

"But there is a problem. We have nearly no income now the company has been—"

"Blown to bits?" Jessie asked from the doorway.

I smiled at her sudden intrusion despite our predicament. "You and Amy are certainly best friends—that sounds like something she would say."

"We share a brain from time to time," Jessie confessed.

Amy grinned, then rolled her eyes and said, "Yesss. You can borrow the communal brain for tomorrow's quiz."

"What's a BFF for?" Jessie asked with a laugh. "So. All this . . . ?"

"Family meeting," Max pouted.

Amy patted his head and *tsk-ed* at his grumbling.

"And I wasn't told?"

I shrugged. "I did not think either of you needed to be involved."

Jessie pointed at Amy as if to say, *But she's here.*

"She all but stalks Max."

"Hey, I'm just doing what I do best."

I raised my hands. "Okay, okay. Let us get back to business. We have a serious problem. We do not have the income to continue our current lifestyle—or *any* lifestyle—after next month concludes. We need a game plan."

"Aren't you still . . . ?" Max left the question dangling in the air, giving only a faint hint as to the unsavory moneymaking method I occasionally indulged in.

Americans called it *hustling*.

I called it building a nest egg.

Jessie and Amy pinned me with their gazes. Neither of them knew how I traveled from pool hall to pool hall and card game to card game—there were a remarkable number of both in the area, considering the relatively small size of the population—but then, too, there were numerous bars, an understandable surge of gambling and alcohol following the recent rise in unemployment. I lifted one shoulder in a shrug. "I am a gambling man."

"Remember how he gambled with our lives?" Max added in a way that was both cold and casual. "This way at least he's the only one at risk."

"Unless you tag along," I retorted. "Then the entire establishment is at risk."

Amy looked at Max, the pressure pouring on. "Explain yourself."

"I have not *tagged along* in several weeks."

Her left eyebrow arched, and he raised his hands between them to erect a wall, surrendering. "You need to stay out of trouble, mister," she said, the serious set of her mouth sliding into a slow grin.

"*Then* what will I do for fun?" Max asked, one of his eyebrows rising to match her own as his voice lowered, softening into a faint rumble.

Instantly Amy stiffened, her flirting cooled, and she abruptly spun back to face me.

Max's gaze fell from her face, the arm that had rested across the back of Amy's chair dropped, and he stared at the table, more uncomfortable than I'd seen him act in years.

If Marvin hadn't already been dead I would have *wanted* him dead just for *that* moment—for the awkward space his violence against Amy put between her and my little brother.

I cleared my throat and pushed past the thought. "We must all now pull our own weight—contribute to the family cause and work together, if we intend to stay."

Max leaned back in his chair, his eyelids heavy. "So what do you suggest, brother?"

Before I could say a single word, Amy had turned on him, her head cocked, eyes flashing. "That you get a job."

I nodded, holding back the smile edging at my lips.

"A job?" Max mused. "And what are werewolves—ex-werewolves," he corrected snidely, "good for?"

"Bussing tables," Amy quipped.

"Waiting tables," Jessie suggested.

"Taking tickets or working the concession stand at the theater, or sweeping up in the theater."

"Retail."

"Fast food."

I crossed my arms and watched Max, Pietr, and Cat grasp the seriousness of our predicament. They had never held jobs before, but then, we had never been in one place long enough to hold jobs. I picked at the tablecloth. This might require more paperwork—more forgeries—unless they all worked, as they said, "under the table."

Cat gave a long, slow blink. "Dear god," she whispered. "Retail? *Pravda?*"

Jessie and Amy snorted and said in unison, *"Pravda."*

"I'd offer to try and get a job, too, but I'm as busy as I can be with the farm . . . ," Jessie apologized, reaching out a hand to Pietr's.

He nodded. "I'll keep doing odds and ends at the farm," he offered. "That is a small something. . . ."

"A small something will not pay the bills," I said firmly.

Amy toyed with a fork left on the table from lunch. "I'm living here now, so I should contribute. I think I can get something—maybe even temp work with one of the local agencies."

"Temp work." Jessie nodded. "Probably filling in at Aphrodite, but a temporary gig at a factory's still better than nothing."

"Okay," Amy said with the groan that meant she'd made up her mind, "I'll put in as many applications as I can—hit everything. And you"—she punched Max in the arm, the most physical affection I'd seen her easily display in front of us for quite a while—"will fill out every application I give you. Happily."

"Gladly," he muttered.

"Gleefully," she added.

"Gleefully?" His eyes slid to catch hers and he groaned. "Must it be gleefully?"

"Yes," she said, all serious. "I'm afraid gleefully is the least I'll accept."

"There is something above gleefully?" he asked her, a hint of fear coloring his tone. This was how they played now: carefully. Awkwardly.

But it was something.

"Of course there's something above gleefully," she said, her voice somber and low. She spun to face Jessie, startling her just enough so she jumped in her chair. "Jessie," she hissed melodramatically. "What's above gleefully?"

Jessie's head hit the table in response. "I used up all my words with the lit assignment," she apologized. "I could add Sarah to your speed dial, though . . . ," she offered slyly, her hand creeping across the table toward Amy's ever-present phone.

Amy smacked it definitively, grinning at Jessie's overacted yelp, and whipped back around to Max. "I'm sorry to report that although I am absolutely certain there is something above gleefully, I have no current means—and want no *new* ones," she added over her shoulder to her best friend, "to tell you what it is precisely."

"So I have to take your word on it?" Max asked, reaching up to stroke his stubbly chin in thought.

"Yes. I'm afraid so."

"Then that's what I'll do," he conceded, but the subtext between them was much deeper than a discussion about linguistics and job applications. I had the definite feeling he was promising her something more. That he was promising to take her word on everything—every question he asked.

Relieved by his reply, a certain tightness in her shoulders released and she leaned back in her own chair, peering at Max a moment.

"Excellent strategy, Amy," I congratulated her.

"And I'll help Cat get some applications in at places that'll suit her tastes," Amy offered. "Think clothing stores, Cat," she said with a wink.

"Oh! The shoe department," Cat replied.

"*Da*, there is hope for everyone," I muttered.

Marlaena

We'd been bedded down in the same place for two days when the sharp scent of woodsmoke filling the old house and leaking past its tattered curtains and out broken windows woke me. A welcome smell until my nose pricked and my eyes watered. Uncurling, I stretched and swallowed up my wolfkin side, feeling the fur pull back into my flesh like a million tiny pinpricks that woke my human senses more fully.

They stared at me, eyes stroking along my naked form, some curious, some hungry as I stepped to the fire's side. They'd stacked firewood hastily in the center of the tile kitchen floor and lit it as safely as they could.

"Is there no fireplace?" I asked the group resting with snouts on their paws, my voice still gruff from both waking and the change.

Most of them were younger—timid things I'd picked up along the road, lost, wounded, or abandoned and still shy in their human skins and barely playful in their furs. Shyness was a luxury. The hard fact was the quiet ones had less chance of survival in our world than those of us who learned to be bold.

Gabriel's mouth stretched in a long canine yawn and he changed from the boy in the nearly fox-colored wolf pelt to the man he kept trying to prove he was. He stood before me, as naked as I was, his shoulders back and head held high, green eyes glinting. Bold and as unmarred as he was now, I'd seen him at his lowest—whimpering in a ditch, bullets from his adopted father's handgun riddling his flesh.

We were the lucky ones.

Survivors.

"Flue's blocked—can't unjam it," he explained coolly.

"So building the fire in the kitchen—"

He sat slowly down, his eyes never leaving mine and full of the spark of challenge and hunger. "Allows a better way to circle and enjoy its heat. The smoke can't be helped." He stretched out, lounging—basking—in the warmth and glow of the fire.

It was weird how easy it became to ignore nudity once you'd seen so much of it.

Crouching, I thrust a nearby stick into the fire, holding its tip in the flame until it kindled, fire licking greedily along its end. Standing, I held the burning brand before them. "What does this fire have in common with us?"

There was quiet from my pack as they shifted to forms more capable of speech, some reaching for their scant clothes or the moth-eaten blankets Gabe had rummaged for us.

"Stop," I commanded. "Be not ashamed of your forms, either human or animal. We are made in the image of God— doubly so because we admire both Fenrir, the dark and dangerous wolf destined to devour the sun, and Loki, the light-bringer and trickster, his father."

They paused, hands sliding away from cloth for the moment. At my bidding. My command. Perhaps listening to Phil preach hadn't been a total loss after all. They were hungry for the Word—even if the Word was mainly of my own construction. Wasn't the Bible made by ordinary men supposedly inspired by God? Why couldn't *I* be likewise inspired if it helped empower others?

Where was the harm?

I shook the stick at them. "Tell me: What do we have in common with this flame?"

"Some of us are *hot?*" Gabriel's eyes swept across my form, pausing on key locations that piqued his interest.

I growled at him and shook the stick again.

"The flame is as hot as the fire that burns within us," a soft but steady voice responded, and my eyes caught Darby's—a cute strawberry-blond girl who'd had little of the trauma most of us had endured. I'd found her in San Antonio near the River Walk, tired and hungry, the police chasing her away for begging from tourists. She'd worn out her welcome at the local homeless shelters and was as lost as anyone could be.

Until I found her—recognized her for what she was and brought her to the pack.

"Damn right—what else?" I wiggled the stick again, watching as embers tumbled from its tip to be licked up by the flames nestled a few feet below.

Red eyes glowed from one dark corner, and a voice deep as the noise of the nearby train rumbled out of the darkness. "It burns brightly when tended, but never long enough."

Gareth. The eternal optimist. The man meeting our group's quota for tortured hero.

My mouth twisted into a grin. "So we tend our inner fire—our wolf—and remember that just because life ends too soon it doesn't mean we shouldn't make the most of it. We seize each day. Make it ours. And why is *that*?" I asked them, looking from face to face in the wavering light the fire cast.

"Because the Wolf is the Way!" Kyanne led the cry.

Grinning, I threw my head back, let out a howl, and joined them in the chorus of "The Wolf is the Way!"

I reached into the blaze and pulled out two sturdy branches, thick with flame. Tauntingly, I jabbed the torches toward my wolves, watching them grin and dodge. I stood as straight and tall as I could, watching the flames flicker and creep closer to my hands.

When the tongues of fire were so close the fine hairs on

my hands curled in the heat, I raised the torches over my head . . .

. . . and set the ceiling on fire.

Grabbing odds and ends we ran out into the snow, mostly naked but fully alive—and laughing.

Except for Gareth, who merely raised a heavy eyebrow in my direction and shook his head at the growing blaze. *Wanton destruction*, he'd once accused me of. I strode over to him and, with a smile, I bent over to slowly pull on my jeans.

When I rose I knew his eyes only bothered to meet my eyes—that they never strayed to any other bits of me.

Because between Gareth and me, there was only one of us who was ever wanton. So I laughed again.

In his so very serious and disappointed face.

CHAPTER NINE

Jessie

"Seriously? You're going to play Dungeons & Dragons?" Amy raised an eyebrow skeptically at me. "Why do I feel a need to stage an intervention?"

I laughed. "Well, I'm tempted to agree with the intervention idea, but it'd be aimed at Pietr since he's initiating a family game night and it seems we're going on a quest. . . ."

"I'm so sorry for you."

I snagged her wrist. "Oh, don't be sorry for *me*—you'll be joining in the fun."

"What?"

"You're the one suddenly tossing around terms like *grand mêlée* in the midst of a snowball battle."

"So I'm being penalized for improving my vocabulary?"

I began to drag her toward the dining room as she sputtered out her protests. "I'm really not a gamer. . . . I don't know the first thing about this stuff. . . . This really isn't my thing. . . . I . . ." But her mouth shut when she saw Max sitting next to an open chair.

She shook free of my grip and straightened.

"Hey," she greeted him. "Jessie was just telling me about this quest. . . ."

"Great," he muttered, pulling the chair out for her. "Then you can explain it to me."

"Jessie!" I heard someone call from the other side of Max. Smith leaned around him, waving to catch my attention. "There's a seat open here . . . ," he said, pointing to a spot located conveniently at his side.

Luckily it was also at Pietr's side.

"Thanks," I said, slipping into the chair between the two of them and right across the table from where Hascal and Jaikin sat, fully mesmerized by the existence of Cat—who was looking as nervous as her namesake in a room full of rocking chairs.

Alexi lounged nearby, his chair tipping back haphazardly as he texted on his cell.

"Nadezhda back in the States?" I asked him, noting how intent he was on reading and replying.

He spared me a glance and a grin—all I needed to answer my question. Then he returned to what he was doing.

"So," Smith announced, clearing his throat and rising from his seat, "the first matter of business—"

Amy groaned, *"Business?* Isn't this supposed to be fun?"

"Just the turn of a phrase," Smith assured her, looking her over skeptically. He had a gift for occasionally backhanding someone with a wry cynicism, but I knew he'd keep his mouth shut about Amy.

He knew she was my best friend.

And I knew—god help him—he was still crushing on me. *Hard.*

It was flattering, really, having a guy with a full scholarship to nearly anywhere—based on his brain alone—crush on you, especially when it appeared Pietr had nearly become his geeky doppelgänger.

I did a double take.

Well-combed hair, button-down shirts, downcast eyes . . .

I was sitting between two studious, bright (and decidedly pale, I added to the checklist—Pietr was going to need some light other than what bounced back to him off his computer monitor's screen) guys. One who'd crushed on me since we started our frequent flirters club in the school van taking us to and from our Service Learning project, and . . . Pietr.

And as clever as they both were . . . I would've accepted a less studious Pietr if he'd just returned to studying my lips. Or my neck. Or . . .

I straightened, suddenly warmer than the room should make me. I looked at Pietr. He was looking at a paper. The same type of paper Smith thrust in my direction.

". . . character design," Smith concluded.

I gulped, hoping I hadn't missed anything vital.

The next twenty minutes were a blur while I tried to catch up and fill in the blanks that had gaped open while I'd fantasized about Pietr kissing me. And holding me . . . Maybe Pietr was exactly all he could be as a simple human. Maybe if you wiped all the alpha out of any of us you were naturally left with someone gentle and kind and too willing to please and study and . . .

Focus, Jessie, focus . . .

Dice were rolled, numbers were scrawled on my paper by

a doting Smith, and people began babbling knowledgably—even Amy and Max—about a game I was already struggling with.

Smith seemed a bit disappointed in my lack of focus, but he coddled me, repeating things more slowly—and was he using simpler words?!—than with everyone else.

Dude. I was frustrated, not stupid.

Finally my character sheet was filled out and approved. By none other than Smith: self-appointed Dungeon Master. Where was Amy with a snide remark about the odds of *that?*

But leaning against Max and looking as comfortable as I'd seen the two look together in a while, Amy merely yawned and asked, "What time is it?"

"Ten-seventeen," Max reported as Pietr pushed up a sleeve to check his wrist.

Pietr raised wary eyes at his brother and nodded at the accuracy of his statement.

"Sounds like time to call it a night, boys," Amy said, slowly rising from her chair and stretching. "Some of us"—she reached down and tapped Max's stubbly chin—"should call about the status of our job applications in the morning."

I froze, astonished by how focused she'd become on something other than Marvin's funeral.

Also in the morning.

"And on that note . . ." Alexi tucked away his cell phone, rose, and looked at the character sheet sitting before him. "Am I supposed to do something with this?"

Amy snorted. "Give it to me, Sasha. You're enough of a character. I'll make you into something new and shiny."

"Shiny is overrated." Alexi looked at Smith. "Smith," he said after a long pause that told me he was working on remembering the name, "thank you so much for starting us on what will surely be an exciting adventure of the imagination."

I blinked.

Smith knew a dismissal when he heard one and clambered to his feet, quickly collecting his things. He cleared his throat, managing to get Hascal and Jaikin to look away from Cat. For a moment.

"Oh." They both stood, both apologized, both stumbled over themselves telling Cat what a pleasure it was to meet her . . . and both headed to the door, Smith lingering a moment longer to wish me good night.

"It was a great deal of fun introducing you to the realm of D&D," he said. "I hope we can make this a weekly event."

Oh, god.

Pietr rose and came to where we stood in the foyer. "I intend to set a schedule of that sort," he announced.

"What if you get a job and have to work?" I asked, silently hoping. It sucked to spend a Friday night without Pietr, but if it meant spending a Friday night without Smith's awkward advances and playing a game I somehow missed the point of, I'd send him away.

"I'll make it work," Pietr countered.

Smith nodded and the three of them left, leaving Pietr and me alone in the foyer.

He reached over and gave me a hug, pulling away as soon as I started to relax in his grip.

"You'll make it work, huh?" I asked, looking up into his eyes.

"*Da.*"

I hoped the game night schedule wasn't the only thing he'd find some way to make work.

I waited a few more minutes after Smith, Hascal, and Jaikin had gone and I cleared my throat to get Amy's attention. She looked up from where she sat beside Max, playing with his hair, tugging at individual curls just to watch them spring back into place.

Her lips pursed. "I know," she muttered.

I shrugged. "It has to be your choice. If you want to stay here tonight . . ."

"Sleep all alone," she added, her lips turning down at their ends.

Max leaned back and shook his head. "We've had this conversation."

"I just can't," she whispered. "I don't know why. . . . I trust you, but I can't sleep in a bed with you. Even though I know nothing's going to happen."

He shrugged. "Like Jessie says: your decision."

"I'll pack a bag." She brushed the hair back from Max's eyes and then headed to the basement.

I pulled out a chair and looked at him. "Hey."

"Hey," he agreed, resting his head on the dining room table.

"Are you going tomorrow?"

"To her rapist's funeral?"

I waited.

"You really need me to say it?" He rolled his head so that he could peer at me without lifting it off the table. "Let me say it like this: If he wasn't already dead, I'd kill him."

"You nearly did before."

"*Da.*"

"So you won't go. You won't be there for her."

"I can't. I'd tear the place apart the moment they started saying nice stuff about the bastard." He raised and lowered his shoulders. "I know my limits. At least in this."

I nodded slowly. "We always deify the dead."

"*Da.* Asinine. What is it I've heard Amy say: 'Call a spade a spade'?"

Again I nodded. "So you want to be remembered accurately when you die? Not glorified in any way, shape, or form?"

"*Da.* Let the priest number my sins—at least it will give him material for an interesting sermon. . . ." He smiled at me with a wicked turn of his lips. "I've made mistakes. Bring them up at the end," he rumbled. "I've always done the best I could—*he* didn't."

"What if he did?"

He drew back from the table, his eyes narrow and cruel. "Think before you speak," he warned. "He raped your best friend."

"I know." I reached forward to roll a die that had been left behind in the nerds' scramble to leave. "But what if he was so damaged . . ."

"*Nyet.*" He leaned back in his chair and, crossing his arms over his broad chest, glared at me. "Just because you're damaged doesn't mean you must damage others. You have choices. We all make them every day."

I blinked. "Good point."

"Free will. It sucks because it means we're responsible for our actions. There is no destiny, just difficult decisions."

"That's one way to look at it. . . ."

"I'm ready," Amy announced from the foyer as she dropped a duffel bag onto the carpet. "Heyyy, what's got him looking like Mr. Grumpy Pants?"

"My fault," I said by way of apology.

"*Da*. Free will at work. You have a choice, too, Jessie," he added, rising from his chair to give us each a hug. Amy's was much longer than mine.

"My mother would've wanted—"

He shrugged again. "I'll drive."

We rode in an uncomfortable silence, his words in my head. When we finally got to the farm and stepped onto the porch, he lingered, watching Amy. Worried. "And I will see you back at the house—back home—tomorrow afternoon?" he asked her.

"Yes," she assured him, slipping her arms around him and resting her head on his chest. "Tomorrow afternoon can't come soon enough."

CHAPTER TEN

Jessie

My mother would've wanted me to go. My mother would've wanted me to go.

That's what I kept telling myself standing before the bathroom mirror, fists balled and pressed on the countertop, staring at the brown eyes studying me—eyes that'd turned more red than brown with stress, anger, and tears. I was dressed in my black "Sunday best" as my mother would have joked: a long-sleeved blouse with subtle satin trim and a modestly cut skirt.

I tried adjusting the emphasis of the words: *My mother would've* wanted *me to go.*

Damn it. So why wasn't I already downstairs waiting by the door? The funeral service for Marvin started in forty minutes. People were waiting for me. Downstairs my father was probably already standing by the door, watching Annabelle Lee as she put her coat on and braced against winter's chill.

And Pietr would be there, too, knowing that it was the proper thing to do. Even after everything, Pietr still tried to do the right thing.

My elbows were locked, my shoulders stiff. But I tried again. *My mother would've wanted me to go.*

"Jessie! Hurry up!" Dad yelled. "We have to go."

Max's words popped into my head.

I pushed them down.

I sighed and forced myself away from the mirror and out of the bathroom. Down the short flight of stairs I went trying to keep my new mantra in my head. *My mother would've wanted me to go.*

Max's words swam through my brain. Free will. I could decide for myself.

At the bottom of the stairs, I paused, realizing what made me hesitate from actually attending Marvin's funeral.

Amy stood there, dressed in sun-bleached black, her long red hair pulled back and tucked under into a conservative hairstyle to mark the formality of the occasion.

Drawn tighter than her hair was her expression.

"Jessie," Dad said. "We *have* to go."

I stepped forward, my hand reaching out to Amy. Taking her hand in mine, I searched her face, noting the stress that made her look so much older than eighteen. The words played in the back of my head, rushing to repeat themselves until it became a dull hum, a new mantra: *So much more than eighteen, So much more than eighteen* . . . "No, Dad," I said. "We don't *have* to go."

Dad looked at me, his jaw hanging open in surprise. "Your mother would've *wanted* . . ."

"I know." But I couldn't live my life according to my mother's desires. I could only live my life knowing what she would've wanted and making my own decisions based on what I and the ones still left alive *needed*.

And in the back of my mind I knew plainly what it was that held me back from going to Marvin's funeral.

It was my redheaded best friend. And the irony was it wasn't Amy's intention to stop me at all.

Had Marvin died a few months earlier—before I knew how he'd treated Amy, before I'd seen the bruises that colored her body everywhere that clothing covered—I would have gone. I would've cried and mourned the loss. But I realized willing myself to move forward—to act as if he never raped Amy—was impossible.

Darn Max for being smarter than me.

A knock at the door signaled Pietr's arrival, along with Alexi and Sophie. They were later than I expected. But even they understood the social convention of an entire town attending one teen's funeral. But more importantly they understood Amy would need me and I would need them to make it through this event.

Slipping my arms around my best friend, I said, "Do you *want* to go?"

She blew out a breath like she'd been holding it forever and shook her head so hard strands of red drifted free of her bun. "No," she admitted, looking only at me. "No. I don't want to go."

"Then we don't go." I linked my arm with hers and guided her to the kitchen.

Everyone else stood, stunned, in the mudroom.

"Decide if you're coming or going," I said over my shoulder. "You. Sit." In the breakfast nook I pulled out a chair for Amy and went to the pantry to drag out our old game of Scrabble. "Wanna play?"

"God, do I," she replied, tearing at her hair until it fell free around her shoulders.

In the mudroom a conversation went on without us.

"I'm going to get set for players to draw tiles . . . ," I warned as I dumped the box onto the table and helped Amy flip tiles facedown and slide them around.

Pietr stepped in briefly and leaned over my shoulder. "Alexi and I will go to represent the family."

I shrugged, fighting disappointment. "It seems appropriate," I agreed. "Soph?"

"I love Scrabble," she responded, dragging a chair over for herself.

"Annabelle Lee Gillmansen?"

She groaned at my use of her full name. "Count me in. I will thoroughly trounce you."

"You boys okay without me?" Dad asked. I looked back toward the mudroom. He was pulling his coat back off and hanging it up.

Pietr and Alexi nodded.

"I'm just afraid I'd say somethin' that might call into question the Brodericks' parentin' skills. . . ."

And five of us sat down to play Scrabble, all dressed in black but much happier for exercising our free will and not blindly following social convention. Today we'd play by the rules that felt right to us.

Or what my mother would've wanted *me to do,* I realized.

Alexi

I folded the newspaper and set it down to showcase the headline:

Strange House Blaze at Edge of Town

I did not like seeing the term "strange" in the local newspapers—especially if I had no idea what the real story was. Now that Dmitri had left Junction and the company had been routed, it seemed strange—no, *bizarre*—to see so many odd little things still cropping up in the area. Abandoned houses did not just go up in startling blazes for no reason.

I thought back to the other recent headlines:

Graffiti Colors Junction

Vagrants Spotted Near Caves . . .

Something strange was definitely happening in Junction. I grabbed my coffee and considered my options.

I could call Wanda and ask what she thought of the new anomalies. My stomach curled at the thought. She was again making herself scarce—though there was no reason for her to be stalking us now: All her questions had been answered, and she knew we were not in a position to just leave Junction on a whim, not without help.

I could call Nadezhda, but that would be more pleasure than business. No matter what she knew about me and regardless of her father's intense curiosity about my family, I did not like the idea of entangling her further into the troubles we continually encountered stateside. So much the better if I could keep it that way.

The one who would know the most and make the best guess regarding the most recent oddities because she was local was also one of the youngest in our number: Jessie. Her curiosity and willingness to do sound research had given us an edge before.

Rising from the table, I stalked to the dining room window and considered the convertible: cherry red now dusted with the white of last night's additional snowfall.

"It looks like some fabulous dessert," Amy said, sneaking up beside me. "Like a decadent cherry pie sprinkled with powdered sugar."

I nodded. "It is lovely, *da?*"

"Yes."

"Perhaps too lovely."

She switched her focus from the car to me. "What are you thinking, Sasha? And don't reply with some clever modification of something from *Pinky and the Brain*—they're clever enough," she said with a fleeting smile.

"*Pinky and the* . . . ?"

"Never mind." She waved the idea away. "What are you thinking?"

I took a long sip of coffee. "That Pietr does not know how to drive stick. That I am a poor teacher and that Max would surely compare driving a stick shift to something so overtly sexual anyone listening would blush."

"So there's no one to teach Pietr to drive the car?"

"*Da.* She does not get good gas mileage, and money is tight. And her body is far more fiberglass than steel. . . ."

"You're thinking of selling her."

"*Da.*" And thinking that I would never again enjoy driving her knowing she'd transported Mother's body to an unmarked grave and taken us to an event people called a funeral but was more truly a celebration of a rapist's life. No matter how Max might shine the convertible up, she had lost her appeal for me. "*Da.* I should sell her."

Amy disappeared a moment and returned with the paper. "Place the ad. We can find something cheaper," she assured me with a shrug. "It can be hard to let go," she muttered, "but sometimes it's necessary."

As she often was, Amy was correct: Two days later we found a used car that fit our budget and thoroughly offended any sense of style we shared. *Or any sense of style at all*, I thought, regarding the vehicle with disdain.

But Mr. Gillmansen looked under its hood, kicked its tires, took it *for a spin*, as he said, and finally announced, "She's good to go." Receiving his approval we drove it home: our less than impressive, three-color Volkswagen Rabbit. Fitting the entire Rusakova family inside made it look even more like a clown car.

But finding a buyer for the convertible would mean a huge savings for the family.

Marlaena

I paused in the shadow of the thin tree line by a river, a bridge spanning its width not far from where my furred toes itched with cold. A girl was out for an evening jog, her hair—a flash of red proving to be a shade or two darker than Gabriel's when she passed by a streetlight—flew behind her in a long ponytail that snapped in the growing breeze.

She paused on the old bridge, letting the darkness that puddled between lights swallow her up. Her hair fought the band binding it, tendrils of red dulled by the dark. Did it sting her face? A small branch tore off a nearby tree as the breeze changed direction, tossing clumps of snow into the air once more and uncovering a few brittle leaves left from

autumn. They rattled a moment on the branch before snapping free and flying into her face with a crunch.

She barely flinched, barely blinked. "I've had worse," she
snarled into the wind, daring it to hit her with something
harder. "Come on—take your best shot!" she dared, gripping
the bridge's rail and pulling herself up onto her toes to lean
more fully into the biting breeze.

I liked her attitude. The sharp way she challenged even
Mother Nature. The girl may not have balls, but she acted
like she did. That I could respect.

For a minute she froze there—a statue against the wind,
casting her gaze into the swirling water far below.

Pieces of ice ground along the bridge's support columns,
one minute sounding like old men mumbling over a game of
cards, the next squealing against one another like piglets
sent for slaughter. They danced in the frigid froth of the tu-
multuous and inky waters beneath the bridge.

What was she thinking?

Did she wonder what would happen if she just leaned over
too far . . . ? Did she wonder if she plunged into the swirling
water how long it would be until her absence was noticed?
Who would miss her?

Her foot moved, sliding closer to the wall, the toes of one
sneaker stroking up its rough edge.

I caught my breath, the fur on my shoulders prickling my
flesh as it stood.

What if she just stepped over? Leaped off? Ended everything? Would anyone wonder—would anyone mourn her loss?

The only way to find out was if she did it. . . .

Against the cutting wind I lowered my ears and narrowed
my eyes, unable to look away, my heart racing. *Do it,* my
heart repeated with its rhythm, *do it, do it . . .*

But she sighed and stretched back, pulling against the rail and lengthening her cooling muscles before they cramped up.

Shit. Not even impending death was easy. Couldn't people just commit to action anymore?

"Hey."

I focused on the word that slipped along on the breeze—deceptively casual.

The girl hopped, her head snapping to the side to see who else would have come out in such nasty weather. Squinting against the wind that threatened to pull tears from the corners of my eyes, we saw him at the same moment—leaning against the bridge's rail as if he'd stood there the entire time. Watching and waiting to step in. To come to the rescue.

Big as a wall, the only softness about him was his mop of midnight hair—slightly tousled curls the wind dragged its fingers through teasingly. The shadows chopped him into a series of hard lines and sharp angles, making him look every bit the description of a man who took no prisoners.

The air wheezed through me, and I forced myself to breathe normally again. He was no Gareth, but he wasn't hard to look at, either.

"Hey," the girl echoed weakly. "What are you doing out in this?" She turned back to the wind, letting it tear the words from her lips.

He moved closer. Perhaps better to hear her?

But the wind caught their scent and pulled it past my cold-stung nose and my interest in the pair ratcheted up.

There was a werewolf on that bridge.

I changed my position to get a better look.

The girl was flexible and her movements were fluid, but the guy . . . the way the shadows clung to him and the way his eyes let anyone watching know he wished the girl would do the same . . .

He was one of *us.*

He ignored her question, letting his gaze rake over her body, taking in her runner's outfit and the fact that she frequently shifted her weight from foot to foot to ward off the creeping chill.

"Let me take you home," he said, the request as solemn as the expression Gareth normally wore. Regardless of the fact there was no *r* in any word he uttered, I recognized the faintest growl in the sentence.

Yes, he was most definitely one of ours. The one I'd smelled by the pool hall.

And the fact one was so close but blocked by the presence of a simple human girl . . . It made me tremble more than any slap of cold air could.

"Let me take you home," he repeated.

"How many girls have you said that to?" she asked.

He blinked. Stunned? His lips curled into a slow smile, and he shrugged—such a simple move of his broad shoulders . . . Dimples hiding at the edge of his mouth appeared, deep and dangerous. He tilted his head to the side, watching her, his eyes glowing just beneath the shadow cast by his curls. For a wolf he could appear very sheepish—just a boy. The next words were carefully measured for effect, his eyes never leaving her own as he delivered the truth. "Enough as of now." He shrugged. "And this last one? She deserves a repeat of my request."

"So have you kept count, or do they blur together?" she snapped. But I doubted she was angry at him specifically—more likely angry at the world, or at least at one of the world's inhabitants that had recently hurt her badly.

"Math's not my strong suit," he responded, the dimples smoothing out, the smile sliding away. His arms crossed and his stance widened, impervious to the wind and the venom she spewed.

He would make an excellent addition to the pack—bold and powerful and quick on his feet.

And the girl? She was gutsy but not so impervious—at least not to the cold. "Fine." She ground out the word from between clenched teeth. "Take me home, Max."

Max. *That* I could remember.

With a move that surprised her so much she squeaked, he swept her up and over his broad back, resting a hand on her ass.

I nearly changed just to laugh at them in my human skin.

"What the—?" she yelled and struggled, reduced to nothing but a sack of potatoes slung over his shoulder.

"You didn't say *how* I should take you home. So I improvised." There was no apology in his tone, perhaps a streak of arrogance instead.

I liked this one.

And the girl did the oddest thing: She laughed.

As a chuckle built in his gut at her response, they walked away. I slunk along the shadowed edge of the bridge's wall and watched them fall into a waiting car. And that was when I took my chance and raced into its shadow, following them for as long as my legs held beneath me.

I dashed after the sleek red convertible, feet quick and sure on the road, still wet with salt and grit from combating the most recent snowfall. We went through the circles of white light the streetlights stained the ground with and for a while I kept up easily.

He was cautious with the girl in the car—something I hadn't expected.

He used his turn signals even though there was no traffic behind him. He slowed down well in advance of any turns. And, if my guess was right, he never pushed beyond the speed limit. It was strange at best and—*unnatural* at the worst. Our kind was bold—verging on reckless. . . . Was it odd I expected that of our breed, that I thought a werewolf driving a sexy car would speed and only pause briefly at stop signs without committing to a full stop—unless it was to benefit from stopping short?

We pushed from the edge of the town through its brick-walled and concrete-sidewalked heart—shop lights still glowing in display windows though signs on the doors clearly read CLOSED. The streets rolled themselves up early in Junction.

Maybe it was like the time I spent in Catholic school—the lack of opportunities led to rebellion and wilder choices. Maybe the town shut down early, but somewhere kids roamed free or partied beyond the prying eyes of parents at well-hidden raves.

A girl could hope. . . .

But something stopped me beyond the fact that a werewolf and—his *girlfriend*?—had just parked the car behind the ugliest four-door imaginable to head into a well-appointed house in the suburbs. There was something odd here. I ran my snout along the ground and then pushed it into the air, searching the breeze. There was a scent that was off somehow. Like the sickly sweet scent of disease . . .

Something was wrong here—*someone* was wrong here. . . .

I crept closer to the house, slinking along the shadows until I nestled in the darkness at the base of the porch.

The door flew open, and a man dashed out with a flashlight. That was all I needed to end my voyeurism. I had found the place once.

I'd most certainly be back.

Alexi

I blasted the flashlight's beam in Max's face, prepared to scold them about some imaginary curfew, but something caught my eye instead. "What was . . . ?" I ushered Amy and Max inside, closing the door as my eyes fought to focus on a smudge of darkness zipping across the lawn. My light was too slow to catch it, and Max set Amy down inside to step back onto the porch. I would have sworn I saw his nostrils flare, but that made no sense.

If he was simply human.

CHAPTER ELEVEN

Jessie

If you say something often enough, you might eventually believe it. Maybe that was part of why I said "I love you" to Pietr so frequently now that he'd changed—now that he was far more human than animal. Maybe I needed to hear it so I could better believe it. Standing there, in his doorway, watching him study, seeing him so far from the impulsive and powerful hero he'd once been, made me pause.

The final stanza from T. S. Eliot's *The Hollow Men* came back to me, and I wondered if maybe it was the same way love ended . . . not with a bang, but a whimper.

Why didn't my heart race anymore whenever I was around him? Why didn't he make my breath catch? He was still just as handsome—chiseled features and high cheekbones, a strong jaw and dramatic eyebrows framing beautiful blue eyes. . . . Although I could recite the things that made him beautiful, and they were still present, there was something missing.

The same something that used to make me so hot for him.

The spark.

I'd wanted normal and now I had it, in all its calm, understated glory.

Quiet. Normalcy. Time filled with movie nights and board games, Dungeons & Dragons and double dating—like normal people did.

Well, maybe not so much the Dungeons & Dragons. . . .

And as much as I craved normalcy when I feared for my life and struggled for answers, now . . . I missed the fighting, the outright passion that was part love and part lust, peppered with the thrill that came from danger.

It was petty. I got what I said I wanted and so much more. In so many ways, Pietr was great. Verging on perfect. He always returned my calls promptly. He wrote me cute notes and sent me funny texts and occasionally surprised me with flowers. He never tried to cop a feel. He'd become exactly what every girl hoped for: a handsome, smart, sensitive, and giving boyfriend.

He was *absolutely* dependable.

Dad loved him.

And it was killing me.

I was *so* bored. Part of me itched for trouble, hungered for action—for something exciting to happen in Junction once more. For my life to be more than the wrapping up of loose ends in what felt like the fourth book in some roller coaster of a paranormal novel series.

I sighed—a soft sound that just a month ago he would have heard even across the room.

But now he didn't.

So he didn't realize when I'd gone, either.

Or that I'd ever been there, watching and hoping to feel something reignite.

Marlaena

"Watch—there and there." I pointed out the cameras posted high on the store's walls. In the darkness at the edge of the Supercenter's parking lot a few of us huddled together and watched a couple cars leaving.

The place was nearly dead.

Gabriel sauntered up, snapping the gum he chewed. "Blind spot. There," he said, grabbing my hand to adjust where my finger pointed.

"Jackass. *Here*," I countered, yanking my hand away and pounding a fist into his chest.

He grinned, blew a bubble, and cracked it in my face.

I hauled back my fist and felt my lips pull away from my teeth. "I swear to—"

But Gareth's hand wrapped around mine. "We've had this chat," he whispered in my ear, and my bones dissolved at his proximity. "You believe in nearly nothing, so who can you swear to?"

"Sons of *bitches* . . . ," I seethed, pulling away from them both and fighting to catch my breath.

Gabe laughed so hard he nearly choked on his gum. "You're probably right with that assessment." He grinned. "We're sons of something, must be a bitch in there some-where."

Gareth shook his head. "So we've established a blind spot. . . ."

"And a desperate need for money," Kyanne added, looking at Gareth. "Everyone's hungry."

"We could do another liquor store . . . ," Gabe said with a yawn. "Worked well for us before. . . ."

"No. There's drawing attention to ourselves and there's drawing *attention* to ourselves."

"Says the hot redhead pyromaniac," Gabe teased.

Gareth put a hand on Gabe's chest and my shoulder just as I lunged for him. "Stop. Focus on our goal. Feed the pups."

"Arrgh!" I growled, hopping in frustration. "Fine. You, *you* though," I said, thrusting a finger in Gabe's face, "need to stay off my back."

He raised an eyebrow and grinned at me. "I haven't been on your back. *Yet*. But I look forward to the opportunity—"

I hit him so hard a tooth flew out of his mouth. "Remember your place, dog," I demanded. "You're *under* me."

"I can do it that way, too," he assured, rubbing his jaw.

I rushed him, took him to the ground, and hit him again and again until Gareth and Kyanne got a good enough grip on me to pull me off.

The whole time Gabe kept laughing. Laughing and bleeding.

I wiped the blood coating my hands onto my jeans and faced the row of vending machines. I thrust my open hand out. "Crowbar." Feeling the cold weight of it in my palm was reassuring. "Kyanne."

"Ready," she said, holding a crowbar to match my own.

Behind us I heard Gabe sit up. "Don't forget that blind spot!"

he called as we jogged across the parking lot. I nearly turned back to hit him again, but I gritted my teeth and thought about the hunger rumbling in all our guts and sped up, eyes on the cameras and the damn blind spot he'd identified.

"What'd ya do without me?" Gabe chuckled in the dark.

CHAPTER TWELVE

Alexi

The newspaper again confirmed my suspicion. A new situation had arisen over night—nothing major, just the vandalization of a bank of vending machines lining the east wall of the Supercenter.

Someone was getting desperate if they were knocking over vending machines to get spare bills and change. A situation of such desperation and foolhardiness could certainly escalate. . . .

Why could things not be normal around Junction?

I thought I might once like to sip my coffee in peace and read about simple things like drunken college students ruining their chances at a decent job by mooning city officials at a dinner party. A little mindless and reckless stupidity—something that did not link to anything else, did not make my brain sputter guessing how it might all interrelate—that was what I wanted.

But *I* had to live in small-town America, where everyone *thought* they knew everything about everyone and nothing was further from the truth.

Jessie

"Hey, look out. New kids," Amy said, directing Sophie and me with a dart of her eyes.

I bit my lip, recognizing the guy with the fox-like features and short red hair. The thief from the Grabbit Mart. The two girls who accompanied him were blond and nearly identical, right down to the way they wore their long hair—which was almost exactly the same length.

We were far from the only ones watching them—it seemed everyone had turned to see where Junction High's newest additions went. That didn't normally happen. . . .

So I studied them more intently. They looked rough, with worn jeans—and not in the factory-created way—and bad-fitting hoodies. Like they'd gotten some harshly used hand-me-downs and were still waiting for them to fit.

I reminded myself I wasn't judging them based on their clothes, I was judging them based on *his* actions. "I don't like new kids," I muttered.

Amy choked. "Yee-ahhh. That's why you went ga-ga over Pietr."

"Just trust me. We don't want to get mixed up with that guy."

"There's a story here. . . ." Amy leaned in.

"Isn't that how it should be for reporters?" Sophie asked with a wink.

I looked down; "Not now . . ." Too late. "Oh. Hey."

"Hey," the redhead said, pausing with his entourage by our table. "I remember you."

"Great."

"But I don't think I got your name last time."

"I didn't give it."

"Burned," one of the blondes said.

The redhead's face started to match his hair.

Amy stood up, though, and reached out a hand. "I'm Amy," she said. With narrowed eyes she watched the way he took her hand, shook it, and then straightened back up.

And in that moment I saw it, too. The fox-like features weren't fox at all. He moved like something far more powerful. Something we were all familiar with.

Wolf.

"Amy," he said. "You must be the polite one in the group."

"If Amy's the polite one, then we must all have slipped into an alternate reality. Or it's Opposite Day."

Sarah.

Amy turned the hand she'd just shaken to expose one particular finger for Sarah's close inspection.

"Cuh-lassy," Sarah responded before offering her own hand to the guy. "Sarah Luxom. And you are?"

"Gabriel."

"How angelic," Sarah said, setting her tray down at our table. The twins leaned toward each other, cupping their hands around their mouths and whispering. Before Sarah'd gone psycho on us, it would have been nearly acceptable for her to join us at lunch. But now Amy just pushed her tray back and mouthed: *No.*

Sarah shrugged and picked the tray back up.

"Very nice to meet you, Sarah," Gabriel replied.

"You say that now . . . ," Amy murmured, sitting back down.

"And you, Amy. But, you, my friend from the Grabbit Mart. What's your name?"

With a groan I said, "Jessica."

"Jessica. Good to know. Girls?"

The twins bent forward and introduced themselves.

"Jordyn."

"Londyn."

"Hey," I said. And then I realized the guilt from letting him get away with his petty theft was keeping me from what usually came most naturally. Asking questions. "And where are you all from?"

"All over," Gabriel said with a smile.

"Most recently—"

"Chicago."

I nodded. "It has to be a big change going from Chicago to Junction."

The girls nodded eagerly. "We had—"

"Motivating factors that—"

"Encouraged a change of venue."

"That's always the way." *With werewolves*, I thought.

The doors to the cafeteria opened as the remnants of the Junction Jackrabbits entered, a draft flowing around us.

The twins eyes sparked and turned to Amy, then to Gabriel. "Should we—"

"Tell—"

Gabriel glared at them and looked pointedly at Amy. "There's nothing *to* tell. Yet."

Amy and I exchanged a glance.

"We look forward to meeting more of you," Gabriel said. Smiling in a way that made me queasy.

I just stared at him, waiting until they felt uncomfortable enough to leave. The girls reacted first, becoming noticeably nervous.

Gabriel wasn't so easy to dominate with a simple look. But he didn't strike me as an alpha, either. Finally boredom worked to my advantage and he turned away.

Amy tried the same tactic with Sarah, but she was less likely to feel pressured to leave by simply being looked at. Instead, she basked in the attention.

"You should go," I finally said to her. "I'll call you later."

She gave a dainty snort. "Maybe I'll answer." But she left.

Amy looked at me. "That was—"

"Weird," I concluded for her with a wink.

"Should we tell Pietr and Max?"

"What? That there are werewolves hanging around? I say no. It's not like they can do anything about it now. Really. And it's probably a lucky thing. Wouldn't there be some weird thing about territory if our guys were still wolves?"

"I guess . . ."

"You do know I'll eventually fold and tell one of them," I admitted.

"I'm counting on it," Amy replied.

I poked at the milk container sitting on the tray by my brown-bag lunch. As far as I was concerned, after finding out what we had about the origins of the school lunches, everything in the cafeteria was suspect.

Sophie pierced her brought-from-home drink bag with a sharp straw and began quietly sucking.

Amy just glared at her apple. "We need a plan of action."

"What?"

"This sucks—packing lunch every day," she muttered.

"Okay, I totally agree," I conceded, "but we have to be smart about all this. We have no idea how far up—or down—the figurative food chain this goes."

"Good point. It does seem like everyone in Junction has a secret to hide. Who woulda thought small-town America was so—"

"Creepy?" Sophie asked.

"Troubled?" I interjected.

Amy looked at me and nodded. "Troubled. There's nothing normal about this supposedly normal town."

"There's bound to be a way we could incorporate that into the school motto, too," I suggested.

Amy stuck out her tongue. "So we agree? We need to find a way to cut off the food distributor serving Junction High."

I nodded.

Sophie just stayed still. Quiet.

"Well, Soph? You in?"

Pietr, Cat, and Max approached the table, making me wrap things up quickly.

"Oh," Sophie responded, looking over my head to the wall and the clock that I knew hung there, thanks to Pietr's obsession with time. "Sorry. I need to get back to my research project."

"Wait—Soph—"

But she grabbed her tray and dodged away as the Rusakovas joined us.

I glanced at Amy. "Do you have any clue what research project she's talking about? I feel like I'm missing something."

She shook her head. "I think we're *both* missing something."

Max settled in beside her. "Could it be me?"

Pietr and I groaned in unison.

But Amy's smile made it totally worth our suffering.

CHAPTER THIRTEEN

Marlaena

My stomach tightened, vibrating out a growl that rocked my rib cage and trembled against my spine, matching anything my throat had ever uttered. My nostrils flared, testing the breeze, sharp with a cold so cruel it was a thousand tiny pins pricking the inside of my nose all at once.

Eyes stinging, I swung my head and tipped up my muzzle, the breeze growing into a wind that brushed the bristling hairs on my upper lip and chin, tickling my snout.

But I had found what I'd come for and I turned my head into the smell, willing my stomach to silence.

The pups needed to eat. And Gareth and Gabriel might or might not be successful in their hunts. But for me—there was hope of sharing a morsel of meat with my pack.

Rabbit.

I forced my ears forward to listen for any movement and padded out on silent paws, snow working up and between my toes, chilling my feet as I kept my scent downwind of where the smell came from, my mouth lathered with saliva at the thought of its fur, flesh, and blood slipping between my scissoring canines. . . .

There was no doubt. The musky scent of something living in the earth's gut, nested in its own fur and warmed by its dung, was unmistakable.

But better than the smell was the sight of it—a small silhouette huddled against the breeze, eyes closed and ears snug against its body.

And facing away from me.

Belly to the snow, I crawled forward, a methodical shifting from one side to the other as I shortened the distance between us in increments of inches.

Hunger gnawed at me, but desperation fueled me far beyond the reach of hunger's chewing jaws.

I rose up, muscles coiling beneath my skin and toenails digging into the frozen ground as I readied to spring—my mind racing in anticipation of the connection of jaws to flesh and bone.

But the wind shifted, betraying my position, and the rabbit rocketed forward in blind panic. I launched after it, jaws snapping closed on empty air as it twisted and turned and tested the limits of my flexibility.

I followed it through hairpin turns as it wove nimbly through the briars. And I locked down that invasive human part of me.

I am wolf. Built for the hunt—made for the kill. Designed to deal death and walk away from victory with a full belly and a howl of joy quivering on my bloodbathed tongue.

Brambles tore at my face, sticking in my fur and biting into my flesh, tiny sabers sinking in and stinging. I ripped through them, uprooting the least of them and racing after my quarry.

The rabbit bent in midair, twisting back the way we'd just come, and I stretched my neck, jaws closing on silky fur. Bones crunched between my jaws, and I skidded to a stop, paws throwing up snow and bits of buried underbrush.

It struggled in my grip, and bracing myself I shook my head, twisting my neck sharply from side to side and squeezing my jaws until my skull ached and my teeth wanted to pop from the pressure.

The rabbit stilled. Went limp. All soft and giving flesh, warm and ripe . . .

My tongue quivered, tasting blood, hot and rich as fine, dark chocolate, and I fought back the wolf to keep from consuming my prey all alone—stripping the meat and cracking the bones to suck out the marrow. . . .

The alpha in me cried out: *This* is my right—this is my destiny—to have all I want, anytime I want it.

But the girl in me . . . I dropped the corpse and shivered into my human form, luckily not far from my discarded clothing. The girl in me remembered the pups waiting—their eyes full of hunger.

And hope.

I slid on my worn jeans with not even a spare coin to jingle in my pockets and settled my stained sweatshirt over my shoulders. Brushing off my feet before wedging them into my boots, I shrugged into the denim jacket I had found discarded on a playground nearly a year ago in Philadelphia.

My hands shook from the rush that came with the chase and the kill. I picked up the rabbit and tucked it into my jacket, buttoning up, the rabbit's fading warmth against my belly a tease. My stomach grumbled again.

The hike back to the new hideout took longer than I wanted, so I sprinted the last hundred yards, arm tight against my jacket, cradling the rabbit.

The scent of wood smoke hit me, and my eyes blinked against the soot in the air. But the smoke glazing my eyes was secondary to the scent of chicken roasting. For a heartbeat my victory was forgotten. Over our humble campfire a makeshift spit turned, bowed in the center from the weight of three plump hens hanging there, glistening in their fat as they cooked, shining in the firelight like greasy stars.

Gabriel leaned away from the fire, turning the spit slowly with one hand, a sly smile splitting his face. "Welcome home," he said, announcing my arrival. The pups greeted me, their mouths full, cheeks bulging with freshly cooked meat. He raised a plate with his other hand. "Chicken?" he asked.

"Where . . . ?" But I knew. There was a farm not far from our new position—a production farm selling eggs by the truckload. Regular humans didn't smell the fat, laying hens living so close to one another inside, but I—we—did. Easily. "You'll get us caught, you idiot."

He shook his head. "No. The farmer won't miss a thing. I made it look like someone forgot to latch the cages. And four birds out of a thousand . . ." He shrugged. "The pups are fed. That's what matters."

"The pups would've been fed without your theft," I muttered, dragging the limp rabbit from my coat. Such a small thing. Thin already from winter. I saw that once hunger wasn't blinding me.

And so did Gabriel. His smile twisted at one end. "Rabbit's tasty," he agreed. "But barely a mouthful to it."

Someone stepped up behind me, the solid weight causing the floorboard to dip just the slightest amount. The scent of cloves and far-off places drifted to me, and I knew Gareth stood as my shadow at the firelight's edge.

"Did you . . . ?" I asked over my shoulder.

"Nothing," he whispered back.

Gabriel's grin unfurled, the arrogance clear. "Chicken?" he offered again, and I wondered if he meant something else by the single word, something about our unwillingness to steal out from under a local farmer's nose.

With a grunt, I willed my fingernail to a sharp claw and beheaded my bunny, trimming along its hind legs and belly. My grin grim, I held its hind legs in one fist and pulled its fur free in one swift move. Another careful slice and the entrails dumped out, still steaming. The pups' eyes sparked red. "No thanks," I replied. "I'm good."

Both Gareth's and Gabriel's gazes locked on me, confirming the accuracy of my statement.

As I cooked my meat I knew that just as dangerous as the threat of hunters and hunger was the threat Gabriel posed to my leadership and the pack's stability.

And as sure as I was of that, I was even more certain he'd brought us to Junction for reasons of his own.

CHAPTER FOURTEEN

Jessie

Sophie and I were headed to the school library to grab a resource on an article for the school paper—as normal a pursuit as I could imagine—when I heard them in the hallway not far from us.

"I said no thanks." Even without seeing her signature red heels, Counselor Harnek's voice was unmistakable. "Your type of help is exactly what got us all into this mess in the first place. We were supposed to locate the gifted, not feed them stuff that makes them go crazy or explode. . . ."

"That was the exception, not the rule."

Vice Principal Perlson. The lilt of his voice and its unique rhythmic quality made it impossible not to recognize him.

"They're *all* exceptions—don't you see that? Every single kid here—they're all special."

"*Now.* Before the company came to town, you were just making assumptions about anomalies and adolescents experiencing abnormal situations—which, ironically, *is* the norm. There is not a normal adolescent in the world."

"But none of those non-normal adolescents are as far from normal as these kids are now," she argued.

"True, true. Which is why we need to take such good care of what we have. And why you should give all your test subjects the special supplement."

"I don't have test subjects. I have students. Confused students. A whole frikkin' school of them, if you haven't noticed."

"I've noticed. And I require better details regarding the group you're training."

Seriously? I looked at Sophie. She just stared straight ahead, her back flat to the wall.

"What do you think you still have to know about the group I'm training?"

"I want to know what precisely you are training them for. I want details."

"The only details I'll give is that I'm training them as was previously agreed. When I am finished with them they'll be able to do everything we hoped for and more. And the more of them you give me access to, the more of them will be safe, functional, and accurate. But drop the issue of the supplement. The kids are already having enough problems from their reactions to the school food."

"But only at about a level of approximately twenty percent of the total student population," Perlson pointed out. "You and I both know that barely exceeds the percentage dismissed as chance or the odds."

"You show me any other place where twenty percent of the student body is exhibiting the powers and nasty side effects that our kids do and—"

"Montgomery Beach Middle School, California."

"What? Montgomery Beach?"

"Now unfortunately nicknamed Monster Beach. But what can you do? Kids can be *so* cruel." He made a condescending *tsk-ing* noise.

"Shit," she exclaimed.

"Now, now. We must remain professional about all this. This is not only the future we are working with but also a highly competitive business venture."

"Oh, I'll be professional, don't you worry. But if you even try to get that supplement into the student body, I will go on the warpath. I will *destroy* you. We're here to give these kids a brighter future—to empower them—not to ruin their lives and destroy their hopes."

"Sometimes one thing needs to be sacrificed for the benefit of the others. We can empower them, but it will take a little more risk."

"No. Absolutely not. I'm doing what I signed on for here—long before you came on the scene. I'm going to study the anomalies and protect our students. And don't ever make the mistake of trying to come between me and my goals." The clicking of her shoes, fading as she walked swiftly, let me know she was headed away from us.

I held my breath, hoping Perlson did the same thing in his loafers.

For once we got lucky.

Soph and I let out sighs of relief. "Wow," I said. "Who'd have guessed that she'd stand up to him to protect us? I mean, I like her, but . . ."

Soph nodded slowly, her voice going soft again. "Yeah. Who'd have guessed?"

"So where do you think they're being kept?"

"Who?"

"The kids Harnek's training? Can you imagine? Training a group of kids to use special powers?"

Sophie shrugged. "What are the odds? In Junction?" She grabbed her book bag and headed to the library.

I caught up to her. "I'm going to find them."

"Who? Perlson and Harnek? They went thatta'way," she said with point and a roll of her eyes.

"No. The kids."

"I wouldn't bother if I were you."

"Well, then, I guess it's a good thing you aren't me. Because I'm going to bother. Someone should look out for these kids."

"Yes," Sophie agreed. "Someone should."

Marlaena

It wasn't a big store, but then again, it wasn't a big town. The parking lot was the most remarkable thing about the little strip mall—all sleek and recently poured macadam, black as a new moon night and smooth as satin. Snow fluttered down, only showing briefly in sharp contrast to the blacktop before it vanished, white absorbed by the black. The buildings were standard fare—something new filling the façade of a franchise store that stood here earlier—its architecture proclaiming its original intent, but its strange choice of colors showing new ownership.

Judging the space I guessed the mall had been started in the nineties, hit its heyday then, and soon started to tumble into the faint signs of disrepair and a failing economy that still marred it now. A few roof shingles hung awkwardly, some mismatched from more recent repairs. The sidewalk rose up at an odd angle where a tree's root worked to reclaim the earth beneath it, and the brick face, its corners chipped at bumper level, was in need of a good powerwash.

Gareth tugged at my hood, tucking a stray wisp of my hair back into its dark depths. "If you'd take my advice and dye it," he whispered—his breath so close I fought a shiver— "we'd all be safer. Brunettes are a dime a dozen. But redheads—ya'll are memorable."

"Aren't I memorable for something more than my hair color?" I asked, feeling the alpha in me slip away as I searched for his eyes in the falling gray of dusk.

He rolled them, his lips pressing into a long, firm line. "Come on, Princess," he drawled in that slow Southern way of his that always seemed to say no matter how fast our lives rushed by—no matter how hard we bled out—that *this* was the only moment that mattered and it needed to be savored. Gareth sucked the marrow out of life without even trying— just by *being*. I envied him that. He looped one arm around mine. "Stroll with me."

"I'm not the strolling type." But with Gareth beside me, I couldn't imagine anything else. "You're brunette and you're far from forgettable."

"I'm as brunette as they come," he said, flashing a smile full of white teeth that contrasted beautifully with his rich skin tone—so much like freshly made cocoa, and capable of warming a person just as much. An ebony curl danced near one of his pale lavender eyes and I resisted the urge to brush it back as he'd tucked mine away.

His mama was a white girl with freckles dappling her face and shoulders and his daddy was a dog as dark as midnight, he'd once said as we all had huddled together, sharing tales around a campfire beneath a bridge in some now-forgotten city miles away.

They may have been in sharp contrast to each other, but when they'd come together they'd bred one amazing wolf, in my opinion. So Gareth carried her cheekbones, pale eyes, and freckles and his father's dark skin, broad shoulders, and amazing lips. He coughed. "Focus, Princess."

But I *was* focused. On *him*. The heat of his body matching mine, the way my breathing fell into a perfect rhythm with his. . . .

"We're here to do a job," he reminded.

Caught. "I am *very* well aware of that," I sniped, turning my head away from him to look at the stores, observe the people, and note the time. Things appeared to be winding down. More people were leaving the store than entering it. And thanks to my ever-present internal clock, I knew it was nine twenty-five. According to the handwritten sign hanging on the store's door, they closed at ten.

Gareth stiffened slightly beside me, and I followed his gaze, noting the video cameras.

"What are the odds they're actually on?" He knew as well as I did that some stores used fakes to try and keep people honest—just empty shells or dead cameras no longer capable of recording anything their blind eyes were turned toward.

"I don't like taking the chance that they are . . ."

Ever since Mississippi, Gareth had become cautious. A werewolf caged was no werewolf, he still occasionally mumbled. He hadn't spent much time imprisoned—but some was much more than he ever intended to see again. So now, no matter how hungry or desperate we were, we plotted and planned. *How can I protect the pack if I'm kept from them?* he'd asked me once.

And so he'd become the cautious one, keeping my impulses—*all* of them—firmly in check. Sometimes I wanted to kill him for it.

But most of the time I just wanted to rub up against him and make him focus on nothing but me. "We have a can of spray paint," I reminded him.

"True, true," he agreed. "We can give it a nice ol' black eye. . . ."

I shivered, the breeze turning and cutting into me suddenly.

Gareth pulled me close, slipping his arm away from mine to encircle me with it instead. And although my heart sped at the move, my mind knew it meant nothing. Gareth would have wrapped *any* of the pack members—male or female—into his warmth if it meant making them comfortable or happy. Besides, we were playing a part—pretending to be a couple. And as much as I wished it weren't pretend, I knew better.

It only had to be believable as we scoped out the place.

Gareth didn't want me. He followed me to protect the others *from* me.

"Let's go that direction," he said, pointing with his chin. "We don't wanna hang too long in front of one store and draw attention to ourselves."

So we strolled away, I clinging to the side of him and enjoying his strength, his warmth, and the solid power of his body, and he? Too cautious and careful to notice the way I fell into beta mode around him.

Because even if he didn't always agree with my style of leadership, Gareth was the first to admit our group needed a firm leader. And since he didn't want to be an alpha . . .

That left *me*.

And Gabe sniffing around the pack's edges, hoping for a way in—a way to lead at my side. As my equal.

My mate.

Gareth led me down the sidewalk to the Blockbuster and opened the door, holding it for me like a true Southern gentleman should. It had taken me months to get used to his little courtesies—and the fact that he held on to them so tightly after so much discourtesy had been done to him.

Together we wandered down the aisles of DVDs and Blu-ray discs, my finger trailing lightly along the shelves.

He paused in the horror section.

"They always mislabel these," I remarked, picking up a few favorites. "*Ginger Snaps* isn't horror, it's drama." I set it down again.

"And *Blood and Chocolate*?"

"Romance," I stated.

He released me and drifted farther down the row to where the foreign films began. "*Brotherhood of the Wolf*?"

"Tragedy."

"*The Twilight Saga*?"

I shivered. "That's horror. Stark and terrifying horror."

His full, dark lips slid into a generous smile. "I sort of liked them," he admitted. "Using a minority to represent the wolves. That was clever." He winked at me, and I pursed my lips in reply.

"You're such a dork sometimes."

He shrugged. "A dork . . . a romantic . . . ?" He shrugged again.

"What's romantic about the girl choosing the wrong guy? Jacob should've totally won Bella. He deserved to get what he wanted. He was passionate, protective . . ."

"The boy had abs of steel," Gareth remarked.

"Nothing wrong with that," I agreed, reaching out to pat Gareth's tight stomach. I fought down the tremble that launched through my bones at such simple contact.

A gentleman, he said nothing, but his eyes darkened slightly in warning, and I pulled my hand away.

"Besides, 'truth is stranger than fiction,'" I quipped.

His smile was fleeting, but it was better than nothing. "We'd better go back out and finish watching. The pups are probably starting to miss us," I added, leading him from the store. "You know how crazed they can get when they're this hungry."

He nodded, the darkness still staining his eyes. Did he remember the time they broke into a fight over the last piece of beef jerky and Tembe nearly lost an eye? I blanched at the memory of Tembe's eye hanging from its socket. Nearly *lost* an eye was exactly what I meant.

We did fine if everything remained in its place—damage was often fixable by our natural means and occasionally a splint or brace. But a part gone was . . . a part gone. Forever.

We weren't starfish—we couldn't regrow parts.

I shook my head, clearing it. That had been an unpleasant night. I rolled my shoulder, feeling the pain still nestled deep in it.

Gareth caught me and looked at me, his eyes full of concern.

I ignored him. Doing our job here and returning promptly to the pups was important when hunger stalked so close behind.

"There's still the homeless shelter," I reminded him.

He nodded grimly. "We may have to split the pack and try it. Let's hope we find another way, though."

"Yeah. Homeless shelters don't seem to suit our type."

He blinked at me, waiting for me to continue.

"But petty theft and larceny does." I shrugged. "It's the system that works."

His silence spoke volumes.

"You're judging me again," I hissed.

He raised his hands, palms out. "I do not judge."

Damn him, he was right. He was the least judgmental person I knew. He made Christ look hypocritical. "It's our system." I sighed.

"You do not need to justify it to me. It keeps them alive and gives them a family and hope."

"But you wish things were different, don't you?"

"Don't *you?*"

I turned back to the store we'd been watching and let him pull me against him, wrapping me in his powerful arms as he acted the part of the snuggling lover and carefully kept us just beyond the view of the camera.

A slender man followed a final customer to the entrance and waved her out before turning the sign to read CLOSED in the door and clicking a single dead bolt into place.

10:02.

"Here we go," I whispered, leaning into Gareth so that our two hearts pounded impossibly close together.

10:03. Lights flickered off in a pattern running the length of the store, so fast there had to be a bank of switches that could be flipped quickly and leave only one set of lights glowing. Near what we knew to be the office.

And the safe.

10:04. Faint movement near the office. If Skipper's was like most smaller businesses, now would be the time for counting out, evening out the cash register drawers and prepping the deposit for the bank.

The curious thing would be to see if the money sat in the store's safe overnight or if the owner stepped out to his car to drive it to the nearby bank and make a late-night deposit. If it stayed in the safe, we'd need to adjust our slowly forming plan on how to get access to it. But if the owner headed to the car with it . . . I held my breath, noted the time, and kept watch.

At 10:12 the same man approached the door again, key in hand and something tucked up beneath his arm. Taking a long look at the parking lot, he undid the bolt, opened the door, and snapped it shut again, sliding the key in and twisting with a well-practiced move. The store locked behind him, he headed across the parking lot, clicking a button on his keys so that the lights on a nearby car flashed in response. Then he slid the hand holding the keys up to grasp the zippered cash bag—a plump one—under his arm.

I watched him climb into the little car, heard the locks activate, and the engine start as we slowly walked to the car Gabe had recently obtained for us.

Sliding into the passenger's seat, I let Gareth drive. Stealthily, we followed the man's car until we knew what bank he was using and what roads and hiding places there were between the store and it.

CHAPTER FIFTEEN

Jessie

We paused between classes—I'd finally succeeded in luring Pietr to a stairwell where we'd spent some time in the past. Kissing. Reaching up, I tugged his hair forward, pulling it across his right eye like he used to always wear it.

He looked at me, puzzled, and swept it back so both his eyes were clear.

I sighed and, looking up into his pale blue eyes, I said, "I love you."

"I think you say that too lightly," Pietr complained.

"What? What am I saying too lightly?"

"*Nyet.* Ugh. Don't get me wrong. I love to hear it, but you say 'I love you' all the time."

"I do not. . . ."

"Every time you hang up the phone with your sister or father—no matter how good or bad the call—'I love you.'

Every time I head to a different class, or the bathroom," he griped, " 'I love you.' "

"So?"

"At what point is it habitual and less meaningful?"

"Never," I protested.

He looked away.

"You don't believe me."

"You developed quite a reputation for lying," he pointed out.

"Yes, Captain Obvious," I growled. "But I don't lie when I say 'I love you.' Ever."

"Do you need to say it so often? Doesn't that—cheapen—the effect?"

"Does my love seem cheap to you?"

His eyes widened in realization. "Oh, shit. *Nyet* . . . there's nothing cheap about you. . . ."

"Quit backpedaling and tell me this: How much time do we have, Pietr?"

He checked his watch. "Three minutes before the tardy bell."

"No. I mean how much time—overall—do we have, Pietr. You and me. In our lives?"

He paused and swallowed.

"A decade? A year? A month? A day maybe?" I pushed. "Do you know what tomorrow will bring?"

"Of course not," he snarled.

"Neither do I. I have this moment and maybe the next, if I continue to be lucky. You've taught me that life is short."

"You've taught me that life is precious."

"Then understand. This is my mother's influence. She did this same thing—telling me she loved me so much, spreading it around like the words were nothing. I called her on it, too. I called her on it, Pietr. I told her that. That all her little 'I love you's' were shit because she tossed them around like nothing. Do you know what she said?"

He shook his head.

"She reminded me we're farmers and said it takes a lot of shit to make something beautiful grow. And after I'd shut my mouth, totally stunned, she explained that she always figured if she said those words often enough that when she was finally gone, although I'd doubt and I'd forget a bunch, at least I'd remember she told me 'I love you' a few times. And you know what, Pietr? Now she's gone, and all I want is to hear her say those words. Again."

"I didn't realize," he whispered. "I'm so sorry. I didn't know." He gathered me to him, and we stood silently together in the hallway and just let the tardy bell ring.

Alexi

I'd taken the VW Rabbit to Johnny Bey's to try my luck with the Tuesday night crowd. As the convertible was not quick to sell, nor was Pietr quick to find work, I reverted to what I did best: watching people, examining their strengths and weaknesses, and playing a role that'd get me an opportunity I needed to win money at pool. In short: hustling.

Although I was quite a good player, I never challenged the men I judged to be the best at the tables—they did not have egos that needed proving like their more mediocre counterparts. An ego that needed proving was often backed up by large amounts of money.

Amy would have called such action "overcompensating," which only reinforced the fact that I liked Amy.

Men who overcompensated believed they were unbeat-able. Or at least *said* it. Saying it with cash was good enough for me to be willing to put them to the test.

I was observing the action and trying to choose a target when the wolf walked in.

I drew back, leaning into a shadowed corner by the long, slick bar, and watched her stalk around the edge of the pool tables.

Long-legged and slender, with a tiny waist, she had a build like my sister's if Cat had been stretched out another four inches.

She wore a short top that exposed just a hint of her stom-ach, and tight blue jeans that were scuffed at the knees and ended in black high-heeled suede boots. Long red hair fell loose around her shoulders, and I wondered if what I was feeling seeing her stalk the room was a modicum of what the man in Farthington felt for my mother.

Nothing in her body language hinted at insecurity: no stoop to her shoulders, no slow stride as she walked, no dart-ing of her large and shining eyes. . . .

She knew she owned every room she walked into.

I was certainly not the only man to notice.

I was observing a female alpha.

A female alpha who was, as Max would say, "Off her chain." She wore no necklace or what Cat called a "collar" to dull the intensity of her allure. That fact was nearly as frightening as the beast she could become at will.

Thankfully, being raised by wolves had granted me a soft immunity to their charms. Unfortunately the other men in the room did not have that same advantage. They were noth-ing more than prey animals with no idea they were the ones being hunted.

She ran her fingers lightly over the bar's sleek wooden surface, smiling at each man as she went. Where they saw sex and flirtation, I read *danger*. She was as much shark as wolf, circling the smoky room slowly and drinking in the scents of alcohol and the haze that pervaded everything.

She was waiting to scent blood in the water.

The way she took in her surroundings, I had to presume if she found no blood, she would make someone bleed simply to satisfy her desires.

I was so intrigued by her I nearly missed the man who trailed her silently at a distance. If I had not known wolves, I would have thought they had come separately and arrived at the same hunting grounds as a matter of coincidence.

But there seemed no coincidence in Junction.

He moved with the same quiet animal grace that she did—a grace and power others would wrongly mistake as leonine. Those who had never seen a wolf in action, a wolf in the wild, no doubt would misjudge him as a lion among men.

Though they moved in a similar fashion, he was as unique as she. Dark, African, or Caribbean in descent, the red that lit his hair muted among the rich brown and ebony he wore in lengthy dreadlocks. He was as broad across the shoulders as Max and nearly as tall as Pietr. The men in the pool hall were smart enough to give him wide berth as he passed by.

A few men boldly stood taller or threw back their shoulders and puffed out their chests, but I could not be sure if it was in response to her or the threat of him.

Remaining in the shadows, I watched and waited for a moment to slip away unnoticed.

When she finished her round through the pool hall, her companion not far behind, and went to the bar for a drink, I headed for the door.

"Don't I look twenty-one?" she asked the bartender, and I glanced over my shoulder in time to see her motion down the length of her body as if it were all the ID she needed.

"You look amazing, hot stuff," the man replied, wiping at the same spot on the bar he had been rubbing with great intensity since she'd walked in, "but if I get busted for serving minors, I'm screwed. No card, no Coors."

Her friend joined her, his hand on her shoulder. He leaned in and whispered something. She pulled away from him, her hands balling into fists that rested on her hips.

"I deserve a drink," she snapped.

"Come on, George, there aren't any cops around . . . ," someone called from the end of the hall.

"And it wouldn't be your ass in a sling if there were," the bartender replied.

"Here," another man said, reaching across the bar, "I'll help you myself—"

"What the—" the bartender hit him with his towel. "What are you thinking?"

"They're thinking they want to buy me a drink." She laughed.

"And I said *no*," he shouted. "You need to leave."

Fists started flying, and I ducked out the door. I had been in enough bar fights with Max to know how things would end—with broken chairs, tables, and maybe a broken arm or a leg for some participants. I had no interest in being a part of that.

I looked around the parking lot, wondering what car they had come in. If I knew where they were from, it might give me some clue to their destination or their goals.

If they had goals.

Finding their vehicle might also help me determine their numbers.

What if there were more than the two?

If Wanda had been along I would have asked her to run license plates, but my stomach tightened at the thought of getting more help from Wanda.

The way Mother had called her a traitor when Wanda helped us rescue her—there had been such vehemence to the word it was hard to believe it was merely the dementia of a dying wolf. . . . What if Wanda had betrayed Mother in the past?

I slid into the car, still contemplating the vehicles crowding the lot. A few motorcycles, some standard two-door and four-door cars, and an old box van. A lot of wolves could fit in an old box van.

Starting the Rabbit, I thought about how few of us fit in it. Amy already joked about needing a shoehorn or a better understanding of the game Tetris to get Max in and out of the vehicle.

Backing the car out, I hoped both wolves had squeezed into the tiny two-door I saw parked near the lot's back.

And I hoped they needed no more room than that.

Marlaena

Gareth found me in the old farmhouse's kitchen, opening cabinet doors and rummaging through drawers. "Even mice are in short supply here," I muttered.

"I don't think this is a good idea," Gareth warned, his eyes soft with worry.

"Searching an abandoned home for odds and ends?" I teased him, knowing he was dragging up the bits of Gabriel's recent suggestion to make a connection with a very questionable character.

He pressed closer to me, his face grave. "The Russian."

I pushed past him and through the doorway to the tiny living room. I looked at the pups in their faded hoodies and jackets, all huddled together in the best corner of the building. There was no denying they were cold and hungry. No denying they were my responsibility. I was their alpha. "He offered money?"

Standing in the other entrance, watching me, Gabriel nodded slowly.

"How much?"

He shrugged.

"How much is your safety worth?" Gareth asked over my shoulder.

I shrugged and remembered how it felt as a pup on the run with a stomach grumbling all the time. "And he's not some wolf hunter?"

"He's like nothing we've ever dealt with before," Gabriel answered.

"And he's not some perv with some bizarre kink, right?"

Gabriel raised an eyebrow at me, the smirk sharp on his already crisp features. "Are there such people?"

"You have no idea," I muttered. "So. Freaky Russian dude with money wants to meet a werewolf and talk business."

"You sound intrigued," Gabriel said, approval clear in his voice.

"Intrigued?" I shrugged again, noncommittal. "Curious? Yes."

Margie—not my mother but the woman who signed papers

and claimed motherhood in the name of a wicked tax deduction and the ability to then call herself a philanthropist—was fond of warning, "Curiosity killed the cat."

If she thought curiosity was rough on felines, she had no clue how hard it was to deny in canines.

Besides. Freaky Russian dude? What harm could possibly come of it?

Of course, cats got nine lives. And werewolves? Just one.

And a short one at that.

CHAPTER SIXTEEN

Jessie

Pausing outside the boiler room door, I thought about it. I'd searched for Harnek's group of special students during my homeroom and study hall for a few days now. What were the odds that the something weird I was searching for was going on down there? Just because boiler rooms were some of the creepiest places in movies—besides the spiderweb-filled attic or basement of somebody's cat-obsessed aunt . . .

I twisted the door knob and—to my surprise—it opened easily. From somewhere under the staircase, lit by a soft glow of light from below, came the sound of steam and liquid passing through old pipes and beyond that—the sound of voices.

I paused on the first step. I could go into the heart of it alone or—I touched the cell phone I kept in my hip pocket—I could call Pietr and ask for backup.

Of the decidedly sensitive sort.

Dammit.

He'd overthink things and slow down whatever progress I might be able to make by just going in and exploring. I could jump in feet first and figure things out as I went.

But . . . I could get hurt.

Killed was even an option.

Pietr would want to take the time to lay out a cautious and concise plan. There'd probably be at least one carefully created chart. . . . Maybe a Venn diagram.

That did it.

I hurried down the rest of the stairs, stooping to see as much as I could as fast as I could.

Desks were arranged haphazardly and at a decent distance apart, one student at each one, all focused intently on something in front of them.

I descended another two steps.

With her back to me a petite blonde was verbally railing against one student who seemed to be struggling to complete whatever weird assignment would bring you to a makeshift classroom in the boiler room of Junction High.

"I said, *Do it again!*" she bellowed, nearly doubled over, fist and clipboard at her sides.

"Sophia?" I squeaked, finally recognizing the blond hair and slender form.

She whipped around to look at me, confirming my suspicion as to her identity, her eyes wide. The kids scrambled to—they pulled out books and homework—appear *normal?* In the boiler room. Well, we all tried our best to seem less than strange. . . .

Sophie smiled, her voice changing from the drill-sergeant shout and sinking back into the soft near-whisper I'd become so used to. "Oh. Hey," she said. "Come on down."

She turned back to them as I came down the last few steps and said, "It's okay everybody. Go back to what you were doing—it's only Jessie. Hi, Jessie."

"Hi, Jessie?" I repeated, stunned. "Just: 'Hi, Jessie'?" I waved at the room of students focusing so hard on their separate tasks—oddly reminding me of the aspiring Hogwarts wizards, minus the feather-stuffed wands, robes, and strange hats. I looked at one particular kid and corrected myself. Okay, so at least one of them had a strange hat.

Sophie shrugged and turned back to watch them, jotting down quick notes on her clipboard as she began to wander through the awkwardly arranged desks. She had to know I'd follow.

I peeked over her shoulder at a girl who focused on an orange. "What's she doing?" I whispered, but Sophie waved me to silence.

The orange wobbled, rolled down the slanted desk . . .

"Gravity works," I muttered.

The girl cursed in frustration and stuck a hand out to grab the orange as it tumbled off the desk's edge—but suddenly it was hovering just above her hand. She cursed again and it quivered in midair, rising a few more inches.

Soph made a *tsk-tsk* noise with her tongue. "If you use that same passion, the emotion behind that cuss that just singed my ears—*twice*—you'll have it floating in no time. And not get stuck with detention," she said with a sigh, tugging off a pink slip she'd just filled out.

I looped an arm in hers and towed her to the side of the classroom. "Whoa. Soph. So, you're, like, what? Coaching these kids? We stood in that hallway listening in on you-know-who—"

"Voldemort?" she teased.

"Might as well be, considering the level of crazy we're all mired in," I returned. "And you—what are *you*?"

She stood nearly nose-to-nose with me, keeping a wary watch over my shoulder to make sure nothing went wrong. "I sort of coach . . . I'm more like an enforcer? An overseer?"

"I guess I'm—"

She shouted over my shoulder, "Sam—don't close your eyes—"

BOOM.

—just a little too late.

Sophie leaped past me, clipboard clattering to the concrete floor as she grabbed a fire extinguisher and doused the desk that had suddenly burst into flames.

"Stunned," I concluded.

"Next time, keep your eyes open when you try to set something on fire—it's called *aiming*," Sophie said, shaking the stunned boy's shoulder.

"Next time," the girl with the orange said, waving her pink slip in the air at him, "aim that blast right here."

Sophie shook her head and whispered to me, "I'd hate to be around when Samuel starts staring at some pretty girl and thinking, Man, she's *hot*. . . . She might suddenly be hot in a far more literal fashion." She rolled her eyes. "Okay, everyone. I think it's time for a break. Pull out your silent reading books and take a seat."

"Really? Silent reading?"

"Reading opens your mind to possibilities," she justified. "Until a couple weeks ago—maybe a couple months, in your case—none of us had any clue that any of this was even a possibility. But now?"

"Yeah," I agreed, thinking back. "I guess that makes sense.

So, are all these kids affected because of the school lunch program?"

She shrugged. "At this point that's our best guess. It's not impossible that a few students with latent abilities would've triggered with the onset of puberty, but we think even those have been greatly enhanced by whatever's being fed to the students."

"So it connects back to the food."

"Yes."

"Anything else we know about the food and its impact on the students?"

"That on days they serve burritos, Sam's fireballs become a touch more . . . *explosive?*"

"Everyone gets a bit more explosive on burrito day," I quipped, "regardless of the suspicious nature of the additives."

She pursed her lips.

"And the other part of the *we?* This is Harnek's pet project, right?"

Down the stairs I heard the click of high heels coming and a moment before I saw the woman, I identified her by the signature color of shoes she favored.

"Ms. Harnek. Hunch confirmed."

She froze a second, assessed the situation, and then allowed a smile to cross her lips. "It shouldn't surprise me that someone like you has stumbled into our midst, should it, Jessie?"

"By someone like me, do you mean *nosy?*"

"I prefer to think of you as tremendously inquisitive." She winked. She surveyed the room again and held her hand out for Sophie's clipboard, trailing her gaze along the list of names and notes. "Interesting. Dear sweet Samuel." She shook her head as she headed toward him. "I know what the cafeteria was serving today and it wasn't any product with a significant bean count. Explain your lack of control."

He looked up from his copy of *Firestarter* and started to open his mouth, and my attention returned to Sophie.

"So. Harnek?"

". . . has an intriguing history," Soph admitted.

"I hear you," Harnek warned over her shoulder.

"I thought teachers and staff were only supposed to have *eyes* in the back of their heads," Sophie retorted.

"You mentioned my intriguing history," Harnek quipped. "Let's not bring my ex-husbands into this."

"Ha!" Soph grinned. "I like working with you, you know?"

"You'd better, because there sure as heck isn't a paycheck coming with this gig," Harnek returned. She turned her focus back to Sam, her hands clutching the scorched desk as she leaned over to have a private conversation.

"Harnek was one of the last staff members in part of a special—and very hush-hush—Duke University program that ran in conjunction with the Rhine Research Center. It was designed to identify and train teens and preteens with special abilities. Harnek got placed here as a counselor—"

"Which I'm *more* than qualified to be," Harnek added, clicking her way back across the concrete to us, "but the idea was I'd hang out here a while and scout the locals. Even then, Junction had a higher than average number of reports of the paranormal kind. . . . Ever hear of Susie Fenstermacher?"

Oddly enough, I had. "The kid who could produce socks out of thin air?" I snorted.

"The same. Some kids cry glass, some dream-walk,"

Harnek pointed out. "But Susie manifested socks. And not just any socks—matching pairs—talk about a useful, but weird, ability." She shrugged.

"I could've used her on laundry days," I muttered.

"I've seen you shoeless on days other than laundry days. You could've used Susie a lot," Soph muttered.

Harnek continued. "Anyhow, researching Susie was one of the main reasons I got this gig."

"Seriously?"

"Susie was a viable point of study. Hey, it was the eighties—there was so much aerosol in the air from maintaining big hair, it's a wonder anyone could think straight."

"I've seen pictures."

"I've *been* in those pictures—and I *liked* it," she reported with a smile that snapped into place.

"So you came to Junction to track down the weirdness and study the people?"

"It was that, and a bit more. The government—well, the military specifically—has always wanted to know about every single asset we could possibly employ: the more bizarre, the more covert, the better. So psychic studies and paranormal research were hot. Sure, people imagined some of the stuff we encountered, but mostly its existence was only rumored. And the idea small-town America, full of the salt of the earth—the common people—could be so rich with paranormal diversity . . . well, we *hoped* but we never guessed there'd be this much. That's the amazing thing: Fact truly is stranger than fiction."

I pointed to the students who'd gradually put down their books and returned to testing their newfound abilities. "Is this what you expected—what you hoped for?"

"No," she admitted. "This was never part of any plan I was aware of. But it's happened. Kids have been affected. So now they need to be trained."

"Trained for what? Military usage?"

She shook her head. "I hope not, though I think that may be in the works. It's not on my agenda, though. Here I'm just trying to get them to use their powers enough so they can control them. So they can be safe." Looking down at the toes of her brightly colored shoes, she added, "Beyond that, they can train for whatever. To fight oppression, to defend democracy—"

"An assault against terrorism using floating citrus hardly sounds do-able," I said. "I mean, have you seen the price of oranges recently?"

Harnek blinked, but the smile never strayed from her lips. "They don't need to be our heroes. We shouldn't expect that sort of dedication or sacrifice from anyone but ourselves." She shrugged. "You of all people know that there's far more we don't know than what we *do* know. And these kids"—she looked at Sophie—"*all* need the best chance they can get. At survival. We've tampered too much with things. I'm just trying to make our mistakes survivable."

"Are they?" I asked. She had to know I was referring to the girl who was wheeled into Pecan Place on a stretcher and exploded. "Are these mistakes survivable?"

Her eyes darkened. "I hope so. All I can do is my best."

"Tell them not to eat the school food," I suggested.

Harnek looked at Sophie.

"I don't eat it," she confessed. "I'm still doing what I was doing."

"But you were pushed by Derek. He was your catalyst. That's gotta be different. What if once you've been triggered, that's it?" I asked. "What if you don't need to keep being exposed to the catalyst again and again? What if overexposure is . . ."

"Deadly," Harnek said, her voice soft. "You aspiring authors and your what-ifs."

"You need to put an end to this. You told Perlson no about the additional supplement—face him down about the additive, too," I urged.

Harnek pressed her lips into a thin line.

Sophie whispered, "What if coming out so openly about all this gets her removed from the picture?"

"Killed?" I asked Sophie.

Harnek paled. *"Killed?"*

I snorted. "You're running with quite an organization, you know? I've been shot at a bunch. Grazed, even."

"I meant they'd *fire* her," Soph said with a roll of her eyes. "Make it look like a budget cut."

"Like they'd ever remove a guidance counselor from a middle school or high school," I muttered. "Parents are the first ones to say their tweens and teens need help."

"Schools cut teachers all the time, and what are schools supposed to be doing? *Teaching*," Sophie responded.

"Good point."

"So let's not wrongly equate the needs of the students with the designs of the administration—or any school board."

I shrugged, agreeing. "So she might lose her job. Wouldn't it be worth it to warn the student body about something so potentially dangerous?"

"Still standing right here, girls. Besides, losing my job would make it harder to keep up with the students and make sure they're taken care of. Now, at least, I'm in the *heart* of the operation."

The boiler grumbled.

"Or its unruly gut," Harnek muttered. "You have to excuse me, girls. This whole thing can make you a bit crazy. I'm definitely at the 'If I don't laugh, I'll cry' stage." She sighed. "Besides"—she signaled us to lean in—"there haven't been any more deaths since that one at Pecan Place. I truly think this can be handled."

"As long as Perlson doesn't sneak in the supplement," I said.

Harnek's eyes narrowed. "You were right before."

"About what?"

"About being nosy." But she reached out to us and threw her arms around us, drawing us away from the other students. "But that nosiness? It might be an advantage. . . ."

Alexi

I pulled into the broad parking lot and took a deep breath before looking at the building that sprawled ahead of me, marked by one large sign that read GOLDEN OAKS ADULT DAY CARE AND RETIREMENT CENTER.

Over the weeks I had grown bolder, driving the car a row or two closer to the entrance before parking and sitting in a contemplative silence.

It was just a building housing many older people. Why should I even care?

I glared at its stoic brick face.

Although I did not know why I cared, I knew at least that I *did* care. That although Hazel Feldman was far from being the mother I knew and loved, she was my mother. Should that not count for something?

But I was not ready to meet her or speak to her. I was not able to yet face the truth enough that she might see it and know it. That I did care. It showed up in my anger and frustration. In the way I warred with Max over petty things, some part of me always remembering that *he* was the eldest Rusakova.

Some part of me remembering I was merely a fraud.

But how could I meet her and not accidentally let her know that even in abandoning me she had still *affected* me? Deep down I knew that eventually meeting her was inevitable.

CHAPTER SEVENTEEN

Marlaena

I'd never been much for sticking to the shadows, especially in my human skin, so the request to get together in a dim alley sucked. "You wanted to meet me?" I raised an eyebrow at the man in the shadows, his attempt at anonymity in the poorly lit alley nearly worthless considering my superior night vision and my sense of smell. And this man's scent was distinct: humanity tainted with cheap cigarettes, cheaper cologne, and vodka—*lots* of vodka. I'd recognize him just by his stink. His scent coated the inside of my nostrils like pollution crawling into carefully maintained airducts.

"*Da*," he said, his eyes scanning me.

"Well, here I am." I clapped my hands in front of me and pushed out one hip to rest a hand on it.

He blinked, startled but unimpressed.

"You are one of them?" he asked.

"One of who?"

"The oborot."

"Ober-*what?*"

"Oborot: ones transformed." He stepped into the light. Muscular and significantly older than me, he had short-cropped, salt-and-pepper hair, and eyes that looked like they had seen everything life had to offer—good and bad—twice. "Werewolves."

"Ohhh. *Werewolves.* Yeah." I straightened. "Yeah. I'm not just *one* of them—I'm the *best* of them," I said, shooting him a narrow look. "But before we go any further, exactly who are *you?*"

"A man with significant ties and money who is looking for some people—*independent contractors*—with special abilities and a desire to make some fast cash under the table."

"Under the table. Of course. Go on."

"Things will be dangerous."

I crossed my arms over my chest and nodded.

"Certain situations will become violent."

I shrugged.

"There may even be a need—from time to time—to break a few laws." He went silent, watching me with hooded eyes.

A few long minutes passed.

"Did I tell you to *stop* talking?"

He barked out a short laugh. "So we shall do business?"

"You keep my pack sheltered, clothed, and fed—well fed—and I think we can reach an agreement."

This time he clapped *his* hands together. "Excellent. Then perhaps we can get started." He motioned for me to follow him out of the alleyway. "Let us get something to eat. You look hungry."

My stomach rumbled at the invitation.

"The first thing we shall discuss is my suspicion there are more of your type here. In Junction. Parading as simple humans."

"I'm not a fan of hiding what you really are."

"Excellent. Have you met the Rusakovas?"

"My scout mentioned them, but no, I haven't had the pleasure. They're your over-whatevers?"

"Oboroten. *Da*. But they may no longer be."

"What?"

"They have taken a cure—a medicine of sorts that denies the wolf its grasp on them."

Sick. And not in the that's-so-amazingly-awesome-I'll-call-it-sick way. In the that-thought-makes-me-wanna-puke-kittens-sick way.

"I want to know that the cure works. That it is unbreakable—permanent. If it is permanent, they have gone against their nature. They should be destroyed, *da?*"

I glared at him. "Totally *da*. The Wolf is the Way."

"I knew we would see eye to eye. Bring them in if they are not cured or the cure is not permanent."

"And if it is?"

"Kill them."

"I'm not so big on killing."

He glared at me, his jaw set.

"I didn't say we *wouldn't*, just that I'm not big on it. Besides, I know why *I'd* be pissed at wolves opting for some dumb-ass cure, like *this*"—I ran my hands down my sides—"is some sickness. But what's it to *you?*"

"I invested a great deal of time and money in Pietr Rusakova to extract a promise from him."

"A promise?" I nearly laughed. Life was littered with broken promises. "So he screwed you out of something."

"*Da*. His services."

"Huh." Weird Russian dude was willing to off people who didn't meet his expectations. Hardcore. I cracked my knuckles. "How soon does my pack get taken care of?"

"Just say *yes* and I will take care of everything."

"I'm not as dumb as this Pietr guy. No promises just yet."

He looked at me with rage simmering in his eyes, but we both knew his options were limited. There weren't enough werewolves to go around, it seemed.

"Let's talk food and shelter." Thrusting my hands in my pockets I pointed out of the alley with my chin. Unlike the Russian, I realized my pack suddenly had a bunch of options opening up.

Alexi

Although I struggled to trust Wanda, it still seemed she was doing her best to allay my fears. Standing outside her flat, I knocked quickly.

She opened the door and gave me a welcoming smile.

"I never thought an officer of the enemy would so gladly invite me into her flat," I remarked as Wanda ushered me in. "Why do I keep thinking, 'Walk into my parlor said the spider to the fly?'"

"Because you have significant trust issues when it comes to older women?"

I cocked my head and thought about it a moment. "*Da*. A point for you."

"Look, I just figured since you guys are going to be in a bit of a financial crunch now with the Mafia gone and the company blown to smithereens and since I need to head back to DC and elsewhere to discuss my job options and get a few things straightened out—"

"Being sold to the highest bidder still does not sit well with you?" I asked, remembering how she came to be a part of the company when she still believed she was working for the CIA.

She blinked at me. "You could say that. . . . Anyhow. There's a lot of stuff it seems I accumulated in a short amount of time."

"How very American of you."

She snorted. "And it's stuff I don't need, but your family might find a use for."

Slowly we made our way through each small room and I did indeed find a few items here and there that my siblings and household might benefit from possessing.

In the bathroom (a spot we were still refurbishing, thanks to Max's destructive final change), half-packed boxes revealed a curling iron for Cat (she had two already, but seemed to lust after others, saying barrel size was as important in curling irons as guns), a set of matching bathroom rugs and curtains, and a set of cups and a toothbrush holder.

Wanda flopped down on the couch. "If you can convince Max to help you move this," she said, motioning to the blue plaid upholstery beneath her, "you can have it, and the recliner, too. I have no idea what's going to happen with my job. Or where I'll wind up. And I have no desire to pay rental for a storage unit I may never come back for."

"So that's it, then," I asked, sitting in the recliner and testing it out. "You're leaving with no intention of coming back?"

She leaned forward and flipped through a box of picture frames.

"Are you seriously leaving for good? Leaving Leon?"

She paused, seemingly examining a photograph of something. "I don't know where my job will take me."

"So do another job."

She snorted. "It's like telling a tiger to change its stripes. This is the only job I've ever really had—except for that one sandwich shop when I was seventeen." She shook her head, ponytail whipping. "I don't intend to go back to making subs."

"You have had other jobs," I protested. "Your cover jobs. Librarian, what else?"

She smiled faintly. "If we include my cover jobs, I can honestly say I've worked in nearly every type of industry in the past dozen years."

"You had training to appear competent—to blend in—with all of them, *da?*"

"Of course. That's the only way you maintain cover."

"So you have options. You do not have to work for the CIA anymore or any of its wayward branches. You can return to Junction. Live the life you really want to live, with the man you want to live it with. You are no longer a slave to your employment."

"My employment—even with the company—provided decent benefits like health care. I can't get that making sandwiches or selling shoes or fancy soaps."

"Would you rather have health care provided or be provided with the sort of care that will help keep you healthy physically, emotionally, and mentally?" I smiled at her.

"Who the hell are you?"

"What?"

"What'd you do with Alexi—you know the guy: bitter and cynical, struggling with life and his family. Always smells of smoke or vodka? Where'd he go?"

I laughed.

"I swear to god, it's like I'm talking to a pod person."

"Life is not so bad when you are not on the run or wondering when your big secret will suddenly come out and things will blow up in your face." I shrugged.

"So how is the White Crow?"

I froze and looked at her carefully. "As beautiful and intelligent as ever."

"You're in love with her."

"I have been for a while now," I admitted more easily than I expected I ever could.

"Does she know?"

I shrugged again.

"You're gonna louse this up."

"*Nyet*—why would you say that?"

"Where is she? Right now?"

"Samoa."

"And who is she with?"

I shrugged. "I would presume she is with a partner."

"She went Interpol, didn't she?"

"She and I have yet to talk the details of her employment, but it would be the most effective way to thoroughly piss off her father and announce her own special brand of independence."

She nodded solemnly.

"What are you thinking?"

"That pissing off a mob boss of her father's level is never a wise idea—even if you are blood and part of a clearly oppositional force."

"It is dangerous work, *da*. But she is quite clever. And well trained with weapons."

"Do you know anything about her partner?"

"*Nyet.*"

"Have you told her how you feel about her?"

"Not in so many words . . ."

"It only takes three. And they're short ones." She stood up and looked at the last wall that had things hanging on it. "I don't want you to screw this up, Alexi. People like us . . ."

"People like *us?*"

She nodded and lifted a picture off its hook. "Yes. Like us. World-weary. Out of luck and fighting falling in love. People like us don't get many chances at love."

"So what do you propose I do?"

"Get to her somehow. Tell her what you think and feel. And do it soon."

"In short: You are instructing someone who is taking your old things away in a trash bag to produce the amount of money to fly internationally to say words that could be spoken over the phone?"

"In short: *Yes.*"

I rested my head in my hands. "And how do you suggest I accomplish such a grandiose gesture?"

"I'll give you part of the money when my deposit comes back to me. Should be soon. Call it an investment in our friendship."

I balked, straightening suddenly. It was not so much the idea as the term she used. *Friendship.* Mother called her a traitor. . . . "I don't take money from friends."

"Has anyone else offered?"

I looked down at my shoes. "*Nyet.*"

"Then accept *my* offer. You can even pay me back, if it makes you feel better."

"I would." I lowered the footrest and stood. "I will think on it," I assured her, picking up the items I had already secured. "I will be back to pick up a few things in a day or two."

"Sounds good to me," she replied, motioning to the door.

Jessie

Alexi wasn't home when they came sniffing around. Amy and I got to the door first and paused in the foyer, recognizing Gabriel. "What's *he* doing here?" she hissed at me, her face scrunched up in concern. "We should tell Pietr or Cat."

My suspicion about Max's recent behavior—his quick moves and uninterrupted intensity—made me think he was best suited to deal with wolves at the door.

Gabriel knocked again.

"Damn it." Amy yanked the door open. "Yo, Gabe. What's up?"

"Or maybe the question should be: 'What are you doing here?'" I asked.

"Isn't this a Russian-American household?" A woman stepped into view. "Is there no code of hospitality?"

Yeah, Max could've handled this much better. No one expected manners from Max.

"It may be a Russian-American household, but the door's been opened by two American-American girls. Like yourself, I'm guessing," I added. "And our current international reputation is far from showcasing our hospitality to suspicious visitors."

She laughed. "We're suspicious," she said to Gabe, with a congratulatory sneer. Yeah, not a smile. Totally a sneer.

"Oh, Gabe's not suspicious. I *know* he's trouble," I corrected her. "But you're suspicious by association."

"I might like you." But her expression added a dangerous note, as if she'd meant to say: *I might like you roasted slowly on a spit.* "Life's short—let's cut to the chase."

Amy and I folded our arms and tilted our heads. "Go," I said.

"You aren't stupid."

"Thank god," Amy muttered.

"You know what we are."

"I know what *he* is," I specified. "A thief. Among more paranormal things," I added. "I guess you're the same."

She shrugged. "We know the ones who live here are the same as us."

I blinked.

"Not quite." Max came up behind us and wrapped his arms around Amy protectively. "We're not thieves."

The woman leaned forward. "Ah. Max," she said.

"'*Ah, Max*'?" Amy said, looking up at him.

"Do we know each other?"

"I watched you together. On the bridge."

"Okay. Totally creepy," Amy muttered. "There's petty theft and then there's stalking."

"Geez," I muttered. "If someone starts to sparkle, I'm going to worry I'm part of some author's crazy series."

"Max," the woman said. "It is so good to meet one of our own."

"I'm not anyone's *own*," he corrected.

She pursed her lips and cocked her head.

Pietr and Cat joined us.

Gabe's gaze flickered to Pietr, some odd bit of recognition lit in his eyes, and he turned his face away, submissive.

But the redhead on the front porch showed no such respect. She stepped right past Max and appraised Pietr with bright green eyes, letting her gaze travel the length of his body.

. Boldly.

As she took him in, I watched them both with equal fascination. And I realized I was comparing myself to her as she stood there on the porch. Her waist was narrower. Her neck longer. Her cheekbones more defined.

Pietr was frozen as if he recognized her somehow, though he'd never mentioned her before. Someone from Farthington? An ex-?

I had the feeling I wasn't going to like the answer.

She drank down his scent, her expression even more intimate, no—*indecent*—than when her eyes had paused while traveling across his body. Her eyes narrowed, her nose wrinkling for the briefest of moments before she schooled her features once more and smiled, her lips turning in a way I could only describe as languid.

"Pietr Rusakova," she said, clearly impressed. And—a bit puzzled?

"*Da.*"

"I am Gabriel's alpha," she said.

Pietr pulled me around in front of him, tucking me against him. Possessively. "This is—"

"Jessica Gillmansen," I reported, offering my hand.

She just looked at it and then back at Pietr.

"Marlaena," she said, reaching out a hand for Pietr.

I took it and gave it one hell of a shake.

She pulled back, disgust twisting her features.

She didn't like my touch about as much as I didn't like her—*everything*. Yeah. I simply did not like her.

"We need to talk." Her gaze grazed my face to fully lock on Pietr, who kept his mouth near my ear.

Pietr's voice was strained. "Say what you must. We are very busy here."

"We are two different packs that might perhaps consider an alliance."

"I believe you are misinformed. We *were* a pack. But now we are cured. Human. Healthy."

"Really? *Cured?*" Her eyes widened. "You're no longer wolf?" Her eyes shifted from his face to Max's.

Max looked away.

"*Nyet*. We are no longer wolf."

"Why would you do that? Why strip away the greatest part of you?" she whispered, her voice thin. "You do not *cure* a wolf—you embrace it. 'The Wolf is the Way,'" she proclaimed, her eyes bright.

Pietr's voice deepened and darkened, a dangerous quality creeping into it. "We choose to *live*."

"But how can you live when you deny your nature?"

Pietr shook his head. "There is no need for an alliance."

"Then will you try and force us out?" Gabriel asked.

Marlaena's eyes sparked at the idea, and she tilted her head to peer at Pietr from beneath her long bangs.

"*Nyet*. Why would we do that?" Pietr asked, his head tilting in an odd mimicry of her posture.

"Because we are on your pack's territory," Gabriel said, stepping forward, his lip lifted from his teeth.

Max and Pietr blinked at each other. "We do not have the same belief system, it would seem. As long as you do not threaten our family or the people in this community, you're welcome here."

Marlaena's brows drew sharply together. "You are not like the alpha of a normal pack." Her eyes flickered, and for a moment held mine. "Oh, Pietr." She reached out to brush his cheek with her fingers, whispering, "It's her fault, isn't it?"

I slapped her hand down, and Pietr thrust me behind him protectively, doing his best to snarl at her.

Still, her hand brushed down his rigid cheek. "No one's taught you how blessed and beautiful we are."

"Leave now," Max ordered, his attention split between what was happening between Marlaena and Pietr and the perplexed expression on my face.

"You must come, meet the pack, and see the truth before you deny it," she insisted.

"NOW." Max moved between Pietr and Marlaena, forcing her back out the door, Gabe stumbling behind her.

The door slammed shut on them, and I wrapped my hands around Pietr's waist, pressing my cheek to his back.

He just stood there a moment, stunned into inaction.

"She'll be back." He pulled me around to his front, holding me so tightly I thought my joints would pop. "I want you to stay away from her—from him—from all of them. I don't want her to come back here," he whispered into the top of my head. He inhaled sharply, sucking down as much of my scent as a simple human could, as desperately as a man dying in the desert sucked down water.

But I wanted to see his eyes.

To know what he wasn't telling me.

CHAPTER EIGHTEEN

Alexi

I could not believe I was taking Wanda's advice. But I called a
local travel agent and began making arrangements to book a
flight to Nadezhda. It was more than I would have liked to
pay, but with the money Wanda was giving me, I could just
cover it. I needed to see Nadezhda face-to-face. I needed
to say things to her—things as powerful as the feelings I
had—things connecting us across continents and huge water-
ways.

Jessie

Somehow I was surviving another session of Dungeons &
Dragons. It amazed me that my survival was possible, considering how lost I was. Again.

Luckily, Max's and Smith's characters kept stepping in to

save mine, but I knew I was all but doomed the moment Hascal suggested my character be given a red shirt to wear. Even *I* got that particular reference.

Amy, well, Amy was kicking ass and taking names. Maybe not names as much as loot and levels. Once the biggest opponent to playing D&D, she'd become a convert. When the game finally wound down and Smith began packing up his notes and books, she pointed out that it was a good idea to close the game up early, as Max actually had work.

There was a faint growl that aptly expressed his opinion regarding a return to the movie theater that had decided to employ him. "It wouldn't suck so badly if I just got to watch movies all the time, but they actually make me work, too," he said with a slowly uncurling grin. "And it's harder to sneak a hot chick into a dimly lit theater than you'd think. . . ."

Amy slapped his arm. "Who're you trying to sneak into dark theaters?"

"Why don't you meet me at Exit 3 tomorrow at twelve fifteen and find out?" he said with a wink.

Amy grinned. "Maybe my weekend's looking up."

I nodded in support. I wanted her to have an amazing weekend. But I wanted one, too, with *my* boyfriend. That same boyfriend who was being evasive about why he thought Marlaena would keep coming back until we all went to see her pack in action.

Alexi

I had returned to Wanda's flat, as I'd arranged, to pick through a few more odds and ends before bringing Max over for the heavy lifting.

"Good enough." She set a photo on the coffee table. "Come back tonight with Max to get the couch and anything else you need." She pointed. "Coffee table?"

I glanced at it, but my eyes focused on the photo in the frame that now rested on it.

Wanda. Holding a little dog and dressed in a jogging suit. Odd, it seemed somehow familiar.

"*Da*. Coffee table," I agreed, my mind racing.

"Do you *want* the coffee table?" she clarified.

"Ohhh," I teased, though my heart suddenly wasn't in it. "*Da*, Cat would probably like it. When did you have a dog?" I asked.

"A little more than a year ago," she responded, a bit too slowly for my taste. "Why do you ask?"

"I noticed the picture. . . ."

She looked at the frame I held in my hand, her expression nearly devoid of emotion. She was hiding something. Then she smiled and stepped forward to take it from me, giving it a look herself. "That was Geoffrey," she said. "A cute little devil. A very common breed, but an uncommon character. I had to have him put down. Cancer." Her expression dropped away again.

Maybe that was all it was then. She had a little dog of a breed I had noticed before and it was euthanized. Perhaps that was all I was reading from her tone and expression.

"I am sorry," I said.

She nodded and slipped the picture frame into a box and closed the lid on it. "Oh—I have good news." She turned and picked up her purse. "The deposit's back early because my landlord said I'm so honest and a great tenant."

I did not flinch.

"So here, take this and go see that girl of yours. Make her

understand the way you feel. Otherwise . . ." She shrugged. "You don't want to lose someone you love, do you?"

"*Nyet*." I had loved my mother. And lost her. "I never wanted to."

She handed me an envelope. "I have a box of some kitchen stuff Cat might like practicing her cooking skills with. It's by the door. And take all the curtains and blinds as you go," she said, pushing a garbage bag filled with them out of her bedroom. "You all can sharpen your claws on them, for all I care."

Nodding, I grabbed the bag and the box and headed for the stairs, my mind on everything but what I carried.

Marlaena

Gareth took the lead, slipping into the store at exactly nine fifty-eight. The owner shot him a glare and looked pointedly at the clock hanging above the door.

We knew the time, intimately.

Gareth's shoulders slid up in a shrug as if that were apology enough and he headed to the cash register, where he appeared absolutely entranced by the selection of gum and candy.

And while attention was on him—who could tear their eyes away from him—Kyanne moved forward from the shadows, slid beneath the camera, and leaned back to black out its curious eye from below. Sliding along the wall, she sank back into the night and slipped around to come stand beside me. "How long?"

But she knew as well as I did. "Watch," I commanded.

The man escorted Gareth out, and Gareth smiled, waggling a pack of gum at him appreciatively.

It was the last distraction we needed for Gabriel to take his position.

The door closed, the lock clicked into place; the sign flipped over.

CLOSED to the store owner meant OPEN FOR BUSINESS to us.

Gareth sidled over, withdrawing one slender stick of gum. He looked at me, tilted his head, and offered it to Kyanne.

"Thanks," she said with a grin that made her cheeks plump up and emphasized her expressive eyes. Garr. I wanted to pluck the gum out of her hands and shove it into my mouth just to chew it up and spit it out—*on Gareth's shoe*—but I shifted my weight instead, a close eye on the store.

Lights popped off.

Movement in the back.

A shadow headed toward the front.

A bag tucked under his arm.

I stiffened, eyes finding the thin outline of Gabriel's sleek form as he stood in heavy shadow by the door, waiting to snatch the bag and run.

It'd be easy. Gabriel was quick on his feet as a wolf giving chase to its favorite quarry. More slender than Gareth, I'd found myself thinking of him as more fox than wolf many times. His coloring made that even easier to imagine. He leaned tight against the store's front, tucked into a slight alcove between the brick face of the storefront and the broad stretch of glass that made up the main display window.

A flash of color showed in the reflection of the glass and the man was there—a quarter-inch of glass separating Gabriel from him—separating Gabriel from the money we needed to survive.

Need drove us far harder than *want* ever could.

Maybe I should've taken the deal with Dmitri. But to give him so much control . . . We needed control of our destiny as much as we needed food.

That need was the thing that made us stand there, still as rabbits—our breath burning in our throats—as the lock turned, the door opened, and the man stepped outside the safety of his store and within Gabriel's reach.

Gabriel rushed him, his hand snaking out in anticipation of the bag's location.

The man's eyes widened when Gabriel plowed into him, reaching for the bag he cradled up under his arm. I nearly laughed at his shock and surprise. Junction wasn't a place you worried about getting robbed. He must've thought that same thing as he pulled back from Gabe, determination fierce on his face. Was he betting Gabe was just a kid—so what were the odds Gabe was armed?

Way less than the odds the man was armed.

The crack of gunfire sounded, and Gabriel stumbled backward, his eyes wide and frightened, his hands clutching at his chest as blood poured from a sudden wound. I pulled free of Gareth's grip, but Kyanne was ahead of me, just a few strides, making a headlong rush—to catch Gabe as he fell or snatch the prize from the shop's owner. . . .

The second shot knocked her back, too.

I reached the man, hit him so hard his eyes blinked shut and his head rocked back on his neck with a cracking noise that reminded me of Phil husking walnuts at Christmas. The man slumped to the sidewalk, his head landing with a dull thud as the bag fell free and I snatched it up, looking for Gareth.

He'd already slung Gabe's arm around his shoulders and

snaked another around Kyanne's waist, hauling them both up and urging them forward with kind words.

I snagged Kyanne, twisting her arm over my shoulders so I could lock it with my own. She yelped as I pulled her to her full height. "Step it up, Kyanne," I commanded. "Step it up or die here—next to *him*," I added, looking down at the store owner's body, limp by the door.

Gareth shot me one of his totally-appalled-by-my-behavior looks. But there was no time to call me out. Together we half-dragged, half-carried the two to the waiting car and pushed them into the backseat. I slammed the doors and slid into the passenger's side, my hand slapping down on Gareth's thigh.

I didn't have to say the word, but I did, anyhow. "Drive!"

With a squeal of tires we roared away from the scene of the crime, blowing through the town and its assortment of traffic lights and stop signs like we were color-blind.

If anyone had cared to take a look at our current vehicle's mismatched parts, they would have had another reason to assume.

"Get back there," Gareth said, looking at me as I unzipped the bag.

"What? Back where?"

"In the backseat—take care of them."

I yanked my mirror down and looked at the two of them, their legs tangled, blood weeping from their wounds. Their ribs heaved. "They're breathing. . . ."

The look he gave me . . .

"We're werewolves," I justified, "damn near invincible!" His glare didn't soften—it seemed to intensify the next time he pulled his gaze from the twisting country back road. "Damn it," I muttered, crawling into the backseat, prying the two of them apart to get a better look at the damage.

One shot to the chest for Gabriel. Wide of both heart and lungs. I patted his face, and his eyes opened. "Hey, angel," he said with a sloppy smile.

"Gabe's hallucinating," I announced. "Or he's proclaimed today Opposite Day and decided not to let any of us in on the joke."

Gabe grabbed my hand and held it until I tugged it free of his grip.

I turned in the seat to look at Kyanne. A shot to the shoulder oozed blood across her T-shirt. Her eyes were unfocused but somehow fierce. "Kyanne," I said, touching her good shoulder.

"Thanks so frikkin' much," she snapped. "Pull me out of one gutter to get me shot in another."

"Wow," I replied.

Gareth was again the voice of reason. "She's in shock."

"The hell I am," Kyanne responded, her normally sweet demeanor dropping away. "I'm seeing things clearly. *She* wasn't first on the scene to help Gabe because she didn't care enough."

I whipped around to face her. "How dare—"

"How dare I? How *dare* I?" She shook her finger in my face.

"What about *me?*" Gareth asked.

Kyanne stopped short, hearing his softly spoken words. "What do you mean, what about you?"

"If you're going to say she's guilty because of when she arrived to help, then I'm even guiltier being three steps behind you when she was only two."

"Darn it, Gareth," Kyanne muttered, looking down at the

hand that a moment before had been in my face and now had fallen limp in her lap. "Why are you always so quick to fall on the sword?"

He refocused on the road, but I could glimpse just a bit of his face—hardened by some pain he never spoke of—in the rearview mirror.

I tried to find a socially appropriate response. "I'm sorry if you feel I'm letting you down, Kyanne," I tried.

"Geez. Have you ever listened to yourself? You're 'sorry if I feel' like this isn't your fault, like it's the fault of *my* emotions, not *your actions*. That's one of the most retarded phrases I've ever heard anyone say. It ranks right up there with 'because I said so.'"

Evidently Kyanne wasn't hurting too badly. At least not physically. I had more important things to deal with than her emo spaz out. I turned my attention back to Gabe.

"Kyanne, you need to relax. It looks like you're still bleeding badly," Gareth tried.

"Well, of course I'm bleeding badly. It's a gunshot wound. It also hurts like heck, if you didn't know." Then her voice got soft and the compassion crept back in. "But I think that you do know, don't you, Gareth?"

Gareth's eyes again focused on the road. Fiercely.

I tugged at Gabe's shirt. The cloth stuck to the drying blood.

I looked out the window at the countryside flashing by. Even with my keen nighttime senses, I couldn't accurately judge our location or the distance we were from what now served as our home.

"I should've just taken the deal."

"What?" Gareth asked.

"The Russian. This'd be different if I'd gone along instead

of thinking about it. Damn it." I pressed the button on the door handle and watched the window roll down with a soft whirr. The wind rushed in and I opened my nose and my senses to the night.

Gabe muttered something like, "Glad I didn't steal the Rusakovas' red convertible. . . . It'd suck trying to get this much blood out of a real leather interior. . . ." He closed his eyes and dozed off under the weight and warmth of my body.

Gareth glanced back at the three of us, Kyanne still grumbling angrily, and me all but curled on Gabriel's lap. . . .

He smiled.

And it made me just the slightest bit angry.

CHAPTER NINETEEN

Alexi

We climbed the stairs to Wanda's flat, and she opened the door just before I had a chance to knock on it.

"Hey, guys," she greeted us. "Grab whatever you want."

Max looked at me and shrugged.

"We will start with the coffee table," I suggested, thinking about its glass top.

Max followed my lead, heading for the center of the room. "Ready?" Max asked, hefting the coffee table. "You get the doors. I have this."

I opened each door and spotted him on the stairs and all the way to the door, but the picture from earlier—everything about it—seemed to overlay real life in a strangely surreal fashion. I had been there before.

I knew it.

Back we went for the recliner. And then the couch.

On the way down the stairs I suddenly remembered and

slipped toward Max, my ass hitting two steps as I bounced down the staircase and was nearly crushed beneath the couch.

Max snorted. "It is only a couch. Why must you wrestle with it?"

I stood and, wincing, got a grip on the couch once more. "Do you remember what color the houses across the street from us were?"

"Where?" he asked with a grunt as he rested the couch on his hip to get a free hand to open the last door.

"Farthington."

"There was that tan one. And the white one. And that strange one. It always looked pink if the sun caught it wrong."

I kept my grip on the couch although I feared I might lose my grip on my mind. "*Da*. The strange one."

We loaded the couch awkwardly in Mr. Gillmansen's truck. "There are some boxes we need to get," I said. "And then I think we will be finished."

"Excellent," Max said. "You just point and I'll carry. Like the man in any couple would."

I shot him a glare.

He responded with a grin.

Back up the stairs we went.

Wanda was back in the kitchen, so I took my chance and stacked two boxes in Max's waiting arms. One that said CRAP and one that said PHOTOS.

He looked at me a moment, and I just shook my head, warning him to silence.

I needed answers now that my mind was filled with so many fresh questions.

All I knew was what I could remember and what I had just discovered. Mother had called Wanda a traitor, something I had dismissed as part of the madness that came with being an older oborot. Wanda had been working in the area when we were in the same area—before Junction.

Mother had gone jogging once or twice a week and mentioned a little rat of a dog. Wanda and her rat of a dog were in a photograph in front of a house that looked oddly pink. A house that stood across the street from ours in Farthington.

The photo positioned Wanda on our sidewalk.

With the photographer standing on our lawn.

With everything loaded, I returned one more time to Wanda's flat. I needed to see her again. To read her face and hope that I was wrong. That everything was circumstantial. That I was making something out of nothing.

Standing before her open doorway, I called her name and she appeared.

"Thank you for taking all that stuff," she said with a sigh. "I hope it makes things better."

"It seems to be what we *do* with stuff that makes things better. Or worse," I added.

She nodded. "There you go again. Thinking."

"It is a hazard of being me."

"Well, don't let it mess up the good things in your life—sometimes overthinking ruins things. And remember what I said: If it'll make you feel better, you can pay me back. But you don't have to."

"*Nyet*," I said, my voice falling into a whisper. "I will most certainly pay you back," I promised. "For everything."

She smiled and said good night and good-bye and I stood there a heartbeat after the door was shut and the lock slid into place before going back down the steps.

Paying her back would be the least I could do. But I doubted it would be the sort of payback she expected now that I knew the truth.

Marlaena

The car pulled around to the door of the abandoned little farmhouse. No need to park in the driveway like a proper family, so we rolled over a few bushes and got as close as we could to our ramshackle sanctuary.

More important than maintaining a lawn was maintaining our lives.

They rushed out to greet us, all grins and laughter—expecting success—until they saw the grim truth tumble from the backseat. Help rushed forward to cradle their friends—their family with a capital *F*—and help to bring them into the house.

Gabriel was flopped onto the nearest couch, and Kyanne fell into a heap of fabric and springs that once—probably years ago—had been a fashionable chair.

I watched a moment, making sure everyone was settled before I left the room and returned to the car to retrieve the zipper bag.

I sat down in the passenger's seat again, setting the bag on my lap.

I tugged on the zipper, feeling it catch on a dollar bill. Or maybe a check. I quietly hoped it was the former. Checks, I couldn't do anything worthwhile with and the only contacts I had who could turn a check into cash were miles and miles away. "Cash," I whispered. "Have lots and lots of cash. Small bills," I added, reworking the zipper so that it finally ran loose.

I pulled it back and opened the bulging bag wide to examine the tops of the bills. I fingered through the stack, ruffling the edges. Not a bad take. Junction might be just one more economically depressed bit of small-town America, but at least this store had a decent day.

Except for the death of its owner . . .

I swallowed.

That was an unexpected consequence of feeding my family. . . .

Killing was new. But if we went with the Russian, it might be necessary. Several times. Killing might become the norm.

Weren't our lives "kill or be killed"?

I tugged the stack of bills free and ordered them neatly so all the presidents' heads were right side up. Then I arranged the bills by denomination, unwilling to count any of it until it all had some semblance of order.

"Was it worth it?"

I jumped at the sound of his voice, nearly dropping the money loose in my lap.

"Jesus, Gareth."

He eased himself into the seat beside me and put out his hand.

I looked from it to the money and back.

"I'll count it tonight," he whispered solemnly. "I want to know what it all comes down to. What's the cost of one man's life?"

I threw it all at him, the money, the bag with some coins in its bottom, and the last bits of attitude I had. But I felt no satisfaction as the bills floated down around his head and landed on the dashboard and in his lap. Even the thwap and clink of the bag and its coins hitting him square in the chest did nothing to alleviate my loathing.

My loathing of him, my loathing of my lifestyle and, most of all, my loathing of myself for not being able to find some other way for all of us.

Survival shouldn't have to be so hard.

"Find out then—tell me what a man's life is worth," I

demanded. "Because I know what the survival of all those lives in there is worth to me, and it always comes out on top regardless of what anyone else thinks or feels. Always!" I slammed the door and stormed away.

Alexi

"I am sorry, Pietr. But you must try harder. Surely there is some work you can find. You are very clever," I added. The fact that the brightest among us was struggling to find a minimum-wage job was frustrating beyond words.

Pietr cracked his knuckles. "I'll ask Wanda and see if there are any openings at the library."

Jessie and I both began speaking at the same time. "She's—"

"Not to be trusted," I blurted out, and everyone's head snapped up, all eyes sharp and at attention.

"Damn," Jessie said, her voice little more than a whisper. "I was just going to say she's out of town for a few weeks."

"Alexi," Pietr said, taking Jessie's hand, "what are you talking about?"

We were all keenly aware of Jessie's father's intentions toward Wanda. They had fallen into a romantic relationship— initially a bit one-sided—as Wanda needed a way to stay close to the students of Junction and being around Jessie and her smart-mouthed little sister provided decent intel considering how girls talked. But Wanda seemed to have truly fallen for Jessie's dad. And Jessie was just beginning to accept the idea.

I should have kept my mouth shut. "It was nothing," I said, seeing the darkness grow in Jessie's brown eyes.

"No," she said, her eyes fixed on me, her gaze full of daggers and, worse yet, the fear that I was right. "Tell me—tell *us*—what you meant. Why *now* can't Wanda be trusted?"

I sat heavily. "I have learned a few more things about her past."

"Oh." Jessie heaved out a sigh. "Her past?"

"*Da.*"

"So this isn't about something she's doing right now."

"Yes and no," I said, struggling to clarify. "It is about her past, but she has yet to come clean about it now. . . ."

"Sometimes there are things in a person's past that no longer matter in the present," Jessie said. "People change and grow. People make mistakes but they can get past them."

Amy watched her, hope in her eyes.

I hated to be another one who dashed her hopes, so I chose my words carefully. "People can change—I believe that. But what she did should have been explained. Although I doubt there is any explanation that could suffice. . . ." I ran a hand through my hair and tried to focus. "She has not told us all about a very important part of her past. A part that ties in directly to our family's past."

"Quit beating around the bush," Jessie urged me. "What did she do in the past that caused you to not trust her now, after all we've been through—the way she fought beside us against the company. What could it possibly be that she did that was so wrong you can't trust her even now?"

I looked at her levelly and licked my lips before saying the words that already lodged in my throat. "She murdered our father."

CHAPTER TWENTY

Alexi

Jessie seemed to stop breathing. She blinked once, a slow move that made it possible to believe I was actually watching the wheels in her brain struggle for traction. "Wanda murdered your father?" she asked.

I knew it was unbelievable. I could not even grasp the depth or gravity of what I had so recently discovered—and what I had finally said aloud. *"Da."*

"Proof, Sasha," Jessie begged.

Had she ever called me that before—ever called me Sasha? "I need proof."

But I knew what she really meant was: *Please let his proof be something I can blow a hole through—please let him be wrong.* Oddly, I felt guilty knowing I was not wrong.

Wanda had saved Jessie's life—had probably saved most of us at least once—which made it even harder to fathom the level of her betrayal.

How much worse to know all the good she had done recently and still know it could not stack up against her cruelest work—taking away our father's life and imprisoning our mother?

"There was a woman that my mother spoke of briefly while we lived in Farthington—a friendly woman with a small, yippy dog. Mother met her when she was out for a jog one day and they began meeting every morning. They were not close friends, but they talked."

Cat leaned forward, resting her elbows on the table. "That was the little dog Mother joked about eating, *da?* 'Just a hairy morsel,' she laughed one day, 'barely any meat—just fur and bones.'"

"*Da*," I agreed. "That was Wanda's dog. The woman? *That* was Wanda."

"I never met the woman," Cat said, confused. Pietr and Max nodded in agreement. "Did you meet her?"

"*Nyet*. But she would have been there that night."

No one asked what night I meant because everyone knew. It was the only night that still haunted all of us—the night our parents disappeared from Farthington.

"This could all be coincidence," Jessie spoke up.

"I am sorry, Jessie. *Nyet*. This is not coincidence." I went to the china cabinet, opened a door on its bottom, and pulled out the photo.

We all saw it.

Cat cursed, and Jessie knew by that I was right.

"It's a good thing she's not anywhere nearby right now," Max snarled.

I nodded. "*Pravda*, brother. Very true."

It was one of the few times recently he did not recoil at

my use of the familial term for him. In this—in anger—we were again united. Kin.

But until Wanda returned to Junction, there was little we could do to mete out justice.

Marlaena

I stalked into the house an hour later, the cold finally edging its way past the protection afforded by my body's extra heat. I paused in the kitchen, watching the candlelight dance eerily along the dusty old curtains. I pulled open the refrigerator out of habit long ago made useless—how many abandoned homes still maintained electricity, or a working fridge?

Dark and empty. As expected. Noise came from the little living room, and I slunk toward it to lean on the door's warped frame.

There he was, Gareth, licking their wounds, so to speak. Soothing and gentle and—utterly Christlike. . . . I wanted to scream. Or crucify him.

How could he be so sharp with me and so loving to them? And so consistently?

Kyanne was gloating at the extra attention he paid her and it didn't hurt the growth of her tender ego that Noah and Darby were seated at her feet, telling jokes until she laughed and scolded them for making her hurt.

My stomach ached to see them like that. So close, and me not a necessary part of any of it. This was my pack. *My* family.

"They heal, you know," I snapped at him, striding forward and slapping his hand away from the wound on Kyanne's arm

as he was being his tender best with her. It disgusted me how
gentle he could be with absolutely anyone.

"Everyone heals faster with a touch of compassion," he
replied levelly.

"Why must you be so soft with everyone?" I snarled, stepping away from the group of them. I could hear him behind
me—feel the heat of him by my back—and it made my
stomach do strange things, made my mind slow. I spun to
face him.

"Why must you be so hard?"

"Damn it, Gareth," I whispered, backing into a wall.
"Survival. That's why I do *everything*. That's how I make all
my choices. It's survival. Needs and some wants. For them,
for you, for me. . . ."

"We *need* to start looking further ahead," he said. "This
simple survival is coming closer and closer to killing us." He
took a step toward me, coming so near I could smell the sweet
scent of his breath.

My head swam and my spine and knees went loose seeing
him so close, so touchable, so soft and kind. . . . "What are
you suggesting?" I whispered, knowing in my head the words
were laced with a request for far more than he was willing to
give. I blinked and, remembering myself, my place, his place,
I straightened and cleared my throat. "Do you have a plan?
Some brilliant idea that could make all our lives perfect?"

"Not perfect. But perhaps stable. Maybe better."

"Stable. How very middle-class American and *human*"—I
let the word twist out of my mouth like I'd said something
foul—"of you." I crossed my arms before me, effectively building a wall between us.

I'd return to the Russian. If my plan regarding the Russian-
Americans didn't work out first.

CHAPTER TWENTY-ONE

Jessie

Having talked to Harnek and spent a little more time with Sophie's wards, I'd come to a conclusion. "It's simple, really," I said. "We just need someone on the inside to warn us if things go bad. Or if there's info we need to know."

"Yeah," Amy gave a snort. "That's simple. How do you get someone on the inside of a group like this?"

"I agree with Amy. We have a strong suspicion of who the local leader is here, but getting access to his files or overhearing any of his calls . . . it's risky, Jessie. He almost never leaves the offices—"

"Unless there's a food fight—"

Amy grinned. "Yeah, some sort of civil disobedience the teachers can't handle."

"And I'm already walking on dangerous ground with"—Sophie cleared her throat—"my other project."

I nodded. "I agree, Sophie. I can't have you involved."

Cat blinked at me.

"You're not in the running, either, Cat. You attract way too much attention still being new—"

"And foreign—"

"And gorgeous," Amy concluded, sticking her tongue out.

Cat's smile spread nearly from ear to ear. "You are all so much trouble, but I must keep you all as a result of that."

"Does this mean we're suddenly kept women?"

Cat snorted. "Have you seen how little the Super Shoe Shop pays me? I could not afford to keep a mouse!"

"And yet I see some strappy new high-heel boots," I remarked, looking at her feet pointedly.

"Ah! They were discounted," she said, stroking her fingers along the straps and their shiny platinum buckles. "Besides," she said with a smile, "making an occasional purchase helps keep my spirits up."

"Then your spirits must have been sky-high after you brought that tiny leather jacket home . . . ," Amy muttered, looking up and away in mock innocence.

"Oh! You are so not being kept!" Cat scolded her.

"Okay, okay," I said, waving my hands for their attention. "Look. I have a plan—"

Pietr's tray clinked down beside mine. "Excellent. I would love to hear this plan of yours."

I barely kept from groaning. Without skipping a beat, I announced, "The plan is: We all meet up after school and hit the mall to do some window shopping!"

On cue, all the girls smiled and nodded or clapped agreement. "It's settled then." I winked at them and finished my lunch.

Because my friends were smart and girls are naturally quite savvy, we met up right after lunch in the girls' bathroom—the only thing close to a fortress of solitude at the high school. The only place Pietr wouldn't barge in and give his two cents on my plans. Not that he barged in anywhere anymore really. . . .

"Okay, some office staff's been let go due to the new budget cuts instituted by the superintendent," I announced.

"Heard he's a drunk," Amy muttered in disgust, looking down at her shoes.

Aghast that she'd be so cold about someone suffering from alcoholism considering her dad's own fragile state, I stared at her for a long minute.

"He's not in rehab," she explained suddenly, realizing I was staring. "It's different because of that."

I chewed on the inside of my cheeks and wondered when a good time would be to point out that as great as it was she thought things could be made better by getting help, she herself still wasn't talking to anyone or seeing a professional about what had happened to her. *Not now,* the voice in my head said.

"So, because of these staff cuts, the office is looking for a couple volunteers to help the ladies out during study halls and lunch breaks and before and after school. It's as close as any of us can legally get to what Perlson's doing. And it may be close enough to find out what's up."

Nods.

"Cat's out. Sophie's out, and I'm out—I have a bit of a reputation with sticking my nose places it doesn't belong and—"

"Breaking the noses of others?" Amy quipped, recalling the fight in the locker room.

"Yeah, that, too. I no longer have angel status." I shrugged. "Amy?"

"I never had angel status and I doubt any of the office cares to help me earn my wings," she muttered. "I'd stick out like a sore thumb."

I had to agree. "So . . ."

They shrugged.

"We need someone in the office—someone working the inside track." I fell silent, hearing the door open and close.

Sarah stepped around in front of me. "I'll do it," she said.

"Nooo." Amy's was the first protest, but certainly not the only one. "She can't be trusted. She's always the first to flip-flop, and there are things she doesn't know—things that she shouldn't."

Cat nodded. Emphatically.

"Buuut," I said, looking Sarah flat in the face, "she doesn't have to know everything as long as she knows she needs to report everything she sees and hears. No matter what."

"Not a problem," she said firmly. "Besides, the office ladies love me."

"Is that love, or is it a deeply seated fear they have of you?" Amy asked.

"At the moment I don't care. Jessie needs help, and none of you can do it. But I can. I have the social graces and ability to maneuver in different social circles—a gift some of you don't," she said, looking straight at Amy. "I have a high-end phone that can snap awesome photos of documents, record at a remarkable distance, and has no problems sending every-thing it gathers to somebody's e-mail. It's the perfect tool for spying."

"You're the perfect *tool*," Amy snapped.

I widened my eyes at her.

"Oh. For. Spying," she concluded sharply.

"Niiice," Sarah countered. "Look, let's be straight here. I'm not doing this to become anyone's friend. Well, Cat, you and I could hang," she clarified, looking at Cat's recent boot acquisition. "You at least have a sharp sense of style. But some of you don't have any sense at all. And some of you are far from sharp." She turned back to face me. "But Jessie basically saved me when anybody else would've thrown me away. She got honest when it mattered most. And she gave me back my memories. Plus some creepy crap I still don't know what to do about. But she tried. For my sake. So I'll try for hers."

I shrugged. "I'm all for it. We need someone."

"And if you're all we've got . . . ," Amy added grudgingly.

"Thanks. So glad to finally make the list."

"Ohhh, you're on my list, no worries," Amy said, wrinkling her nose.

"Stop!" I shook my hands. "We all need to work together to make this work out okay. Sarah, what we mainly need to know is if Perlson starts acting weird—like if it seems he's ready to charge off in any particular direction. And if he says or does anything else weird."

"Vice Principal weird or—"

"Scary paranormal / supernatural weird," Sophie whispered.

"Awesome," Sarah said dryly. "That's what I was hoping you'd say. And when he does—because, let's face it Scooby gang, this is Junction, and weird seems to ooze up from the sidewalks around here now—what do you want me to do?"

"Text us all. Immediately. First Soph and me, then Cat and Amy."

"Heyyy, look who's on the bottom of the list," Sarah remarked, pulling out her cell phone and passing it to me. "Enter the digits."

We all complied.

The door swung open and Max strode in.

Sophie shrieked, Sarah and Cat snorted, and Amy just grinned.

"Lose somethin', Tiger?" she teased. "Can't imagine any reason a guy like you'd be in a place like this unless you'd suddenly misplaced something tremendously valuable to your gender identification."

"I did," he said gruffly. "But she's right here," he added, taking her hand, "and about to be late for class unless we hurry."

"Fine, fine," she said, letting him lead her to the door. "Adjourned?"

"Adjourned," I agreed.

Max paused and looked around a moment. "Why does your bathroom smell so much better than ours?"

"Maybe because we don't spend our time using our *equipment* to try and take aim and hit—and probably miss—some little blue thing that's disgustingly called a *cake*?"

He nodded sagely. "But some of us are good enough with our *equipment* we can write our name in the snow. In cursive. And in Cyrillic."

"I so don't want to ever see that," she specified as they left the bathroom hand in hand.

Alexi

I examined the ticket in my hand. Flight 732 to Samoa. Seat 23A. Across the country and an ocean later I could be in the arms of my love, Nadezhda. I could tell her everything that was in my heart—all my hopes and fears and distant plans for our future together. And she would cover my face in kisses and take my hand in hers and lead me back to some quiet place away from the hustle and noise of humanity. . . .

Or I would find her with her partner and my reality would be cruelly adjusted.

If I returned the ticket and cashed in my dream I could still recoup some small something and better ensure that my family had the money they needed to last a little longer in Junction.

Or to deal with the treachery that seemed to dog us. I could use the money Wanda gave me to somehow bring her down—get the justice my mother and father deserved.

The irony would be sweet, using her own money against her.

Nadezhda and I might be doing fine at a distance. Surely we could keep what we felt for each other alive a bit longer, even just using phones and e-mail and Skype. . . . Could we not?

Da. Of course we could.

Even though she had a partner who probably played the role of her husband in her current undercover operation . . . who stayed in her flat, in her room. . . .

To keep up appearances . . .

It was just a job.

I had an important choice to make: love or vengeance.

I thought about the heat of Nadezhda's kisses and the way her breath cooled the skin of my bare chest one hot summer day in Moscow. . . .

But my mother and father taught me everything I knew about life and love . . .

. . . and loyalty.

I knew in that instant what I needed to do.

I picked up the phone. "I'm so sorry," I explained. "I need to cancel my ticket. I will not be taking this flight after all."

"I'm so sorry to hear that, sir. Has there been some emergency?"

"*Da*—yes," I agreed. "I'm afraid so. Two of the most important people in my life have died."

It was such a simple thing, in the end, the cancellation of an airplane ticket and the return of the funds. I would spend the money well.

Marlaena

I had returned to the Rusakova household and seen Pietr—alone. Making clear my desire to have them join our pack for a get-together, I finally convinced him it was in everyone's best interest.

From my seat by the second-story bedroom window I watched them enter the house. Gabe knocked on the door shortly after they'd been greeted and come inside. "They're here."

"We know," Gareth murmured, flopped across the broken bed, dreads falling across his eyes.

"Shall I introduce you?"

"Yeah, Gabriel. Get 'em all riled up or whatever."

The door closed behind him and Gareth rolled onto his back, even stronger somehow when he submitted.

"What is the purpose of all this?" he asked, rolling his head so his dreads flopped.

I dropped to my knees at the bed's edge and swatted his hair. "I've never known. Care to explain?"

"Not the purpose of *this*," he said with a smile, shaking his hair again. "The purpose of whatever you're doing tonight. With them. The Rusakovas and their not-so-werewolf entourage."

"We need them."

"Since when did *you* need anyone?"

I fought down the words that sprang to mind and choked on 'since I met you.' Instead I shrugged. "They know this region."

"So we intend to stay?"

I shrugged again. "They have connections."

"Which we can make in time."

"If we have them, we don't need Dmitri. We can make things work on our own."

"They were the first ones to tell you *they* aren't our own, weren't they?"

I kept my mouth shut.

His voice grew softer, luring me closer. "Be honest."

"I am. I always am."

"It's because of him, isn't it? Because of Pietr Rusakova. There's something about him that's caught your curiosity."

"No. Don't be ridiculous."

He rubbed his hand slowly across his stomach and was silent for a moment. "It's okay, you know."

"What? What's okay?" My heart raced. Why was I suddenly terrified I was closer to Gareth than ever and still he was slipping away?

"It's okay if you choose him."

"Choose *him* . . . ? What the hell are you talking about?"

"You know. You're an alpha female. You need an alpha male."

"Who am I choosing *between?*" I asked, fighting the sudden panic edging into my voice.

"You know very well who you're choosing between."

"No—no I don't," I insisted, reaching across to grab his hand.

He sighed. "Between Pietr, Gabe, and me."

He kissed my hand and dropped it, sitting up and then vaulting to his feet in a motion so smooth any wolf would envy him.

Then he walked out the door and left me.

"Shit!" I hissed, squeezing my eyes shut. "When the hell did you let *you* become an option for *me?*"

"We were down and out, lost, frightened and alone—misunderstood, abandoned, punished, and brutalized, imprisoned and in fear for our lives. And for *what?* What was our singular crime? Being different! Being stronger"—they cheered—"faster"—they cheered—"and for being more savvy than the humans who make up the least bit of us. Do we have humanity? YES. Will we ever lose it? NO. But we are far greater than that bit of flesh we walk in—*because* we are different."

Gabe was on a roll. Phil would've liked him—would've seen preacher potential in him.

"Hunted, wounded, weakened—we were each at our ropes' ends when she found us and led us—like the lambs we were—to become something greater—something stronger and fiercer—to become her wolves. And who is she, this leader who raised us all from our darkest moments and led us into the full moon's dazzling light? Who is this girl?" he demanded, his voice cracking.

"Marlaena!" they shouted in answer, and my heart shook to hear it on so many tongues. "Marlaena! Marlaena!"

I stepped into the room, my rabid supporters—the phrase always seeming so much more appropriate for wolves, especially *my* wolves—leaning forward to greet me, a fire in their eyes as excitement built and tested the limits of their control, the wolf edging into each of their eyes.

"My wolves!" I shouted. "My war dogs!" I threw my head back and laughed. "Together we have already come so far— we who were once alone and so lonely are now united, one family, one kinship, one pack! And what is the main lesson the pack preaches?"

"The wolf!" they answered me. "The wolf! The wolf!"

"And this wolf—*this* wolf"—I pounded a fist to my chest— "this wolf *is* . . . ?"

"*The way!*" they screamed.

"And what, my cubs, my whelps, my warriors, what are the laws of our way?"

My eyes found our visitors sitting behind the pack's writhing bodies. Each of their forms told a different tale. They were curious, at least one was fearful, and most were doubtful, but they were all listening. That was the important part. If I could get someone to listen to a message often enough, eventually they would believe it.

"The law?" I repeated.

"The law is survival!"

"The law?"

"The law is power!"

"The law?"

"The law is hunt or be hunted!"

"The law?"

"Eye for an eye, tooth for a tooth, claw for a claw!"

"The law?"

"Morality is a luxury!"

"The law?"

"Fortune favors the bold!"

"The law?"

"Survival of the fittest!"

The one called Jessica balked at the last few of the laws, her head snapping back and her body stiffening. She took Pietr's hand, and he patted hers like he'd comfort a child incapable of understanding what they witnessed.

I couldn't have cared less what she thought. Because, for whatever reason, I needed Pietr to buy in to what we were doing. To understand the Way of the Wolf and that the wolf was truly and completely the only way.

"And who is the fittest?" I screamed.

"We are, we are, we are WOLF!"

"And the wolf?"

"The Wolf is the Way!"

And then the real excitement began.

CHAPTER TWENTY-TWO

Jessie

Another wolf, Gareth, led us to a beaten-up barn and told us where to sit. Werewolves carrying makeshift drums and branches came first, the group of them circling Marlaena as she held up a lighter and a stick wrapped with a rag. As her cohorts piled sticks around her feet she touched the torch and lighter together. The torch jumped to life and she lit the pile of wood at her feet and leaped into the crowd as they howled.

There was dancing and more howling and food and more howling and more dancing. And howling.

I picked at the meat that was given to me and watched Pietr. As he watched them. He smiled, his features lighting with far more interest than I'd seen him have about me recently.

I tried to fight down the nausea clawing at my stomach.

These were his kind. In a way. It was natural he'd feel a kinship with them.

I could only hope that sensation of kinship with Marlaena's pack would be overridden by his logical, cool, and very human side.

When things finally died down we headed to the car, Marlaena close behind. "Pietr," she called. "Pietr!"

He turned back to her, and I hung at his side.

"You were just going to leave?"

"We're very tired," he apologized. "But thank you for inviting us to an amazing event."

"Wait—will you not . . . Won't you join us? The Wolf is the Way. . . ."

"But it is not *our* way," he said softly. "We chose to be human, to live longer lives and spend more time with the ones we love."

I reached out and took his hand. "Come on now," I urged, and as we turned away from her, I thought I heard her say, "You made the wrong choice. And now you leave me without one."

Melodramatic werewolves.

As we squeezed into the car to leave, I noticed I was one of the few not exhausted from dancing.

Or howling.

Even Amy complained happily about her sore feet.

None of it was a good sign, in my opinion.

Marlaena

"Go," I told Tembe. "Take the truck. We may not have lost them yet."

He nodded and took the keys from my outstretched hand.

"You know what to do?"

He nodded again.

"Make it count. If they live, they're wolves. And free of nearly all human taint. They'll join us then."

"And if they don't live?" he asked.

"Then I look into another option."

Tembe scurried away, and the truck started with a cough and a wheeze of its engine. It wouldn't matter how good the engine was after tonight.

I caught Gabriel's scent on the wind and turned back to the house—too late.

"Come on, beautiful . . . ," he coaxed, placing one hand on the tree at my back so his bicep grazed my shoulder. "Didn't I do you proud tonight? Got all the pups cheering you on. . . . Haven't I earned a little . . ." His gaze wandered the length of my body, and I knew by the glimmer in his eyes that he liked what he saw.

That didn't matter. I looked flat into his face. "Just because you do me proud," I stated, "it doesn't mean you get to *do* me."

He didn't even blink but tilted his head and gave me a slow nod. "What'll it take then?"

"To get me?" I laughed.

Gabriel was no longer beating around the bush. "Yeah," he said, his eyes narrowing as he appraised his potential prize. "What'll it take to get you?"

"A different man." I shoved him back, pushing past him.

I could've sworn he muttered something like, "There has to be something I can do . . . ," but I was already walking.

For a moment I thought I still felt him behind me, shadowing me, but then, like a ghost, he was gone, disappearing into the trees that stood like skeletal sentries along the old property's edge.

Jessie

"I don't trust them," I muttered from the backseat, sandwiched between Amy and Alexi.

"I doubt any of us trust them, Jessie," Alexi said with a yawn.

Max shrugged and turned left at the light. "They're not so bad. Rowdy. Cultlike. But they sure know how to throw a party, don't they?" He glanced into the rearview mirror at us, grinning.

And that was when the truck t-boned us.

We whipped like rag dolls against one another, seat belts holding us so tight everything else in our bodies was loose by comparison. My spine was loose as a snake's and my head slammed into Amy's shoulder and Alexi's back crushed against me.

And we were far better off than Pietr.

The ambulance and fire department were fast to arrive and faster still to pull us out, check us over, and suggest we all ride to the E.R. to be checked out more completely by way of another ambulance. Pietr was the priority.

The unconscious, *bleeding* priority.

I vomited right there. Someone said that was a sure sign of concussion, but I knew it was more than that. "Help me up," I asked, looking at Alexi. "We need to ride along."

"Sorry. There's only room for one . . . ," the same helpful medic reported.

"Take her," Alexi said, pushing me into the back of the ambulance. "I'm his guardian—do whatever it takes to keep him alive—"

But the doors were already closing and we rushed to the hospital, siren screaming.

It seemed that no matter what they did, they couldn't stop Pietr's bleeding.

Even more terrifying was the moment he stopped breathing and they couldn't start him up again.

I reached out clumsily for his hand. "Damn it, Pietr, not now . . . not like this. . . ." To lose him now because he could finally live a normal life and a normal life span, or to still have more than twenty years with him as a nearly invincible werewolf . . .

What if the wolf was the way and my blood, the cure, had taken it from him? What if I was finally the thing that killed him?

I squeezed his hand so hard I felt bones pop. "Fight, damn it. . . ."

He gasped and the medics shouted in surprise.

The ambulance came to a sudden stop and Pietr was unloaded first. I stumbled out behind, caught up by one very helpful man. "Here," he whispered, seating me in a wheelchair. "He's going to our best doctors. Let's go get you checked out, okay?"

I nodded, tears sliding down my cheeks. "I've been told frequently I should get my head examined," I muttered.

"Well, there you go. Maintaining a sense of humor's an important thing at a moment like this."

Alexi

We were all hurt from the accident, Amy, Cat, and I far worse than Max. I looked at him carefully. He and I would need to talk. *Da*, I had lied to him for years about being an oborot, but this lie of *his* . . .

They wheeled Jessie out to join us. "No broken bones. No concussion," she reported.

"The vomit?" I asked, looking down at my shoes and glad I had been quick to step back at just the right moment.

She looked at me, stricken. "I'm sick with worry. He won't heal up from this, will he?"

I took her hand. "Of course he will. He will be fine. He will heal. Just like any normal Russian-American."

"It happened too fast," Cat whispered from beside me.

"It did happen very fast," I assured her.

"Have you heard? They did not find the truck's driver." She glanced at me. "They have been talking," she added. "No simple human should have walked away from that crash." She hung her head a moment and then looked at Jessie. "Too fast," she emphasized.

"What do you mean, Ekaterina?" I asked, grabbing her hand in mine so she could not pull away.

Cat balked, pulling away in her seat only to find her shoulder pressed against the wall and nudging a crucifix forward on the nail that held it.

I looked from Jessie to Cat and back again.

"The cure is not . . . not permanent."

"What?" I dropped her hand, burned. "What do you mean?"

"I mean precisely what I said, Sasha," she whispered, her

eyes wide and staring. My brief past stint as Rusakova alpha served me well, and Cat submitted to my awkward interrogation. "The cure is only a temporary measure. It is not a guarantee. It is not permanent. If he'd had more warning, he might not be . . ."

"Be what? Simply human? As badly hurt?"

"*Da.*"

"How do you know this? Jessie . . ." But Jessie looked away. "You knew as well and did not tell me?"

Still, Jessie did not meet my eyes. We had all become liars, and though I was not surprised by Jessie's involvement, Cat's willingness to keep such a secret shook me. "How do you know it is not permanent—that he might have . . ."

"I broke through the cure."

"But I have watched you. You do not run, you do not hunt, your animal instincts are low at best," I whispered, my eyes darting as I studied her face and posture. "Your calorie intake is nearly that of a normal human girl."

"And she can stomach chocolate," Jessie added as an odd aside, noting one of the dietary things that had previously been an issue with the Rusakovas in their oborot state. Christmas had been much improved because of Cat's ability to devour the treats stuffed in her stocking (though she complained bitterly of the resulting acne).

"I took the cure a second time—when Mother . . ." Her lower lip quivered a moment before she regained her self-control. "When Mother took hers, and Pietr drank and forced Max to drink. . . ." She looked away. "I took it and I hid the pelt. I could not bear to be the only one in the family so different. . . ."

I turned away, focusing on the EXIT sign hanging overhead.

"It is not easy—*that*," I agreed. "Being different. Especially when you are the only one to know that you are." I rubbed at my face with a shaking hand. "When did the cure fail?"

"When Derek was beating me," she whispered. "He had me down on the ground. . . . I was certain he would kill me. And Jessie. And then . . ." Her eyes met mine again. "I felt something inside of me snap and it was as if a switch had been thrown. I felt the wolf surging through my veins again— uncaged and angry. And I changed."

"The need and the adrenaline," I murmured, watching her eyes. "You have a larger spleen to help with the dump of red blood cells and adrenaline that the change and your fast healing required, so it makes a certain amount of sense that it would be able to overpower something that cannot actually fix your genetic code." I rested my head in my hands and stared at the tile floor. "The cure only masks it then."

"So what do we do now?" Jessie asked.

"We do what every other human family does when someone is hospitalized. We wait and we hope for the best." I grabbed each of their hands and held them with mine. "And, Max, do you also have something to admit?"

Cat, Amy, and Jessie turned to look at him.

"*Da* . . ." He looked up at the ceiling and reached for Amy's hand. "I did not take the cure. I spit it out. I got sick but never went through the final change."

"But the bathroom . . ." Jessie and Amy gawked at him.

"I was angry."

"You broke my favorite soap dish," Cat accused. "And the mirror!"

"An apology is most likely in order . . . ," he admitted.

"Most likely?"

And we came back together even more tightly as a family while we waited to hear the results of Pietr's injuries.

CHAPTER TWENTY-THREE

Jessie

Most of us went home from the hospital that morning. Not Pietr. With a broken arm and ribs and huge bruises along his right side he was being kept for observation. And to get the good pain meds.

Outed about still being a wolf, Max more openly engaged in his wolfish nature, running on nights he didn't work late at the theater and showing off his strength, speed, and agility more often for Amy.

But they fought. She'd already lost people in her life—the idea that Max came with an early expiration date didn't sit well with her.

And Alexi took the remaining car, the convertible, out for a drive every afternoon and always returned looking a little sadder than when he'd left.

———

Pietr was determined to go back to school immediately, although I suggested he stay home, and the doctors had given him notes to allow him to stay out and rest up for more than an additional week.

But he was afraid he'd miss some nuance of what was being taught.

In math class.

The idea of there being any nuance or subtlety to math astounded me. But he returned to and slipped right into bonding with Hascal, Jaikin, and Smith.

And nearly ignoring me.

I gave up my study halls and part of my homeroom and lunch period each day to work with Sophie and the special kids. And I loved watching their progress—as long as citrus didn't catch fire and desks didn't explode in a burst of rainbow-colored sparkles. But I preferred those to the kid who was so freaky he could read minds and the other who could predict the five-day forecast—accurately—without employing Doppler radar.

It was as I entered the boiler room during study hall one day that I noticed Sophie eating something.

"What is that?"

"Supposedly shepherd's pie," she said, fighting to swallow one more forkful of the stuff.

"From the cafeteria?" Alarm colored my tone.

"No, dork, I brought it from home in a sandwich bag." She rolled her eyes at me. "Of course it's from the cafeteria."

"Why—?"

"We need to know what would happen to kids if they've been triggered by some other catalyst—other than the food—and then eat it."

"Does Harnek know you're doing this?"

"No."

"How long have you been—"

"About a week."

"Stop," I demanded, grabbing the fork.

She blinked at me.

Then she fainted.

Alexi

"Allo, beautiful," I said, my feet up on the dining room table as I made myself comfortable for a long-belated call with Nadezhda. Things had been so crazy—for both of us—that we had not spoken in days. But we understood that about our schedules—our duties.

The voice that greeted me was not Nadezhda's. Or even feminine in any way. "Hello, yourself, you stud, you," came a distinctly Cockney accent.

"Wha—Who is this?"

"Kellan," he responded flatly. "Dezzie's partner."

"Dezzie's?"

"Nadezhda's," he said slowly, separating each syllable.

My feet dropped off the table and slammed onto the floor. "I want to speak to Nadezhda. Now."

"She's a bit indisposed at the moment. . . ."

"Now," I said.

"It's your funeral, mate. . . ."

I heard a door creak open. "Dezzie—"

"What are you doing in here?" she laughed. "Can't you see I'm showering?"

My heart stopped.

"I see that quite clearly," Kellan responded.

"Stop it," she said. With another laugh.

"But you have a phone call."

"Unless it's a prime minister or a king, I have no interest in talking," she proclaimed haughtily.

I heard the door close again. "You heard the lady. Shall I tell her you called?"

"*Nyet*," I croaked. I turned the phone off and threw it across the room.

Jessie

I got off the bus at the Rusakovas' having gotten Sophie home sick and alerting Harnek to what was happening. I'd done the best I could, hadn't I?

I collapsed at the foot of the stairs. Max was working, Amy and Cat were AWOL, and Pietr was staying late at school to discuss something that was surely important to someone with Smith, Hascal, and Jaikin.

I needed . . . I looked down the hall to Alexi's room.

I needed to fight.

I tugged my hair back in a ponytail and stalked down the hall.

Alexi

With the cure's failure—*my* failure—fresh in my mind, she showed up at my bedroom door, eyes narrow and hair pulled back into a tight ponytail.

"*Da?*" I asked, but I saw from the way her shoulders and

her feet were set that she needed something specific. Something only I could provide.

She grabbed me by the wrist, tossed my jacket at me, and towed me outside. My feet had barely found my fighting stance before she came at me. She was faster, harder, and fiercer this time than she had ever been before.

"Shit, Jessie," I exclaimed when she nailed me in the gut with an elbow. Doubled over, I held a hand up to make her pause.

She shifted her weight back and forth on her feet, nearly dancing, she was so anxious to come at me again.

"Would you like to talk?" I straightened, caught my breath, and wiggled my fingers at her, the signal we were good to go again.

She shook her head, grunted, and charged.

"I will take that as a no," I whispered, stepping aside at the last minute so that she raced past awkwardly. Faster, harder, and fiercer, maybe, but whatever was gnawing at her was making her dumb.

She attacked again and I took her to the ground. Straddling her and crouched over her stomach, I pressed the heel of my hand into her shoulder and kept her pinned.

"Jessie. Breathe," I commanded as she snarled at me. "This is no good. There is something bothering you."

"God, you're so perceptive, Sasha," she snapped.

"So talk. To someone. Pietr?"

"No. It's about him. And Sophie. She's sick." She shivered. "The school's tainted food . . . it's screwing up so many lives. . . ."

"Do you want to talk to Amy?"

She flinched. "She's hurting right now. I can't take trouble to her."

"Max?"

"He's hurting *for* her."

I rocked back on my heels. *"Da.* I have noticed that. The way they hurt for each other. It is good, in a way, is it not?"

"I guess it is. . . . God, Alexi . . . I don't know what's good for anyone anymore."

"You need to talk this out—it is what girls do, *da? Talk* it out, right?"

"I don't think talking's going to do it this time."

I nodded and adjusted my stance. "I understand. I do not care to talk, either."

After pounding out our rage on each other for about forty minutes, I headed to the kitchen for an ice pack. The sound of someone crying made me freeze, though, and I quietly skulked in the direction of the noise.

Jessie was flopped on the love seat, her body shaking with sobs. Her face was buried in the crook of her arm and the hair had come loose from her ponytail to cover her face. I had never seen her cry.

The situation with Pietr and now this new thing with Sophie and the school food had finally brought her down. I would not stand for it.

So, knowing what I needed to do, I returned to the kitchen's freezer, placed an ice pack on my shoulder, and decided to wait for official visiting hours to start in the morning.

CHAPTER TWENTY-FOUR

Alexi

I picked at the steering wheel's cover. I had sworn to myself that I would never come here again. I had sworn that oath more than a dozen times. But more importantly I had sworn I would never give her the satisfaction of meeting me. How dare she ever hope to meet me—the man I had become—so far removed from the child she had left? Never meet her. That was what I had promised myself. And why should I want to? She gave me over to the people I still thought of as my parents, though we shared no bloodline.

She gave me up.

My parents had been good people. *Da*—they encouraged me to lie. They taught me falsehood until it became my second nature. They raised me to run and hide and fight if it came to it—but not to stay. I had wings, but never roots beyond the scope of my family itself.

They introduced me to the Russian Mafia.

But they did what they did because we needed to survive. I needed to ensure the survival of my siblings.

It was as noble a set of lies as ever there could be.

But she—*Hazel Feldman*—could have kept me. From what I had learned she was no young woman when she had me. She was lacking in no resources. She had some money, she had a home, and a job—if one could call being a psychic any sort of employment—and when she had me, she handed me over to be raised by wolves.

Quite literally.

I looked at my phone. Nadezhda's name stood out starkly against the glow of the screen. I could press one button. Hear her voice.

Or her partner's.

I swallowed hard. If I heard her, it might grant me the strength I needed to face down the biggest demon from my youth—the demon I had not even realized existed until recently.

But would she respect the man I was if I asked for her to share her strength with me every time I doubted my own?

I could do this.

I *had* to do this.

On my own.

The best chance at getting the answers I needed lay with the woman I wanted most to avoid. She knew my grandfather's research better than anyone else. And she knew the connections I needed. I had lived for twenty-two years without needing anything from her and for a number of those years not even knowing she existed.

But I needed her now.

No. Not *her*.

Her *knowledge*.

That was different.

It had to be different.

Sliding out of the car, my eyes never left the building that seemed to grow and cast shadows before me, darkening the distance between myself and it. With a last glance at Nadezhda's name, I turned off the phone and slid it into my pocket.

I counted the rows of parking spaces between the convertible and the door.

Thirteen.

That number showed up too frequently in my life as a Rusakova.

Inside I was directed upstairs to a nurses' station. One particularly patient girl helped me on my way.

The nurse knocked twice on the door, announcing, "Mrs. Feldman, you have a visitor."

There was a rustle and the occupant of the room, a woman dressed in a colorful long skirt and seated on the room's bed, shuffled a deck of cards, drawing a single one before nodding, returning it to the deck, and setting the whole stack aside. "Death," she muttered.

"This is Mr. Alexi Rusakova," the nurse explained.

Mrs. Feldman cocked her head, examining me carefully; the intensity of her gaze made me feel small.

And angry.

I was being judged.

She nodded solemnly. "Thank you, Karen," she said, dismissing the young woman. Feldman peered at me. "Mr. Rusakova," she finally said with a sigh, "please have a seat."

I pulled a chair away from the wall and sat, my back straight and chin up. This was business, not pleasure. I would not relax my guard and let her under my skin. I cleared my throat.

And she waved a hand to silence me before I had even begun. "You realized the cure is temporary. A stopgap method to maintain some semblance of a normal life."

She appeared amused.

I hated her even more. I had not realized until then that it was possible to hate someone more than *completely*.

I closed my mouth, trying to hide my surprise at her very accurate assessment. But it was too late.

The skin at the corners of her eyes crinkled in a smile. "You have grown to be quite handsome," she remarked offhandedly, her gaze skimming my face.

I twitched. No one thought of me as handsome. Especially not when set beside Max or Pietr, who seemed to glow. I swallowed. I would not let her get past my guard. I merely nodded at the compliment.

"*Da*, the cure is temporary. Which gives me a bargaining chip with an important corporation."

"A bargaining chip?"

"*Da*, but my time to use it is . . ."

"Short? Or perhaps running out. It is always that way with the oboroten . . . Alexi." She tried out my name as if the word were a completely foreign construction.

"I did not name you Alexi," she murmured, caught in her own thoughts as her eyes lost focus for a moment.

"You would not have named me anything as fast as you traded me away," I returned, leaning forward so that my elbows rested on my thighs.

"Ah." She sat back and set her gnarled hands in her lap, chunky jeweled rings twinkling on her fingers. "It was not like that. Not at all."

"I do not care *what* it was like," I proclaimed, wishing my words were true. But my heart beat a little faster as my mind raced, wondering just what she meant.

She nodded. "Of course not. Forgiveness is hard to come by in situations like these."

"I doubt there are many situations like these to compare things to," I retorted, pushing back in the chair to show her clearly that I was unfazed by her words—by her utter abandonment. "There are few enough oboroten and fewer with family members secretly transplanted from otherwise normal situations to become their keepers." I folded my hands behind my head and rested my ankle on my other leg. "Of course you may correct me if I am wrong," I teased.

"You are not wrong. Yours was a one-of-a-kind situation. But you exceeded expectations, Alexi. Marvelously so."

"What expectations did you have of a baby being thrown into a wolf's den?"

"You were no baby."

"What?" I pulled up short, my expression open and utterly readable.

"Do you not remember?" She sighed. "Perhaps not. You were only a few years old, after all."

"I was a *few years old* when you gave me up?"

She nodded slowly.

"You hated me that much, did you?"

"No—no, Alexi. I *loved* you."

This time I waved her to silence. "What is it they say: 'Actions speak louder than words'? I am not here to rehash the past. I am a grown man. I am beyond all this. All I need from you is your scientific knowledge. To help my *family*. I have a family, you know. I had a wonderful father, a loving mother, and I still have three amazing siblings. I am here because of all of them. The man you see before you? He is the result of their involvement—not yours."

She swallowed and nodded slowly. "And they are precisely what I could have never provided you with except the way I did," she whispered. "I am glad they have inspired such love and loyalty from you."

"Your scientific knowledge and connections, Feldman."

She winced at hearing me use her last name. Or perhaps she winced because of the way I said it. Venomously.

"Tell me who to see and what to say when I see them."

"What has happened that finally brought you here? Mother is dead—that much I know because Jessie recently came by with Pietr as part of their Service Learning project. But why now? What happened to force you to come to me?"

"The same company that sprouted from the research of your father's assistant is tampering with the local school's food in order to create a gifted group of students. They are taking casualties. Most recently a dear friend of Jessie's has been made ill. I want them to withdraw the food. I need them to. For Jessie and the others."

"Ah. There is only one thing that man would want from you, you know."

"*Da*. The perfected cure."

"And you understand why?"

"*Da*. I do."

"And you would doom future people to save these current ones?"

I glared at her.

"I see," she said. "Lean in. This is what you must say and do and who you must say it to."

Marlaena

The Rusakovas' avoidance had forced me to make a deal I already regretted with Dmitri. But my wolves were well fed and better dressed and staying at the local Motel 8, where we at least had running water. And hot showers. Often.

But the deal meant I needed to keep a close eye on the Rusakovas. It wouldn't have bothered me so much if it didn't also mean Gabe felt the need to keep an even closer eye on me. Luckily, Gareth also shadowed me—but it was frustrating at times, having females gawk at them.

Even when we were doing something so mundane as watching a basketball game at Junction High.

Perhaps what I felt about the girls stalking Gareth and Gabriel was the same thing they thought about the way simple human males watched me.

"What?" I snapped at Gabriel.

He shrugged and scooted over on the bleachers, tilting his head as he watched me watching *them*.

Pietr and Jessica were a few rows below us. She was leaning her head on his shoulder. He was still banged up from the accident—more damage than an oborot would take, but far less than a human at the site of impact. The cure held. So my choices had tightened down again.

Bring him to our side—to Dmitri now—or kill him.

Pietr was trying to watch the game, and—I tried to get a look at the paper and pencil he held—extrapolate some data about the players?

Gabe was still examining me with his eyes, raking his gaze across my face.

"What?!"

"You seem so intrigued by the two of them. And so absolutely curious about *him*."

I pulled back and looked at him sharply. "I just don't get how something like that works," I said, surprised by the disgust lacing my voice. "He seems to have so much potential. . . ."

"Seriously?" His eyebrow rose. "*Him?* We do mean Pietr Rusakova, *geek*, right?"

"That's how he appears to you?" I cocked my head.

"Chyyyeah . . . Have you seen who he hangs with? They make The Geek Squad look like professional athletes."

I shrugged. "So he's geek-by-association."

"Geek, nerd, dweeb . . . whatever you want to call their breed."

I laughed. "There's a difference, you know. Nerds are big on knowing stuff—like, all sorts of stuff—they're the kings of book knowledge; geeks have skills—they're tech-savvy. They can do stuff and fix stuff. Nerds know it, but geeks can *do* it."

His stare had intensified. He was clearly bewildered by my sudden proclamation.

"And dweebs?" he asked.

I shrugged. "I have no idea." I cocked my head to mimic his pose, and he smiled. "But it doesn't matter how you label Pietr Rusakova . . . no label's gonna stick."

"So he *has* caught your attention." Gareth bent toward us.

"Only as much as anything shiny and new," I justified.

But Gabe and Gareth knew I was lying. There was something oddly intriguing about Pietr Rusakova. If I could only figure out what . . .

A "cured" werewolf was one thing—one really strange, disturbing thing—but Cat didn't catch my attention the way Pietr did, so it wasn't the cure.

And regardless of what Max claimed, he didn't carry the same trace scent the other two did. He was the biggest liar out of them all.

Besides, Max seemed to be someone girls needed a cure *against*, not someone in need of a cure himself.

"He doesn't pay you any attention," Gabriel pointed out in that magical why-waste-my-time-on-subtlety way of his.

"He doesn't pay his own girlfriend attention," I corrected. "And I'm not her."

He rubbed his chin, the sound of his fingers across his short but curling beard reminding me of sandpaper whisking across rough wood. Gabriel was thinking. *Hard.* I shifted beside him. He dropped his hands away, reaching for my waist.

I slapped his fingers away.

He shrugged and tucked his hands into his jacket's pockets. "Let's go."

Gareth shrugged. "It's a dull game," he agreed.

I nodded, and together we ambled away from the school and back to the car Gabe had so recently obtained. "When will you ditch this one?" I asked Gabe as he held open my door for me.

"I figure it has a couple more days left before I need to trade it in. It's not a bad one, really. Not what I really have my eye on, though . . ."

I followed his gaze to the candy apple–red convertible sitting in the parking lot. The Rusakovas' car.

"We've been through this. That's way too hot a car to take, and you know it," I reminded him.

He slammed my door shut and slid into the backseat, allowing Gareth to drive. "Look who's suddenly become the voice of reason."

"Isn't it ironic?" I countered.

"Yeah. Ironic you keep your hair that screaming red—highly noticeable—instead of your natural color. Brunette, right? Gareth's told you about it, I've hinted about it, but still—you have to be you, don't you?"

"Gabe . . . ," Gareth warned.

"You have no idea who I really am," I snapped. "Why I do what I do."

"That's because you don't let anyone close enough *to* know you."

"So is that what you want, Gabe? Some deep spiritual connection with me? Do you really wanna *know* me?"

He opened his mouth to answer, but I spun in my seat and cut him off.

"Because what I think you *really* wanna know is what's the best path to gaining control of this little pack I've established. I get the feeling that for you I'm just the means to an end. And I'd bet there's already some twisted plan forming behind that thick skull of yours."

His mouth closed, jaw tightening. From between thinned lips he asked, "Is that what you think of me? Of my loyalty to you? Damn it. If I'm twisted, it's because of *you*."

Gareth silently pulled the car out of its parking space and started down the road.

"You know as well as any member of the pack that loyalty has nothing to do with this. It's normal—even preferable—for a pack to have an alpha of each gender: alpha male and alpha female. You're doing what seems natural—trying to maneuver into the position of top dog."

He stayed quiet, but I knew he weighed my every word.

"It's natural for you to want that, Gabriel," I said. "But it's also natural for me to pursue what *I* want."

"You mean *who* you want."

My lips puckered. "That, too."

"So how much wolf are we, 'laena?"

"What?" I looked from Gareth to him, puzzled by his question.

"How much wolf are we? You always act like we're more wolf than man . . . or woman. What is it you believe?"

"I—" I sensed a trap. No matter how I answered, I'd somehow be wrong. Somehow I'd get tangled into one of Gabriel's weird webs of logic. "We're more animal than man. Or woman. More wolf."

"Of course," he replied, his jaw working. "You do realize that if we're more wolf, the natural order of things really comes down to what the dominant *male* wants. Yes, you can lord over the females, but in a pack, the alpha male rules all."

"Maybe I'd agree if I was truly dealing with an alpha male."

"You *are* dealing with an alpha," he said, slamming a palm against the back of my seat. "He's just not the one you want. Neither is Gareth." He groaned, slouching down in his seat. "And the one you want . . . well, he doesn't want *you*."

I snarled at him, feeling my teeth lengthen to threatening points.

"Don't kill the messenger," he said, holding up one hand. "Pietr doesn't want you, and Gareth doesn't *get* you."

Gareth shook his head, the beads the pups had so recently put on the end of each of his dreadlocks rattling.

"Not like I do," Gabe concluded.

I wanted to scream. "It's not going to happen. You and me—taking on the world together? *Not* going to happen."

"Why not?"

"Because I don't feel that way about you."

"Taking on the world together doesn't require a romantic connection," he stated.

I looked at him sharply.

"Why not view it as a simple partnership?"

I couldn't believe he was being so bold—with Gareth *listening*. And I couldn't believe Gareth was just listening. Maybe I'd been wrong, maybe all I had were beta males. . . . "Because more would inevitably be expected."

"Not by me."

"By the pack."

"So you'll go it alone, shoulder the full responsibility for the pack even though you know I've limited my expectations and that Gareth—*sorry, buddy*—will never fulfill yours?"

"You're speaking of things you don't have full knowledge of," Gareth grumbled at Gabe.

I rested a hand on Gareth's arm. "Leave Gareth out of this. If *that's* the way it needs to be. . . ."

"What do I need to do to prove myself to you? To show you I'm the alpha male this pack needs to survive and thrive? I've fed us, I've taken a gunshot for us, I've connected you to Dmitri. . . . What other proof do you need?"

Then I saw them at a stop sign and in the red convertible— her leaning on him in the backseat as Max drove, Pietr mindlessly stroking Jessica's arm.

And Gabe noticed, too, and growled out his anger.

Jessie

Having forgotten a notebook, I was back at my locker during class when he found me.

"Hey, Jessica."

I turned so fast my neck hurt. I didn't know what it was about the guy, but something about Gabriel told me he was far from his mythologically angelic namesake. Something about the way he watched me and talked to me just put me on edge. "Hey."

"I was thinking about the assignment in Ashton's class and wondered if maybe you had some advice."

I nodded, a slow bob up and down of my head. "Sure. What do you need help with about it?" I glanced down the hall. Why did everyone always seem to disappear whenever I had an extreme sense of distress brewing in my stomach?

"I was just wondering what she meant by this question." He pulled out the textbook and flipped to the right page, pressing the book up against the wall.

Hesitantly, I looked over his shoulder. He was much too close for my comfort.

I tried to work past it and focus on his question. I rested my hand on the page. "Oh. Basically she wants us to—"

And then he sniffed me. Pulled down a deep breath of my scent.

I jumped back from him, releasing the book and letting it drop to the tile floor with a thump. "What are you doing?"

But I *knew* because it was something Pietr had done when I challenged him on that first day of class—Gabriel had taken in my scent so he could track me. So he wouldn't easily lose me again, even in the thickest of crowds or the busiest of cities.

My heart pounded against my rib cage, racing as I ran through the multitude of possibilities this might really mean. He could find me, track me . . .

"Relax, Jessica," he said, crouching to pick up the book with a fluidity Pietr had seemed to have recently forgotten.

"I know what you are."

"Of course you do. So you should also know that's just something we do. You don't need to get so defensive."

"Fine," I said. Totally defensively. "I'll believe it's just a thing you do. Although Cat and Max have *never* sniffed me like that," I added belligerently. "But I'm *not* helping with your assignment."

And I grabbed my notebook, unnerved, and left him there in the hall.

CHAPTER TWENTY-FIVE

Alexi

It was a large building. Sleek metal ribs and a silvered glass skin scraped the gut of a blue sky, disappearing into the atmosphere in dramatic lines that threatened to stab into the rare cloud. The absence of curves or any hint of softness made it even more clearly masculine, sharp lines and angles, hard and dramatic. The Socialists and Communists who pressed Russia's traditional artists into factory molds proclaiming only the glory of the State would have been proud. And yet, everything about it bore a stark testament to one man's gleaming capitalistic dream.

At its very top was rumored to be the living quarters of the man I sought out—his was a prime view, an eagle-eye view, of the city. A place he stayed to be alone and yet intimately connected to every bit of his corporation.

It was a building I could respect. However, it was not filled with men I could respect.

That was exactly what brought me to its front door. Doors, I corrected myself, counting them. Five bold glass doors, two that spun visitors in or out.

I swallowed. This was a big place. A big job.

But I had worked for Nadezhda's father. Although he owned nothing quite this presumptuous, still, he was involved in a multibillion-dollar industry and it was certainly a multinational business.

The Mafia had ties everywhere.

I was not here to make friends. I was here to influence people, and to encourage them to make the right decision.

I checked my hair in the reflection of the bank of windows as I strode into the main lobby.

Inside, granite was polished to such a high gloss it glowed like Italian marble, gleaming up from the floor. Huge exotic plants decorated the broad room—proof that even this far north man could conquer nature and make tropical plants bloom and bear fruit to his will alone.

I suddenly doubted my ability to influence a man of such standing. *Da*, he had been my grandfather's assistant, but whereas my grandfather had died in poverty, this man had broken through the dreaded Iron Curtain, crossed an ocean, and *pulled himself up by his bootstraps,* as the saying went.

This man's building was the culmination of someone's pride and effort—a glorious corporation built on the backs of many workers. My grandfather would have been jealous— *nyet*. I thought back to his journals and notes. Although he betrayed Wondermann, he would not have been jealous of his advancement. He would have been proud. That was enough to make me feel the opposite way as I stood in the midst of the lobby taking in my surroundings.

Hanging from the high ceiling ahead of me was a lengthy

banner that read: BUILDING A STRONGER, BETTER YOUTH TO LIGHT THE FUTURE'S PATH.

I froze. Where had I heard that before . . . ? Was it something Jessie had said?

Directly beneath the banner was a large desk swarming with security officers and special uniforms. The colors of their uniforms appeared to have been chosen to complement the accents lining the walls and trimming out the large frames of paintings of two men. Done in a classical portrait style, one picture showed a man with only a fringe of graying hair, his complexion sallow, his cheeks sunken. Here was a man who had seen better times. Yet there was a brightness about his eyes, a sharpness, an intellect, and depth that even this mediocre painter managed to capture.

Below the first portrait and engraved on a small brass plate was the name WONDERMANN. My grandfather's assistant, coworker, and confidante; the man Grandfather willingly betrayed in the name of the advancement of science—and the embracing of his own agenda. He was the company's founder and now the owner of a multibillion-dollar multinational corporation.

Beside that portrait was another done by the same artist, the style an absolute mimicry of the classic. This one was of a much younger man, still older than myself, but a man with sharp features, narrow eyes, and an unforgiving stare. This was a man not to be trifled with. This was a man with a hunger in his eyes. And certainly a man I was glad I would not be meeting.

Before the opposite wall was a bronze bust of the first man, the founder, Walter Wondermann, a glossy rendition of someone so important—or self-important—that a statue was required in the building that bore his name.

I swallowed hard. How could I broker a deal with a man of this sort? He was rich; he was powerful; and who was I? Just another Russian-American struggling to make a better life for himself and his siblings.

And, evidently all of the students at Junction High School.

So little of what I had become was what I had expected to be.

I forced my feet to move me forward. To propel me toward the security guards who would be the first judge of my worthiness. If they would allow me to pass, I was as good as home free. But if they stopped me . . . ? I blinked as I arrived at the counter. I had not imagined the possibility of rejection.

"Hello, yes, can I help you?" a security guard asked. His hair was thinning on top as much as his middle was expanding.

"*Da*—yes," I stammered. "I am here to see Mr. Wondermann."

He looked me up and down, his gaze skeptical. "Do you have an appointment?"

"*Nyet*—no."

"Not every person walking in off the street gets to see the head of the corporation. He's a very important man with a very busy schedule."

"I understand," I said. "I realize he is a very busy and important man. However, I feel certain the information I have is information that he would want to be aware of as soon as possible."

"Really? So you feel that you are important enough—or the information you have is important enough—that you should be able to just immediately go to the top of the building and see the man who owns everything here?"

"Yes."

"Let's start with your name."

"Alexi Rusakova."

He picked up the phone and punched in a few numbers.

"No—wait. That name might not mean anything to him."

He hung the phone up and glared at me. "So are you Alexi Rusakova?"

"Yes. Yes, of course. But he might know my family better by my grandfather's name."

"Oh, I see. So this is a case of my grandfather knew his grandfather and so now we should be best friends? Hey, Mikey, get a load of this guy. He comes in off the street and he thinks he should be the boss's best friend because his grandfather and the boss's grandfather used to—what?—play cards together?"

Another guard looked at me and pursed his lips. "Beat it, buddy. We get a dozen like you every morning. Everyone knows someone who knows the boss. It's like—what?—seven degrees of separation from Kevin-freakin'-Bacon. The boss is a busy man. He don't have time for class reunions. Especially when it's not with members of his own class—if you know what I mean."

The first guard snorted at his comment and looked me up and down again. This time more pointedly. No. I didn't belong to Wondermann's social class—I had to presume he could afford to make his very own—but I knew he wanted what I had. It was just a matter of getting a message to him so he could say yes and invite me up.

"Tell him I know about the village of Bolkgorod and what happened to the children."

The guard's eyes narrowed. "Are you threatening him with libel or slander? This village, and the kids there—are you some fruit loop trying to make a quick buck by making

some bogus blackmail claim? Because the boss, he has lawyers, you hear what I'm saying? Lawyers that make everyone
else's lawyers look like angels."

"Yeah he do, Benny," Mikey agreed solemnly. "Take a
little advice, pal. You don't wanna mess with the boss." He
leaned across the desk's wide, black counter, cupping one broad
and worn hand around his mouth. "This one guy—he came
here spouting some pretty crazy stuff about the boss and so
the boss said, *Yeah. I'll see him.* So the boss saw him and . . .
well, let's just say no one else *ever* saw him again. If you catch
my drift."

"Geez, Mikey." Benny waved at him. "You'll make the
poor kid piss himself. Look. It's not like the boss is in with
the mob or nuthin', but you don't wanna make him angry.
Got it?"

"I'm not here to make him angry," I assured. "Or to be
fitted for cement shoes."

"Heyyy. He caught my drift. Yeah, the Hudson's lookin'
mighty full already. Don't wanna be chummin' those waters."

"But," I concluded, "I do want you to deliver my message.
I'm Alexi Rusakova. Grandson of Mordechai Feldman. Son
of Hazel Feldman, and I know what happened to the children of Bolkgorod."

"He's a ballsy one, ain't he?"

I merely tilted my head and appraised them both through
slitted eyelids. I would stand my ground. I widened my stance,
threw back my shoulders, placed my fists on my hips, and
made my body language clear.

The guard picked up the phone again. "Yeah, Stewart,
could you deliver the following message to the boss? Yeah. I
know. He's a very busy man. Oh, yeah? In a meeting right
now?" He looked at me, warning hot in his eyes.

I just stared back, daring him to hang up. To not follow through. Thank god I was a better bluffer in conversation than in poker. "That's okay, I'll wait. You'll need pencil and paper. No. Sure. It can be pen. Hey, did you see the Mets game? Yeah, yeah. Of course you did. Quite a last inning, huh? Good. You ready? Here's the message: I've got standing right here before me a guy who says he's Alexi Rusakova, son of Hazel Feldman and grandson of Mordechai Feldman—no, that's not all. No. I know, right? Not often we pass along the whole family lineage. Anyhow. Guy says to tell the boss he knows about what happened at Bolkgorod and the kids there. Says he wants to talk to the boss. Huh. I'll find out." He cupped the phone's mouthpiece with his hand. "You wanna talk to the boss about the kids?"

"In a way. Yes," I agreed. The kids were directly connected to the Rusakova bloodline. And the Rusakova bloodline was connected to the research I could provide. *If* he was willing to stop the drug trials on the students of Junction High and withdraw all his company's supplies to their cafeteria.

"Yeah. He says, in a way, yes. How the hell should I know?" Again he covered the mouthpiece. "In what way?"

"Tell him I know the offspring of those children."

"Something about he knows the offspring of those kids. Yeah. Sure. I'll hold." He looked at me, his eyes going vacant for a moment. "Mikey," he grumbled, "how do we get better music for when we're on hold? This elevator crap's about to put me to sleep. It can't be good for business."

"What would you suggest?" Mikey asked, shaking out a newspaper only to fold it over and scan the lobby once more.

"I dunno. Something cool—something that pumps you up—like Meat Loaf. *Bat Out of Hell* would keep me on the line."

"I'll make a note of it," Mikey said with a grin. But he simply set the paper down, adjusted the flashlight on his belt, and said, "I'm going for rounds."

"Yeah. Sure."

His eyes flashed, and I knew the guard on the other end of the phone was back. "Oh, yeah? Well, I'll be damned. Thanks, Stewart."

He set the phone back down. "Yo, Mikey. Hold up. I need you to escort the good Mr. Rusakova to the penthouse."

Mikey's eyebrows shot up. "Seriously?"

"Very seriously. You gotta key?"

"You kidding me?"

"Yeah, I guess so. Hold on. I'll get it outta the lockbox." He fumbled a minute below the counter and I heard the squeak of hinges as something opened. Victorious, he held up a simple-looking key and keyring.

Mikey took it, an air of solemnity passing between the two. "Come with me."

I nodded and followed him down a hall and to a bank of elevators.

He glanced at the line of them—all identical and gleaming—and then turned down a smaller hall I would not have noticed, and paused outside an elegantly crafted metal gate that fenced in an older, engraved elevator door.

He pressed the single button and the doors pulled apart. Then he motioned for me to step inside.

Within the whole of New York City, it is often remarked that the building with the most elegant elevators is the Flat-iron Building. Having one brief occasion to be inside one, I would have agreed.

Until now.

The walls were lined with mirrors and giltwork, but done

so as to be a fine integration of modified stained glass and mirror shards. It was like standing in the middle of a Tiffany lamp—as if I were the light.

Above my head hung a chandelier that swayed very gently as we left the first floor and made soft tinkling noises as we rose toward the penthouse.

Mikey stood nearly in the elevator's center, which, considering the size of both the guard and the traveling box, still left ample room for me.

"The boss likes his stuff fancy," Mikey explained. "Gold leaf, Swarovski Crystal . . ." He eyed the chandelier warily. "Me? I prefer a single bulb in a simple light—something I don't hafta worry about comin' crashing down on my head." He shrugged, the epaulets on his uniform crinkling. "But I'm a simple guy. The boss is far from simple."

"How so?" I asked.

He shrugged. "He has exotic tastes and a history that's a bit hush-hush. People claim he did some highly illegal things back in the day."

Highly illegal. Like being a very big part of a group that kidnapped children, killed their parents, and experimented on their genes to force them to change into werewolves. No wonder his employees thought his history was a bit hush-hush. Some things you did not want getting out. Of course *some* things were hardly believable if they *did* get out. "What do you think?"

"He's the head of a multinational corporation. Let he who's blameless cast the first stone, you know? What corporate head hasn't done some dirty dealing?"

"An excellent question." I shoved my hands in my pockets and looked down at my loafers. "So. Any other rumors about the boss?"

"The normal stuff. That he bugs every room and taps every wire."

"Prudent behavior in a large company of such value."

"See, that's what I think. You gotta look out for number one and that's just what the boss is doing. Can't fault a man for protecting what's his and keeping control of it."

Especially if what is his was most of the work that went into designing werewolves. "So how old is the boss now? He must be, as they say, *getting up there* . . ."

The elevator rocked to a gentle stop, the chandelier quivering and throwing prisms of light onto the mirror pieces. Disorienting at best.

The doors began their slow slide open and Mikey said, "The boss is a tough old bird. His age don't matter. This is your stop. . . ." With a flourish suiting a doorman more than a guard he pointed me out into what was essentially a large foyer.

More tropical plants lined the broad expanse, filling the space with a humidity and richness of scent the werewolves would have found cloying with so much sweetness. I breathed deep, remembering a brief jaunt to the tropics with fondness and wondering if this was anything like Nadezhda's current location would smell.

"Greetings," a man in a sharp suit and tie said. "I have heard that you are Alexi Rusakova, the son of Hazel Feldman and grandson of Mordechai?" He stuck out his hand and I grabbed it, giving it a firm shake.

"*Da*, I am the same."

"Quite a pedigree you have there—if you don't mind me using the term *pedigree*. . . ."

"It seems appropriate."

"Well, Mr. Wondermann is ready to meet you. We're all very curious to hear about this information you have. It seems you know quite a bit about our operations already."

He stuck out a hand, motioning me forward toward a high set of windows just beyond a large desk with an empty chair.

"Will he be arriving soon?"

"Oh. I apologize." My guide slipped around the huge desk and made himself comfortable in the chair.

I swallowed hard. This was not what I expected. "So, Mr. Wondermann . . ."

"Senior? He's my father."

"Oh. And he's . . ."

"Unavailable. But I know everything he does. And a bit more." He rested his elbows on the desk and steepled his fingers.

I nodded lamely, slowly recognizing my guide from the portrait downstairs, evidently painted a decade earlier. The last ten years had not softened him at all, indeed it appeared they'd done the opposite.

"Please sit." He motioned to a glossy leather seat. "I am very excited to meet you, Alexi. My father and your grand-father knew each other quite well." He studied my face. "Didn't they?"

Again I nodded.

"So I remember my father's version of what happened at Bolkgorod, but I'd like to hear yours." He left the desk and approached me, sitting on the couch's armrest, perched like some bird of prey examining a potential meal. "Tell me a story, Alexi."

So I told him the story of Bolkgorod, but far more

important was what I said when I'd completed my tale. "Your corporation is currently running drug trials on students at Junction High School, just a few hours from here by train."

"Yes."

"I need that to stop."

He blinked at me. "And why should I stop it?"

"You surely have all the data you need already and you're putting your test subjects at great risk."

He shrugged. "Go public."

I knew a dare when I heard one. "We both know no one would believe me."

He smiled.

I set my jaw. "I know how to cure the oboroten."

"Good. And?"

"I'm only a step away from perfecting the cure."

He nodded slowly.

"And if you have the perfected cure . . ."

"I can, of course, reverse-engineer it and make sure the triggering of a werewolf is irreversible."

"*Da.*"

"You would give me that knowledge to save a handful of pimply faced students at a public school that's always at risk of having funding pulled due to mediocre performance?"

"*Da.*"

"Do you imagine yourself some hero?"

"Hardly," I admitted.

"I always thought it might be fun to be a villain—some hero's nemesis. But, if you're no hero . . ."

"Sorry to disappoint you."

"Close to having a permanent cure? Let's say we make this deal. What do you have for me as insurance that you won't go back on it? What do you have of value to give me in good faith?"

"A poem that gives the basic ingredients for the cure." I held out a copy of the page from Grandfather's thirteenth journal. "You stop the tampering and give me a lab and you'll get your perfected cure."

He motioned me forward and, reaching across the desk, took the paper I pulled from my pocket, unfolding it carefully. His eyes lit at what he saw. "How interesting. I do so enjoy poetry." He extended one hand and I took it, shaking it firmly. "It appears we have a deal."

Marlaena

That night I ran for more than the hunt and the sensation of being wild and free. I ran to clear my head and I let my human worries jumble in with my wolf's mind.

Rounding a corner in a trail out near the Rusakova house I caught an odd scent and slowed down, circling back.

A wolf? *Dead?*

At the base of a tree was a lump, obscured by a coat of snow. I nosed at it. Definitely wolf. I began to dig. Past the snow was a thin layer of rocks and dirt. And beyond that was fur. And flesh. I summoned my hands to tug the frozen thing free.

A pelt. My heart sped. A wolf pelt. Sucking down the scent I realized I recognized it.

The Rusakova female—*Cat*. Was this what happened when one was cured? They left behind a pelt? Buried it? Morbid curiosity grew inside me. Then where was Pietr's?

I moved more slowly through the area, nose snuffling a

hairsbreadth above the snow. They were both cured. At the same time . . . ah. His was buried deeper, more carefully, and just down the hill from the house. I drank down his scent, warmth filling my every cell. What was it about Pietr Rusakova?

And twisting faintly around his scent was another. I paced a few steps to the left. Another grave. Also carefully constructed. Here the scent was weaker—older. But . . . I prowled the site. I had to be certain. I breathed as deeply as I could, my ribs aching as my lungs filled to capacity and pressed against them.

There was no doubt about it.

The second pelt was also Cat's.

But from perhaps a month earlier.

How did a cured werewolf have two discarded pelts? And why bury one so far away from the other—and in a hastily constructed shallow grave?

Perhaps Dmitri's concerns were warranted.

Maybe the cure didn't always hold.

CHAPTER TWENTY-SIX

Jessie

I just couldn't understand it—how was Pietr so quiet, soft spoken, and uninterested in seemingly everything? How was it fair that my beautiful Russian-American werewolf was not only less wolf but also seemed to be less man?

Of course, I also couldn't explain the inexplicable draw of the mall. And yet, we were all headed there together. It was a diversion. A needed break.

Sophie was getting better, having stopped eating the school food again; Marlaena had seemingly decided to leave us alone—which only worried me more—and Alexi was spending weekends in the city working on whatever had allowed him to get the company to stop sending the tainted food to Junction High.

And I was spending way more time than anyone should in the boiler room talking to kids, some of whose powers were waning—some of whom believed their powers had been the only thing that made them special.

So the mall was at least a way to take my mind off of that. And put it back on the problems Pietr and I were still having.

Max still flirted, although more gently now, and teased and played, and although some aspects of his personality seemed lessened, somehow it did little to diminish who he really was. It sucked. Amy was still trying to avoid heat and passion, and her boyfriend had some, while I was desperate for a little bit of passion and it had been wrung out of my boyfriend like water from a sponge.

First stop: the clothing shop. And a decision formed in my mind. Amy and Cat drifted through the aisles, hands patting the clothing hanging on the racks as they made little noises of satisfaction and curiosity and occasionally held up something suspended from a clothes hanger. I followed, trailed by the boys and doubtful that I had any need of any new clothing that I couldn't also use on the farm.

Their arms filled with a variety of different tops, sweaters, and pants, Amy and Cat looked at me expectantly. "Come on, Jessie," Amy said encouragingly. "Grab something and let's go back and try stuff on." She reached over to a rack and picked something out for me, holding it boldly up against my chest. "What size are you? Ten? Twelve?"

I took the top from her and turned it around to look at it a moment. Cute, but I was having a tough time getting excited about clothing. "It depends on the manufacturer."

Pietr and Max tried to appear interested in the conversation, but I could see the glaze wash across their eyes as we talked clothing styles, sizes, and companies.

"Let's go, girls," Cat instructed, grabbing our hands and

heading toward the store's back. "We'll have a little impromptu fashion show."

I glanced over my shoulder at the boys and noticed the spark of interest lighting Max's eyes.

"What do you think, Pietr?" I said, turning and waving the top in his direction. "Should I toss this on and hop out and show it to you?"

But no spark of interest popped in Pietr's eyes, even though he nodded politely. "Sure, Jess. I'd love to see you in it." Maybe it was depression. Healing as a simple human sucked.

I contained my sigh and turned to begin the long march back to the dressing rooms, bumping into Amy, who had stopped ahead of us. "What's wrong?"

She glanced from her clothing, low cut and pretty things—things that reminded us that Amy was certainly female—and then looked at Max and swallowed hard. "I thought it was going to just be us girls," she explained apologetically.

Max cleared his throat and jabbed Pietr in the ribs with his elbow. "*Horashow*—good," he said, although I could tell he was lying, "Pietr and I will go over to the game shop and see what new shooter games there are. You girls find us there. Sound good?"

"New shooter games?" Like they didn't have enough experience fighting bad guys regularly. But I saw the look of warning in Max's face and knew what he was thinking. That as much as he would rather see Amy trying on clothes and having a good time, he would easily sacrifice his happiness for hers.

"Oh. Oh, sure." I nodded. "You guys go on. We'll catch up later."

Max leaned forward and kissed Amy gently on the top of

her forehead. It was such a gentlemanly thing for him to do, so unlike the rogue that Max was happy to play, it made my heart hurt just a little bit to see how we all had changed: some because of the cure, and some because of cruel circumstance and the actions of crueler people.

Amy just stood there and tried to smile at Max's gentle show of affection, but I knew that even being given such a tender kiss was somehow killing her.

Pietr looked at me, nodded, noting the distance between us and the fact that Max and Amy also stood in that distance acting as two small walls, and merely said, "I guess we'll see you in a little while."

I wanted to scream.

The guys left and Cat grabbed Amy's shoulders, turning her toward the dressing rooms and our goal of trying on new clothing to change our focus from the way everything seemed to be going. Amy smiled at Cat, trying to wipe away the underlying current of frustration that seemed to shadow her nearly everywhere as we all headed to the back of the store.

"Look," Cat proclaimed, "three rooms all together as if they were waiting for us. Your room, madame?" she asked, giving Amy a gallant bow as she opened her dressing room door with a flourish.

The cashier, who also seemed to be relegated to tending the dressing rooms, just looked at us and sighed. No one got paid enough to do retail and deal with us—that's what I was certain she was thinking.

Cat likewise opened a door for me, and I stepped inside, hanging up my single top on the hook that was still full of recently discarded tops and bras. The floor was strewn with discarded pants and the mirror had seen better days. Seriously? Was that a kiss mark in the upper corner?

Someone had evidently loved seeing themselves in something they'd tried on. . . .

Probably Jennie or Macy . . . I shivered at the thought as I began to tug my shirt up. And then I stopped. And just listened for a minute.

"Knock, knock," Cat said, and I knew she was outside Amy's dressing room door, being playful and encouraging. Just like Amy needed. Not like me, grumpy and frustrated. "Come on, come on," Cat encouraged her.

Cat had become such a good friend to her . . . and I was selfishly falling into my own problems again—problems Pietr had seemed to help alleviate shortly after his arrival in Junction and now problems he seemed to exacerbate by still being in Junction, but not being so much the Pietr I'd fallen in love with.

The door squeaked open and I heard Cat *oooh* and *ahhh* and I felt even worse. "It looks so adorable on you," she said. "Come on out here and give us a spin. Jessie," she called, rapping on my door. "Jessie, come here and see this top. Amy makes it look spectacular."

I stepped out of my dressing room and looked at Amy, standing before Cat, her mopiness slipping away temporarily as she did a little spin so that the hem of the shirt caught in the breeze she made and fluttered slightly. She smiled the smile of someone temporarily forgetting the horrors that had so recently happened. The way she had so recently been brutalized by someone she thought she'd loved.

It was a smile I had been hoping I could sometime inspire. But Cat had managed more frequently. And as grateful as I was that Amy was smiling, I felt guilty that I wasn't the one who had helped my best friend get to that moment again.

"Doesn't she look delightful?" Cat prompted.

"Yes," I agreed. "You look great in that, Amy."

But when she looked at me she must have realized there was something else going on behind my eyes and she blinked, the smile tumbling from her lips. "Are you okay?"

That only made me less okay. I shouldn't have been the one bringing her down. I shouldn't have been letting my problems add on to her problems. Yet there I stood in the back of the clothing store with two of my very best friends and I couldn't be the friend Amy needed.

"I'm so sorry," I said. "You do look wonderful. I just can't . . . I just think I need to go and have a talk with Pietr."

Amy nodded eagerly. "I agree. You two haven't been the same since . . . Maybe a talk would help. Especially if it's the type of talk you used to have before you two wound up at Homecoming together," she said with a wink.

"Yeah," I chuckled. "Those were some great talks."

"Go," Cat instructed. "Whatever is on your mind, you need to get it out. You have your cell phone, and we have our cell phones. . . . We'll catch up."

I nodded, took down the shirt hanging in my dressing room, the shirt I had yet to try on, and hung it up on the waiting rack of rejects.

Then I headed out of the store and down the hall on my way to the game shop, determined to have a long and important talk with Pietr about the fact that the guy I was dating now was far from the guy I had started dating just a little while ago. And that as normal and as gentlemanly and as polite as my current boyfriend was, I missed the less than perfect Pietr that I had become so quickly used to.

And with every step I took, I thought about the little things I missed. The way he touched my cheek with his too hot hands, the way he pressed his lips so eagerly to my own, the way he pushed his body tightly against mine and wrapped me in his arms so much like steel. . . . The hungry way he used to look at me, as if he were all wolf and I were merely a lamb. I wanted all of those things again and so much more. . . . I wanted his focus to be on *me*—so there was no doubt in my mind that I was the most important thing in his world.

It sounded selfish in a way—to want to be the most important thing in anyone's world, the center of anyone's universe—but it was completely honest of me.

We needed to start all over.

With honesty.

So when I came up to the game shop and saw the two of them inside looking at all of the different video game options, I paused. I reconsidered my stance on everything. Because standing there, staring so intently at a video game Max had just handed him, was Pietr. Staring with the same intensity he *used* to turn on me.

It was partly the fact that the very same intensity still existed, and partly the fact that he no longer used it on me but saved it for games and studying for school that made me turn away from both of them and head out.

Out of the store, out of the mall, my cell phone to my ear, I called for a ride. They were fine without me. Sometimes even happier without me. And they certainly deserved a break from me.

So I slipped into a cab and had the cabbie drive me all the way home so I could sink back into what I did best and take some time for myself. Which gave them time for themselves. It seemed to be the least selfish thing I could possibly do.

We slipped through Junction and I let it breeze past me: the storefronts still decorated for the holidays, the snow making everything seem a little bit cleaner—all the little things that usually brought me joy meant very little to me that day. The cab's radio hummed with the song "Sometimes Goodbye Is a Second Chance" and I thought that perhaps the break that the afternoon would give would allow us all to catch our breath and come back to a better and happier attitude when we saw one another at school the next day.

The cab pulled up at the bottom of my driveway, the cabbie eyeing the long, snow-covered mess speculatively. "Don't sweat it," I said, "I can walk." I handed him the appropriate amount of cash—what I would've spent on lunch—and headed up the long driveway and straight to the stables. There was always some work to be done around the farm and at that moment I needed to immerse myself in work, to be with the horses and no one else.

I entered the barn door, slipping between hay bales and a stack of buckets. It was that period in winter when hay actually smelled like springtime. Like hope. In the barn the temperature difference was tremendous. I pulled off my hat, tucked my gloves in my pockets, and unzipped my jacket.

My hand reached for the pitchfork, but my mind flashed back to the time Derek and Pietr got into their epic rumble here, crashing into hay bales and rolling across the paddock outside. My head buzzed with warning, my scalp prickling like Derek was still somehow nearby. Part of him was, I knew—part of him lingered in my head.

Shivering, I pulled myself back to the present and decided no pitchfork. I grabbed the shovel instead.

Rio was the first to spot me and she let out a happy snort of recognition. The other horses likewise noticed me coming down the broad aisle, each responding in their own particular way, with a toss of their mane or a nod of their head or one stomp of their foot—trying to get my attention first.

But Rio always snared my attention immediately. When it seemed no one else was there for me, Rio had been my stalwart companion and friend. She listened to me complain and cry and scream and stomp more than anyone ever had and after each of my rages or depressions was over, she was there to nudge my shoulder or push her snout into my back and make me get up and move forward.

She was more than a horse, more than a pet—she was my best four-legged friend. I propped the shovel by the wall and picked up the brush hanging on a peg by her door.

"Hey, girl," I said, opening her stall door and sliding inside to stand beside her, my hand on her cheek and drifting down her well-muscled neck to trace gently along her shoulder and back.

Brush in hand, I placed my left palm on her rib cage and stroked the soft-bristled brush along her chestnut coat, carefully following the way the hair grew and turned and created sleek and subtle patterns across her body.

"I just don't know what to do," I whispered. "He's different. Changed."

She pawed the floor, straw crackling beneath her hoof.

"I know. He was *supposed* to change—to not be this half-man, half-wolf that was dying as fast as he could live. I expected *that* change. . . ." I moved back to her head and focused on brushing out her mane. "I expected victory," I confessed. "I never thought a single hard-won victory could still feel so much like defeat."

She tugged away from me and I realized I was pulling a little too firmly on her mane.

"Sorry, Rio," I said, carefully adjusting my grip and pressure. "I just had different expectations. I thought I'd get all the heat and the fire that was Pietr but without the danger of him being hunted because he was a wolf. I thought I'd have the passion but not the limitations. But it was a devil's bargain. Maybe it was destiny that he could only be Pietr—this studious boy—or Pietr the quickly dying werewolf. Maybe you can't have it all. Maybe some things can't work both ways."

I focused on separating one stubborn tangle, determined that today something would go right—something would go my way.

"The thing is, I told him I'd never let go. I promised I'd stick by him. And when I said that, I meant it. But it's harder than I thought. He's so very different, it's like he's not that Pietr I knew at all. Like he's not the Pietr that I want."

My cell phone buzzed, vibrating in my pocket and I pulled it out to see Pietr's face and number on the screen.

Maybe he was calling because he was worried. Maybe he missed me and wanted to know what was going on.

Or maybe he'd just realized what day it was and wanted to remind me that our weekly D&D night was coming up.

It was my turn to bring the chips.

As much as I wanted to answer—as much as I wanted *an* answer—I couldn't bring myself to actually accept the call. I couldn't make myself hit the button. So I just turned off my phone and returned to brushing Rio.

It was as I stepped back out of her stall that I noticed a difference in all the horses' demeanors. The barn was suddenly quiet, a strange stillness shrouding everything within. All the horses had turned their attention in one direction and it was then that I saw him standing there.

Gabriel.

CHAPTER TWENTY-SEVEN

Jessie

"Hey," I said, as if it were totally normal to have someone suddenly show up in my barn unannounced and uninvited. *Dammit.* I should have picked up the phone. "Do you need help with something?" I asked.

"Yes. Yes, I think you can help me with something, Jessica," he said, approaching the stall.

I thought about my options. I could go out Rio's back door and wind up in the main paddock and pasture, or I could go forward and through the stall door and wind up nearly nose to nose with Gabriel.

"What can I help you with? If you're looking to learn how to ride a horse, I can probably teach you, but I don't do impromptu lessons."

"Maybe if you come out here, we could talk about the scheduling," he suggested.

"I'm capable of talking right where I am," I said. There

was definitely something wrong here. Gabriel was not looking to learn how to ride a horse. Gabriel was looking for
something else, something that made my stomach churn
and my feet still in the straw of the stall.

He'd sniffed me. He'd tracked me. I'd expected it, and yet,
here I was, unprepared. Darwin would so define me as thoroughly selected against.

"So when's a good time for you to come back and start
lessons?" I needed to buy some time so I could figure out what
weapons were at hand. I looked at the brush. *Awesome.* I could
groom him to death.

Glad I spent time with Alexi keeping up with hand to
hand, I was also very well aware as a werewolf, Gabriel had
a great deal more power than I naturally came by or had
even with training.

He stood at the stall's door, his hand resting on the handle,
his face close to the bars. "Looks like you have a schedule out
here, a calendar of some sort," he said. "Let's look at it together. I'd hate for us to come up with a time that you find
out later just won't work with what you already have on your
schedule."

"Very considerate of you."

"I do my best."

I tried to subtly reach into my jeans pocket and pull out
my phone again, but Gabriel saw the move and yanked the
door open, leaping into the stall.

"I wouldn't do that if I were you," he snarled, grabbing
my wrist to pull me tight to him.

"Ow!" I cried in anger at myself as much as at him.

"I'd say I'm sorry, Jessica, but I'm not. You're the means to
an end for me. You're the greatest gift I could give someone
really, really important. The weird thing is, I don't even

know why you're so valuable. I mean, I get that you're somehow connected with curing werewolves. But none of us
want the cure. We're happy being who we are—that's something most people can *never* say." He paused, dragging me a
foot forward. "And the fact you're dating Pietr? I couldn't
care less. But I think you may still help me achieve my goals.
And I'm very much into achieving my goals. So you're going
to come with me, like a good girl, and you're going to do
exactly what I tell you."

"The hell I will!" I slammed my booted foot down on his
instep and watched him pull back in pain as my elbow caught
him in the gut.

He was barely winded.

I shoved away from him, past Rio, as she snorted and
stomped, and I fell against the door leading out to the pasture. I pushed open the door, the rush of cold stinging my face.
But he grabbed me by the waist and took me to the ground
as Rio danced away, shrieking her distress and struggling
not to step on me as I thrashed beneath him on the floor.

With a quick spin she jumped us and rocketed past, into
the cold and away from any risk of hurting me. The door
swung back and forth on its hinges, squealing, and I pounded
on his face and chest with my hands as I did my damnedest
to whale on him with my knees and feet.

He seemed unimpressed.

So I bit him.

With a shout of pain, blood pouring from his cheek, he
rolled off me.

I plowed into the stall door, forcing it open, and grabbed
the shovel waiting by the wall.

He was back on his feet. With a growl of my own I swung
the shovel and just missed his head. "Damn it!"

"Come on," he coaxed me, reaching his hands out on arms spread wide. He wiggled the fingers closest to the wall.

Pietr and Max learned that as a distraction technique.

I knew it, too.

So when he came at me with his other hand, I struck.

He screamed as the shovel's blade pinned his hand to the wall for a heartbeat. Caught, he struggled, and my stomach twisted when he pulled free in his panic and rage. Two of his fingers dropped to the hay bale below.

"No more scrrrewing around—" he growled, face contorting, teeth growing into wicked ivory points.

Tugging the shovel free, I connected with his shoulder. . .

. . . As his fist connected with my head.

My world went black, and the last thing I heard was the shovel falling to the straw.

And his breath, hot in my ear.

When my eyes opened again, I was greeted by darkness. Something dry and coarse plugged my mouth and tasted the way an old gym shirt smelled.

I'd been gagged.

I tried to pull the thing out of my mouth, but my hands were stuck behind my back, lashed together. I tested whatever held them and felt the fine hairs on my wrists tear away as I twisted.

Not rope. Duct tape? Rope I might cut or untie. But duct tape? It held the world together.

This was bad.

I focused on my surroundings, trying to get some clue about my location. In movies, a victim can sometimes get word out to rescuers about their location by dropping subtle hints.

Granted, I was not tremendously gifted at subtlety, but I was determined to maintain hope.

I'd already survived so much, it'd be tremendously disappointing to not make it out of this most recent scrape, too.

In the movies there is often a ransom note or a ransom phone call. And smart negotiators ask for proof of life. But this wasn't a movie. This was real life.

Plus werewolves.

I was so utterly screwed.

Focus, Jess, focus.

It was chilly where I was. Drafty. I squinted and tried to make out some detail. But in the dark it seemed there were none.

Damn it. Jessie Gillmansen, waiting on rescue.

Again.

This was not good for my self-esteem.

Marlaena

Gabriel found me not far from the motel in an abandoned lot so overgrown the weeds stuck through the snow. "You're a bit more complicated than most of the girls I've dated," he admitted, scrubbing a fist across his forehead. "Some girls like candy, some are into flowers or jewelry—but you don't seem to care about any of that."

I watched him, a sense of dread growing in my gut. I noticed his hand was bandaged. My hands settled on my hips, fingers curling into fists.

"But we're not dating, are we?"

"We sure as Hell aren't."

"And it seems there's nothing I can do to change that. . . ."

He looked at me from the corner of his eye and I thought he was handsome and bright, but all this—our circumstances? They were tremendously cruel.

He wanted me, but I didn't want him. I wanted Gareth, but he didn't want me. Or maybe he did. . . . I doubted even Gareth knew what he wanted. And so it continued, a frustrating circle of wants and denials. Of misplaced love and loads of loss.

I said the lamest two words in the English language. "I'm sorry?"

"Yeah. Well. I don't even know when your birthday is— you realize that? No one in the pack does. That's how distant you keep us all. But I've been running with you for more than a year, so I must've missed it at some point. I think that sucks: missing birthdays. We don't get many, so we should celebrate each one."

"Gabriel."

He looked at me, hope lighting his eyes at the sound of his name.

"I don't want anything from you."

"I know. You're amazingly self-sufficient. But, as you've pointed out, *needing* and *wanting* are different things. And I noticed something. Something you seem to *need*."

I blinked, having no idea what he was talking about.

"I'll admit, I couldn't get exactly what you need, but I think I've actually found the means to an end. I think this gift I'm about to give you—"

My nostrils flared, and I pulled in the surrounding scents and found one that was familiar. My eyes popped wide open.

"Will provide you with a way to get the thing you *really* need." He jogged a few yards away and dragged her back—

Jessica Gillmansen, bound and gagged and trussed up like a Thanksgiving turkey.

He grinned at the look on my face.

Jessica growled, a big bruise discoloring the side of her face. Beautiful. She thrashed, but really, what threat was *she* to any of *us*?

Gabriel threw her at me, and I let her land on her knees. Her eyes rolled at the impact, and she glared at me, hate hard in her brown eyes.

"So," Gabriel said. "Do you like your present?"

I reached down and ruffled her hair, enjoying the way she fought to avoid my touch. "It's perrrfect." And suddenly everything came slamming together like the pieces of some bizarre puzzle. My wants and needs—those of the pack . . . the pelt I'd found buried . . .

Our options had just opened wide again. And all because of Gabe making a bold move. "I don't like it—I *love* it. And I know exactly what I'm going to do with it."

ACKNOWLEDGMENTS

This list's going to be short because I was juggling so many things I didn't have as many folks involved in the creation of this novel as in previous ones.

First, a big thanks to my readers. You all rock! You're the reason I get to spend my time imagining hot werewolves and the trouble they get into. You're the reason I get to do so much traveling and speaking (and why I enjoy checking my e-mails so much). I hope you love this book as much as the rest (or even more).

This time around I only used three betas. It certainly wasn't because my other betas weren't ready or worthy (they are amazing and very talented); it was simply a timing issue. I screwed up on my time line. There's a lot of juggling that goes into a series of books published so closely together! So, a big thanks to Alyson Beecher, who always dives in no matter what time I send a manuscript and always gives great constructive criticism. A huge thanks to Karl Gee, who managed to listen to the whole book in several different stages of development (often while commuting or driving a tractor)—your input was amazingly helpful. And thanks goes out to Anthony Mincarelli, who read the thing while dealing with timing issues of his own and reported "I love it" when everything was said and done. Sometimes as an author that's exactly what you need to hear.

My thanks also goes out to my editor, Michael Homler, who somehow always makes publishing seem less crazy than it really is; my agent, Richard Curtis, who is tremendously helpful and wise; my sales rep, Bob Werner, who is excited about what I do and a tremendous asset; and all of the amazingly helpful and gifted staff at St. Martin's Press. Thanks also to Paula for her copyedits. This publishing house is the perfect home for my werewolves, and I'm so glad!

sometimes being a teenager can lead to some hairy situations...

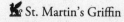